Saxon T

Saxon Throne

Book 9 in the Wolf Warrior Series

By

Griff Hosker

Saxon Throne

Published by Sword Books Ltd 2016
Copyright © Griff Hosker First Edition
Cover by Design for Writers

The author has asserted their moral right under the Copyright, Designs and Patents Act, 1988, to be identified as the author of this work.

All Rights reserved. No part of this publication may be reproduced, copied, stored in a retrieval system, or transmitted, in any form or by any means, without the prior written consent of the copyright holder, nor be otherwise circulated in any form of binding or cover other than that in which it is published and without a similar condition being imposed on the subsequent purchaser.

A CIP catalogue record for this title is available from the British Library.

Contents

Saxon Throne	1
Prologue	4
Chapter 1	6
Chapter 2	21
Chapter 3	31
Chapter 4	45
Chapter 5	54
Chapter 6	65
Chapter 7	74
Chapter 8	83
Chapter 9	94
Chapter 10	105
Chapter 11	114
Chapter 12	125
Chapter 13	135
Chapter 14	143
Chapter 15	149
Chapter 16	156
Chapter 17	165
Chapter 18	180
Chapter 19	189
Chapter 20	198
Chapter 21	208
Chapter 22	218
Chapter 23	227
Epilogue	240
Glossary	242
Historical note	245
Other books by Griff Hosker	250

Prologue

Eoforwic 633

King Edwin was dead. I, Hogan Lann, the Warlord of Rheged, had killed him in single combat. He had been our enemy for many years and the battle of Hatfield had been a surprise victory for us. We had been outnumbered and were an unlikely alliance. Those who write about such things said that King Cadwallon of the Cymri had killed him. It was not true but he led our army and I was happy for him to take the credit. Those who were there and those who were warriors knew that I had killed him. They had watched as I had wielded Saxon Slayer to end his life. It had destroyed Northumbria. The hearthweru had all died with their king. They were true bodyguards and oathsworn to the end. We took away fine mail and weapons, for the Saxons made good swords. The kingdom of Northumbria was split asunder and the divisions of the Saxons became apparent. There were others who wished for the throne but it would take time for them to vie for power. King Penda, our Mercian ally, had taken his army back to Mercia and King Cadwallon exacted revenge from the Northumbrians for all of their raids into his land. Osric, King Edwin's cousin, had claimed Deira and ruled as king. It was Oswald, the son of King Aethelfrith, who ruled Bernicia.

It had been many months since our victory and we had spent the autumn and winter in Eoforwic enjoying the fruits of our victory. King Cadwallon also laid waste to the lands of his enemies. The pleasures were in ale, wine and women. I did not indulge myself but studied in the fine library in that ancient city. The pleasure I took in that ended when a messenger from Wyddfa brought me the shocking news that Irish pirates had raided my land and killed many of our people, as well as enslaving others. This calamity had been made worse by the disease which had followed. My wife and the families of those who had taken refuge in our strongholds had been struck by plague. My wife, Aileen, and Gawan's mother, Myfanwy, had not been enslaved; had they suffered that then I would have rescued them. They had wasted and died. I would not even have the chance to bury them, the Bishop of the monastery at St. Asaph had ordered the bodies to be burned to stop the spread of the disease. One of my wife's ladies wrote and told me the news. They were the second family I had lost. I would not have a third. It was my fault she was dead for I had left her to watch over my people. I should have made sure that she was in a place of safety. My life in my former home was over. I had no reason to rush across the country.

Equally calamitous news was that Myrddyn my wizard and my mentor had disappeared. I knew that had he been at Aileen's side she would not have died but he had disappeared before the plague had struck. Many said he was dead, killed by the disease too, but Gawan, my younger brother who was also a wizard, said it was not true. He was in touch with the spirits but even he did not know where the man who had guided my father and then me to rid the west of the Saxons had gone. The remnants of our people had fled the land. It was now a desolate wasteland. We would not return thither. Each night since the battle I had dreamed of my dead father and Myrddyn. I had dreamed of Rheged and the days when my father had kept it safe for King Urien. Even in my dreams, the sight of my dead father saddened me. The dream was the only thing which kept me going in the nightmare that my life had become.

I began to tire of the King's court. They ate fine foods and they enjoyed women. Since my sister's death, King Cadwallon had been celibate. Now he cavorted and carried on. There were young women who shared his bed. That life was not for me; it never had been.

So, while King Cadwallon and his men feasted and enjoyed all that the Eoforwic ancient city built by Rome had to offer, I mourned. With my father recently slain it seemed that there was just Gawan and myself left from my whole family. There was nothing left for me in Cymru. I decided that when all of King Cadwallon's enemies had been defeated then I would beg to be allowed to rule the ancient king of Rheged. King Cadwallon owed me that, at the very least.

Part 1
Deira and Bernicia

Chapter 1

"You cannot leave me, Warlord, we have not yet rid the land of this Saxon curse. Would you stop so soon? One more push and we can win. I know that Myrddyn if he lives, would wish you to continue."

"Myrddyn does live and I am not saying that I intend to leave you yet, your majesty. It is just that, with Northumbria destroyed, there will be no enemies left. I will not be needed as Warlord. I am asking for the future; when we have destroyed the power of Northumbria then my job will be done. I would like to go home."

"There are Saxons in the south!"

"But the north is my home and the west is yours. There are no Saxons there. And the ones closest to you, the Mercians, are your allies."

"So long as they live in Britannia then I cannot rest."

This was not the man who had been trained by my father and who had fought alongside me more times than I cared to remember. He had changed and it had been the death of Edwin which had made the change. He began to believe the stories that he had killed Edwin. St. Edwin, the followers of the White Christ now called him. He was revered. King Cadwallon was also a Christian but he was not the same man he had been when we had left Wrecsam. Since my sister, his wife, had died he had grown apart from us.

If he would not let me leave, then I wanted the war over. "Then let us set about ending Deira and Bernicia as kingdoms now while they are weak. Osric controls the land to the north of us but it is poor land. Let us strike while it is winter and we are well fed."

"We will do when the land warms up and the grass grows again. First, we enjoy all that this town has to offer!"

"But your warriors become fat and lazy, your majesty."

Saxon Throne

I saw a few of them eye me angrily but none would dare challenge me so long as I had Saxon Slayer, the mystical sword of legend. It was the blade feared by every Saxon.

King Cadwallon did not like my comments. His face darkened with a frown and his tone became harsh. "You go too far, Hogan Lann. Take your wolf brethren and go hunt. We will not stir until the first new grass appears. You have until then!"

"And what of Rheged?"

"When we have defeated the Saxons then I give you Rheged. You can guard our northern borders. You will be Dux Britannicus again. Now go for your sour face spoils the taste of this wine!"

I had been dismissed. I did not mind for it suited me. My wolf brethren were my oathsworn. They were equites all. Encased in mail and with a spear, mace and sword, we were feared by all of our enemies. Even the Saxon shield wall could not stand against us. Wars, age and treachery meant that there were but twenty of us left and our twenty squires. In addition, we had Daffydd ap Miach. He led my archers. There were but twenty of those now and they were even harder to replace than my equites. They would come with us. I would take my men and enjoy the company of warriors once more.

We left at dawn with snow in the air. I had been told to hunt. We would appear to hunt but, in reality, I intended to head for Rheged and see who ruled there now. It had been a generation since we had been driven from that land by the Saxons. I had been but a child. We had campaigned there many times but it had been some years since I had been to the land of my birth. My father had died far from that land. All of his oathsworn were now dead too. The last to die had been Tuanthal who had led my father's light cavalry. They too had perished. The war had cost us dear. It had been my men who had paid the price.

I rode at the head of the column with Gawan. We rode easily for Geraint and his scouts ranged far ahead of us and would ensure that we did not stumble into trouble. My brother had not been born in Rheged. We had fled when he had been born and my father had married again following the death of my mother. Now we were both motherless.

"What do you think has happened to Myrddyn, brother? You are in touch with the spirits. Can you see him?"

"I hear his words in my head which is how I know he is not yet in the Otherworld but I cannot feel him. He is not close. Perhaps the plague made him ill. He has powers but he would retire to a cave and heal himself. If he chose not to be found, then no one would discover him. You know that."

"Aye." We rode in silence.

He shook his head. "Perhaps I am losing my powers. When we were in Eoforwic then my visions became misty. I could read a little of your thoughts but others were hidden from me."

"Others?"

"I have known the King since we were boys and I could always see his thoughts as I saw yours but since the battle..."

I said nothing. I reflected that I had known King Cadwallon all of his life and I too had seen a change in him since we had finally defeated and killed King Edwin.

Gawan smiled, "Aye brother he has changed. Perhaps I needed to be away from Eoforwic for even now my thoughts are clearer. This was a good decision to leave the court."

We were heading for Stanwyck. It was the ancient hill fort where our father had been born. "I miss the old man's advice. He steered our father through some treacherous waters. Even when we thought that our end must come it was the words and advice of Myrddyn which aided us."

"Perhaps he thought we needed him no longer, brother? He saw farther ahead than any. He came not with us to fight King Edwin. He might have foreseen the outcome. We have defeated the Northumbrians and the Mercians are our allies."

"Had King Cadwallon struck as soon as Edwin was dead then we could have ended all spark of Northumbrian spirit. This war is far from over and I may not have your foresight, Gawan, but I see danger ahead. Osric is raising an army."

"How do you know?"

"I had Geraint and his scouts riding far behind the enemy's front lines. There are Saxons flocking to his banner. The embers of war are being fanned again in Loidis and Din Guardi. Besides I have a feeling that all is not well in the land."

Gawan laughed, "And I thought I was the seer. I have had those feelings too. In fact, now that we breathe this upland air I feel it even more and I sense danger. So, big brother, what do you intend us to do?"

"The King has promised me that I can rule Rheged when Northumbria is finished. I would see now what the land is like." I waved a hand behind me. "This is our army now! The blood of Rheged has been spilt to save the men of Cymru. We cannot make more. None of us has families. When we die, it is the end of our line. All that our father did will have been in vain. He sacrificed his life to save me and how have I repaid him? I have lost the army he built up."

"Do not be so hard on yourself. No one could have done more."

We reined in as Geraint waved his hand above his head. It was safe to approach the old hill fort. It had been a hill fort for many years before the Romans had come. Some said it was the ancient capital of Rheged or, at least, what Rheged had once been. The place where my father and his brothers had seen their own family slaughtered by Angles and then fled west had been fought over so many times that no one lived there any longer. It was too dangerous. For us it was perfect. The stream gave us water and the mounds and ditches gave shelter and protection. Half ruined huts remained and it would not take much to turn them into shelters once more.

My men soon had their fires going and food roasting on wooden spits. My archers and squires were set as sentries. The equites first cleaned and oiled their mail and then sharpened their swords. We did this every day even if we did not fight. It became a habit and it was a good habit for it had kept us alive. When that was done my inner circle of family and captains sat with me around my fire.

Lann Aelle was my cousin. He had been my father's squire. The three of us were all that remained from the family. Pol, Dai and Llenlleog were the leaders of my equites. Each led his own knights. Finally, Geraint commanded my scouts while Daffydd ap Miach my archers. Both had served my father and now they served me. After we had eaten they looked at me. They knew that I had a reason to bring them across the spine of the country in the middle of winter.

"I will tell you the real reason I left the King. It was not to hunt although well done Daffydd, the meat was excellent. We must make ourselves our own land. Our days of fighting for others are passing. We are too few now. As my brother tells me, King Cadwallon has almost defeated Northumbria. As soon as Deira and Bernicia fall then we shall have a high king again."

My cousin, Lann Aelle, looked around the firelit camp. "There are few of us to hold Rheged. Our fathers left and took many more than this to Caer Gybi."

I nodded, "But that was when the Angles and the Saxons were on the rise. They are now, in the north, at any rate, a diminished threat but let us see. We come to find what the problems are, Lann Aelle. Let us not create them before we get there."

We had all grown up in a constant state of war. Apart from the time when Pol and I had spent half a year in the east at the court of the Roman Emperor we had fought Angles, Saxons, Hibernians, Scots and even the Welsh. It was all we knew and I could see what Lann Aelle was thinking. How could such a small number continue to fight on against such overwhelming numbers? The fact was we had always done so. My equites were brothers. We fought under the dragon banner of Rheged and we were the wolf brethren my father had created. I could not see myself ever enjoying even a day of peace. This winter journey would be as close as I would get to that state.

We changed horses for the ride the next day. Our mail meant it was hard on our mounts. We all had two horses. It was why we had squires. My father had borrowed the idea from Constantinopolis. Our squires were young men who led our spare horses and whom we trained to become equites. Like us, they fought and operated as one. They were hard to come by and I knew that should the day come when I did rule Rheged then I would need to find a way to recruit such warriors. None of us was getting any younger. Already the first flecks of grey had appeared in my beard. Gawan still looked young but the rest of us wore the faces and bodies of veteran warriors.

The wind blew sharply from the northeast. It made it slightly easier than a wind from the west but as it brought flurries of snow it was a less than comfortable ride. I pulled my fur tighter around me. Geraint and his scouts seemed to bear the harsh weather easier than we and they disappeared ahead of us soon after dawn. After we had crossed the high passes to the west the wind abated a little or perhaps we had some protection from the hills. Had Myrddyn been with us then he would have told us how the spirits were watching over us and making our journey easier. Gawan, our contact with the spirit world, kept his own counsel. He was now our Myrddyn.

As we descended the hills towards the valleys and waters of Rheged I felt peace begin to wash over me. These were not the harsh and savage mountains of Cymru, this was a gentler land. It had softer edges. You could choose when to visit the crags and high places and when to enjoy the soft valleys. We had been happy here when I had lived with my father and mother in the old Roman fort which guarded the road to Civitas Carvetiorum; Brocavum. King Urien, the last king of Rheged had valued my father so much that he trusted him with that task. We headed, now, towards that fort.

Geraint had anticipated my wishes. Even though we arrived before dark and could have travelled some miles further he had set up camp. There was less snow here than on the high passes and the half-ruined walls of the fort afforded some protection. We had rebuilt the fort in my father's time but that had been burned down. It had been rebuilt since but each time it was in wood and wood burns. We used that which our Roman ancestors had built. It had stood the test of time.

As Gawan and I explored the fort I found myself lost in the memories of when I had lived here. I noticed Gawan had the same look on his face but he had never lived here. "Where are you, brother?"

He smiled, "I am with my wife Gwyneth and my son Arturus. I dream their faces."

"Constantinopolis is far from here but at least they were saved from the plague."

"I know, brother, and I am sorry that I have my family and yet you do not."

"I am content. They will be with your mother and she will care for them in the Otherworld."

"Aye, they have come to me in my dreams and they are content. I dreamt well in our father's old home. Perhaps I should not return to Eoforwic. It is not good for my powers. I am pleased that we sent my son to learn at the court of the Emperor. It was *wyrd*."

"It was and now we must put our two minds to this land and how we can make a home for your wife and son when they return in two years."

When we returned to the fire I gathered all of my men around me and addressed them. "We will use this place as our base. The King said we should hunt." I shrugged, "And why not. There will be little game for it is winter but that will hone our skills. However, my real intent is to explore this land and see who lives here. King Cadwallon has promised me this land for my own." I waved a hand around the men before me. "What is mine is yours. We spend seven days here. Daffydd, your archers can hunt while the equites, in five groups with squires, explore. Llewellyn, my standard-bearer shall command the camp and the ten squires we shall leave to guard it."

Pol, my oldest friend asked, "And what if we meet people?"

I laughed, "I hope we shall! There is little point in ruling a land without people."

"But if they are Saxons?"

"If they fight then we destroy them but if they have peace in their hearts then we shall see. I hope that some of our old people remain but it could well be men from Hibernia or Dál Riata. I do not think that we will be lucky enough to find a home without enemies. But we do not come to fight, we come to scout."

I took Gawan with me as well as Osgar, Pelas, my squire, and Gryffydd. We had two squires with us. The numbers would suffice. I rode Star. He was my favourite horse although he was getting, like me, old. I had chosen to visit King Urien's ancient city. The other four groups would range further south and west. We rode without spears but we all had our shields and swords. Saxon Slayer was enough, on its own, to inspire fear in our enemies; all had heard of it. Since it been passed to me from my father it had never been further than a hand span from me. Its spirit was a link to the past and to my father. So long as I wielded the weapon then we would prevail.

I had with me, Tadgh the Scout. He did not range ahead but rode next to me and Gawan. Like all of Geraint's scouts he had been chosen because he was part animal. He did not just look and listen, he sniffed and he felt. Even his hair seemed to discover things we could not. Had Myrddyn been with us he would have had the power to see ahead of us too. Gawan had some of those skills but he was still learning.

"Warlord, there is a village ahead. I can smell it."

"But the wind is behind us."

He smiled, "Nonetheless I can smell it and something else. I hear the clash of iron."

I drew Saxon Slayer and pulled my sword around. "Let us approach cautiously. Spread out in a line. Tadgh, ride ahead and around."

He nodded and, as he rode, began to string his bow. He rode with his knees. We followed silently but with drawn weapons. Our shields had long leather fastenings which allowed us to hold our reins and yet still enjoy the protection of the shield. The Roman Road rose. It was a murky day and visibility was not the best. Even so, I soon heard the clash of iron and I made out shadowy figures in the distance.

It became obvious that this was a village. It had no wall and no ditch. I saw a shadowy figure raise something and bring it down. There was a cry. Someone was being attacked. I kicked Star in the side and he began to gallop. I held my sword behind me. A sweep was an effective stroke when riding a horse. I gripped Star's flanks with my knees. When we fought, we were as one. My men arrowed back from me. I was the point of attack and I would choose our target.

As the murk cleared I saw that these were brigands. They wore no mail and had no helmets but they had round wooden shields, spears and short swords. They could have been Hibernian or from Dál Riata. They were not Saxons. It was clear that they were overcoming the resistance of these farmers and their families. The snow-covered muddy ground dampened the sound of our approach and we were less than thirty paces from them before one warrior looked up, having slain a farmer, and shouted a warning. We were outnumbered; there were, at first glance, more than twenty of them but we were mounted and we were mailed.

I leaned forward and swung my sword horizontally. The warrior who had given the alarm raised his shield to protect his head. I swung Saxon Slayer and my sword bit into his thigh. Bright blood spurted onto the white snow as he fell in a heap. Mortally wounded he would bleed to death. A second warrior ran at my left side with a spear held high. I pulled Star's head to the left and then swiped away the spear head with my sword. I kicked him in the face as I galloped past. We had to keep moving for if we stopped then they would overcome us. I kicked again and Star almost leapt up. The movement made the two brigands who saw the chance to surround me flinch and hold their shields up. I swung Saxon Slayer high over my head and brought it down. Although the shield blocked my blow it was not a good shield and I used every sinew and muscle to put power into the strike. The shield shattered and the blade bit into the warrior's head.

I felt a blow on my shield as the other swung his axe at me. My shield was well made and it held the blow. I brought my bloody blade over Star's head and swiped at the warrior who stepped back out of range. Pulling Star's head around I opened my body to enable me to swing again. This time he was taken by surprise and the sword sliced through his leather shirt and ripped a long scar across his chest.

As another warrior ran at me I saw an arrow appear through his neck as Tadgh began to release arrows. It was the end of resistance. The men I led were ruthless. We had learned to be fighting Saxons. All twenty of the raiders were quickly and efficiently slain. I looked around for more enemies but there were none.

"Tadgh, are we safe?"

"Aye Warlord, none passed me."

I dismounted and, handing my reins to Pelas, took off my helmet. I could see that we had arrived just in time for there were a dozen bodies lying in the village. Not all were men. The brigands had been indiscriminate in their slaughter. Women and children lay slain. I walked over to one of the men I had killed. He wore his hair long and had nothing covering his chest. The amulets and battle rings he wore suggested he came from Hibernia. He had tattoos on his body. I suspected Geraint would know which clan he belonged to but it mattered not.

I stood. A villager with a bandaged head came toward me. He dropped to his knee. "Thank you, lord! It would have gone ill for us had you not reached us when you did."

I nodded, "I would gather their weapons and use them yourselves." Sweeping a hand around the village I said, "If you do not build a ditch and a palisade then this will happen again."

He nodded, "I told Edgar, the headman." He pointed to an older warrior who had had half of his face slashed off and lay in a widening pool of blood. "He said he had paid tribute to Athelhere and that we would be protected."

"Athelhere?"

"He is a Northumbrian chieftain. He lives at the fort called Banna on the old Roman Wall. He comes here in the spring and the autumn and takes tribute from us."

"You are not Angles?"

"No, lord. My people have lived in these hills for generations. We speak the old language."

"Why did you not leave when Prince Pasgen took his warriors south?"

"My father did not wish to leave the land of his birth." He smiled sadly. "Besides he kept hoping that the Warlord would return. He often told us tales of his deeds. My father was slain by a Saxon and we left our home in the south. We lived in peace here for a while and then Athelhere came."

"I am the Warlord."

He looked at me in amazement. "Then you have returned! *Wyrd*!"

"I have not returned to stay but one day I shall. Who will be headman now?"

He looked around, "Edgar and his sons are dead. I suppose that would be me."

"And what is your name?"

"I am Ardhal of the Halvelyn."

"Then until I return I charge you with the building of a wall and a ditch."

"But Athelhere!"

"I shall deal with him. Will you do it?"

"Aye lord."

I mounted Star and shouted, for a crowd had gathered around me. "I am the Warlord of Rheged. Soon I will return and make this land safe from brigands like these and Saxons like Athelhere. Until then Ardhal is headman. Use the weapons you have captured. Build a palisade and a ditch. We go to find this Athelhere. You will pay no more tribute. King Urien would not like it."

They all cheered. It was a beginning.

We rode along the old road for another few miles and saw no more villages. The land was sparsely populated. Rather than returning through the village, we headed back along a more northerly route.

"Tadgh, from which direction did the brigands come?"

"The west, Warlord."

"When we have dealt with this Athelhere we will see if we can find this rat's nest." Just at that moment, we heard from the south and the hills the howl of a wolf. We all turned to look.

Gawan said, "*Wyrd*. I have not heard a wolf since we were in the land of the Cymri. Perhaps it is a sign."

"You are the wizard. You tell me."

He smiled, "I fear I miss my mentor Myrddyn. He was teaching me how to use my skills. I know many of the spells to heal but not as many to understand the ways of the earth and the sky."

"It will come. When I took on the mantle of Warlord I did not think I could do it."

Once back at the camp we took off our mail. I had Pelas clean and oil it. "Put an edge on Saxon Slayer. I think we shall need its edge again before too long."

As the other equites rode in we discussed with each of them what they had found. Pol and his men had come upon four Northumbrians. They had slain three and the wounded fourth had told them before he was despatched, that he was one of Athelhere's band. "I am guessing, Warlord, that this Athelhere is a Gesith, a minor chieftain."

"Then we will meet with him when all of our men have returned. We can do as King Cadwallon wishes and make this land safer for us.

Bors shook his head, "It is a wasteland, lord. There are few people living here."

"That matters not. Ask Gawan. If the land is blighted then nothing grows, neither animal nor human. Nature needs cleansing. The blight is Athelhere and his band. We will scourge the land of them. Then we will deal with a symptom of the disease. The land will heal itself. These Hibernians who treat Rheged as a granary and slave farm, we will teach them other."

"You still wish to live here, Warlord?"

"I do, Kay. It is where I was born. Until Myrddyn reappears I will have to make such decisions."

It was thirty miles to Banna. It would take more than half a day to reach it. We left the spare horses and my squires to guard the camp. I took Pelas and Llewellyn because I wanted them to know who I was. My standard would tell them that. Daffydd and my archers would ensure that none escaped.

We followed the Eden river north until we reached the road. That meant we approached the fort along the Roman Road to the west. We suddenly spied a band of Saxons from Northumbria ahead of us. Rising from a hollow, they were coming from the north and were driving sheep before them. As soon as they saw our horses they ran for the safety of the fort. I waved Daffydd and his archers forward. The enemy had three quarters of a mile to go before they reached the walls. We kept riding at the trot. There was little point in exhausting our horses. We would not be able to catch them before they reached the safety of the fort.

My archers, in contrast, rode their small horses hard and they stopped just a hundred paces from the Saxons. Halting, the archers knocked an arrow each and let fly. Not all of the Saxons had shields. They kept running. The ones with shields survived but five of those without shields were hit. Three stayed on the road. One was dead and the other two had arrows sticking out from their legs.

The survivors made the fort and the crudely made gate was slammed shut. Not all of the original walls remained and, as we rode up, I saw that it could be taken by assault. The question was, did I wish to risk losing men to do so?

My archers ran along the road and slit the throats of the wounded. Those behind the walls hurled stones and released poorly made arrows. I saw Daffydd shake his head at the poor effort. He was a true master of his craft and it appalled him to see such bad archers. The nearby river meant that there was only one way in or out and we had that stoppered.

"Archers, cover the flanks."

We stood in a long line a hundred paces from the walls. At first, they tried a few desultory arrows and stones but when we took them on our shields and they did no damage they desisted. I spoke in Saxon when I shouted to them, "I am the Warlord of Rheged. I killed Edwin, the King of Northumbria. This is now my land. Athelhere, Gesith, if you wish to live, lay down your arms and begin to march east to Bernicia. I make this offer but once."

My answer was a javelin thrown with some force towards me. Star stood stoically and ignored the danger. I fended the missile off with my shield.

"I have given you fair warning. Daffydd, rain death upon them."

My squires stood with their shields as a wall before the archers. My men did not loose them over the wall blindly; that would come later. Instead, they used a flat trajectory. The warrior who had thrown the spear was hurled back into the fort with an arrow in his face. Those with shields quickly brought them up while those without ducked behind the walls.

I dismounted and, taking my mace, headed with my equites, for the crudely made gate. I heard shouts as they spied what we intended. However, knowing what we were about and stopping us were two entirely different matters. Every time a head appeared, or an arm to throw a missile, an arrow sped towards them and found flesh. Gawan and Pol were next to me with Bors. We lifted our metal maces, Bors had an axe and we struck the gate. It shivered and cracks appeared. We struck a second blow and this time I saw daylight as parts of the gate cracked and fell away.

Kay said, "Stand aside, Warlord!"

We stood aside putting our maces in our left hands so that we could draw our swords and Kay, along with three other equites, hurled themselves at the gate. It shattered asunder. We ran in after them. The men of Northumbria did not know what had hit them as eight warriors encased wholly in mail burst in. None of the brigands had armour of their own although a few had helmets. The first five were slain almost contemptuously. Then Athelhere, I guessed it was him, shouted, "Shield wall!" and they hurriedly formed three ranks with locked shields and bristling with spears. It usually worked but not when fighting the Wolf Brethren.

We locked our own shields and stepped forward. The spears jabbed and poked at us. Even had they struck us they would not have penetrated our mail. We hacked the heads from the spears or chopped them in two. A stick is not a good weapon with which to defend yourself. Once the shield wall had lost its defences we stepped back and I shouted, "Charge!"

With our own shields locked and swords held before us, it was our turn to push at the shield wall. As we reached them we punched with our left hands and the Saxon wall reeled. As it did so gaps appeared. I saw flesh and I pushed my sword towards it. It grated off wood and then slid into soft flesh. I pushed harder and twisted. I heard a scream and I moved Saxon Slayer sideways. Then I ripped the blade backwards. The wriggling worms of someone's guts came with the sword.

The man fell and his shield with him. Kay and Bors had killed others as had Pol. A shield wall is only effective if it is not broken. All that they had left with which to fight were their seaxes. A short sword, it was crudely made and when I slashed at the warrior who attacked me I broke his seax in two. He looked in amazement and then his life ended as I ripped my sword across his throat. My archers poured into the fort behind us and arrows flew over our heads to strike those who fled.

Athelhere did not flee. He had a short byrnie and a full-face helmet. He took his sword and ran towards me. He was brave. I braced myself for the impact. With my left leg forward I was well balanced. He went for my head. I raised the shield and his sword smashed into the centre. My shield shivered but it had padding on the inside. I had my sword behind me and I punched forward as I stepped onto my right leg. He flicked his shield to deflect my sword but my movement forward had caught him off balance. He hurriedly stepped back. I brought my sword diagonally over my head to strike at his sword arm. He was forced to block the strike with his own sword and I punched him in the right side with my shield.

As he began to fall I brought my sword down and ripped it across his leg. He wore only leggings and I saw the bright red blood on my blade. He swung his sword at me. Instead of using my shield I stepped forward and turned away from the strike. With his injured leg, he could not move as quickly. I brought my sword around in a wide sweep and caught the edge of his shield. It began to split. There was no metal edge to protect it. I twisted as I pulled out my sword and a large splinter of wood came with it. Even as he tried to adjust his feet I hit his shield with mine. Another long splinter came from the shield. It was now a thick piece of wood only. Feinting towards his shield I spun around in a complete circle and slashed my sword across his back. His mail was as poor as his shield and the mail links tore as though they were not even there. Saxon Slayer bit into his back and more blood spurted. Then it cracked and ripped across his spine. His back arched and he fell to the floor. He shook and he shivered and then he lay dead.

I raised my sword, "Saxon Slayer!"
My men began to chant, "Warlord" Warlord! Warlord!"
We had won.

Chapter 2

I decided there was little point in heading back to our camp. It was late and we had the Saxon bodies to deal with. The other reason was the fact that Roman forts always had treasures buried somewhere. My father had been the first to discover this and, so far, we had found them at every deserted fort or villa. The Saxons rarely seemed to bother looking, surprisingly, but we had learned that they could yield valuable items and useful information. It was how my father had come by Saxon slayer when he was but a boy. Myrddyn had reasoned that he had been meant to find it; it was *wyrd*. First, we burned the Saxon bodies on the opposite side of the road. The wind took the smell and the smoke northwards. While Geraint and his men found us food I shed my mail and explored the fort.

I saw evidence that, at one time, men of Rheged had used it. I saw the marks they had made in the stone to show their passing. However, the crudely made gate and the general condition of the fort told me that it had been some years since then. We had no prisoners and so I could not discover how long this band had been here. Gawan, Pol, Lann Aelle and I went to the Praetorium. At the main office of the fort, there was always a stone disguising the entry to the cellar which was used to store the valuables and money. Sometimes we found writings there too and they were as valuable as gold.

The floor was covered in a patina of dust. I used a pail of water to wash it away. When the water seeped away I knew we had found the entrance. I took the seax I had taken from the Gesith and ran it around the large slab where the water had gone. When we had gouged out sufficient dirt and detritus the three of us put our blades under the edge and began to lever it up. At first, it appeared as though it would not move but suddenly it gave way. A smell of dampness and decay rose to greet us.

"Fetch a brand!"

We lifted the stone out of the way and Pelas brought a burning torch. As soon as the torch came closer we could see that this was not a deep cellar.

"Pelas, drop into the hole. I will light it for you. Lift out any chests, boxes, or weapons you may find."

He dropped down and backed away from the entrance so that he could see what was there. He moved around so that he saw everything within. He reached in and began to lift out the contents. One small chest emerged followed by a large one which took two of us to pull out for it was almost as large as the hole. Then he brought out more treasure; he found rotted bags of caltrops. The deadly spiked traps were as valuable as gold. He brought out handful after handful. Finally, he manhandled a long wooden box to the hole and we hauled it out. When we prised it open we found it contained the nails the Romans used for the caligae they wore on their feet.

"Anything left down there?"

Pelas shook his head, "Just the bones of some dead animals. There is a hole. I think that this is a rat's nest."

"The rats can now have their home back. Llewellyn, find something to put these caltrops in."

I opened the smaller chest first. It contained coins. Most were silver but there were some golden ones in there too. Kay had come over and he rubbed his hands, "If there are those coins in the smaller chest then the larger one will be filled with riches indeed."

"Do not be too sure, Kay."

We broke the lock and opened the chest. To Kay's disappointment, it contained calfskin vellum. It was fortunate that the rats had not eaten through the chest or it would have been lost. We took them out one by one. At the bottom were twenty large gold coins. They were the largest I had ever seen. I recognised the face of the Emperor. They were from the time of Antoninus Pius. He had succeeded Hadrian and I guessed that he had been responsible for the erection of this fort.

The light was fading. "We will read these parchments on the morrow but this has been a good haul." Gawan was thoughtful as we repacked the chests. "What is it little brother? Do the spirits and the gods speak with you?"

He shook his head, "No, brother, Myrddyn. When I picked the parchments up I heard his voice inside my head and I felt my fingers tingle. He is here." He waved a hand around. He did not mean in the fort but in Rheged somewhere.

Wyrd.

Men were not surprised but they were pleased. Like me, they knew the value of our wizard. He was as useful to us as Saxon Slayer. Both Gawan and I were tempted to read the parchments but the firelight would not have been good enough. We would be patient and we would wait.

Pol asked as we ate the sheep which Geraint and his men had recovered, "Does this mean that Myrddyn is dead then and Gawan senses his spirit?"

"Not necessarily. He may well be alive. He could even be close by. I did not sense a dead spirit just the spirit of Myrddyn. He will reveal himself when the time is right."

We rose early for the wind blew from the north again and brought flurries of snow. We were also kept awake by the howling of wolves to the south. We headed back to our camp almost before the sun had risen. As we rode down the Roman Road I found myself looking around. Was Myrddyn watching us? I would not put it past the old man. He had told me that he had dreamed his own death just as he had dreamed my father's. His time was coming to an end but I was certain that he would say goodbye before he left us.

The squires were relieved to see us. The howling wolves had been closer to them than to us. I could not wait to open the parchments. Pol joined Gawan and me as we did so. The first was a map. It showed the roads the Romans had built north of the wall. I had never been any further north than Din Guardi and that had been many years since. My father had been with Myrddyn when they had slain the King who had betrayed King Urien. I was not certain how useful it was but I would hold on to it. All of the rest of the parchments save one were of most interest to Gawan. They were cures for ailments and procedures to heal wounds.

He smiled at me. "This is how I know Myrddyn is near. This is the sort of information he would like. This is the greatest treasure we have found."

I unrolled the last parchment. It was not like the others, it was not on calfskin but it was more fragile. A piece cracked off it as I unrolled it. There were no words on it for it was a map but there was a drawing of a Roman eagle and the number IX could be discerned. It was in the middle of the land. Nor were there any place names but I recognised the crenulated line which I took to be the wall for it went from coast to coast. As soon as I saw that I worked out that the map showed the lands of the Picts, and the barbarians and the picture of the Roman eagle was at the heart of it.

Suddenly Pol reached over and jabbed at the eagle with his finger. "Did we not hear a story, when we were in Constantinopolis, about a Roman legion which disappeared north of the wall and their eagle was never recovered? This must be it."

Gawan opened the other map, the one we had first opened, "And this shows the roads. If we put the two together we can work out how to find the eagle."

I shook my head, "Why would we do that? It is not made of gold and there is no treasure connected with it."

Gawan said, "But brother, we were meant to find it. This is *wyrd*! Surely you can see that. No one else would have made the connection but us."

"Perhaps but we have too few men and the journey would take longer than we have. We will keep the maps and keep the secret, we have more important things to do."

I, too, was intrigued but I had more responsibility now. I was no longer the young equite who could have an adventure and not worry about the outcome. I had a tenuous hold on parts of Rheged and that was my first responsibility. I thought that we had a month at most before we had to return to King Cadwallon. We had only just begun to explore this land.

We headed south in four columns. This time we did take spears for if we had to hunt men in the forests then it was a better weapon. I spread the archers amongst the four columns and once more I took Tadgh with me. I impressed upon our men the need to hunt down brigands and bandits as well as the need to find if our people still lived in this land. My column headed down the valley with the long stretch of water. My uncle Raibeart had lived there. The mountain which towered over it was called Halvelyn. We found a few of the people of Rheged who still eked out a living. It was only when they heard the dragon banner that they emerged, nervously, from their holes.

They knelt when they saw me, "The Warlord has returned! The prophecy is true. Now the land will grow and evil will be driven from the forests."

"Evil?"

"Aye Warlord." The headman pointed to the mountain. "The wolves take our animals and the Irish come and take our children for slaves. Each year there are fewer of us."

I turned to my men. "Then we can rid them of one evil and we can do it now! We hunt the wolves!"

The headman said, "Hunt the wolves? They are fierce, Warlord. All who have tried have failed."

"Then we shall have to be the first to succeed." I dismounted, "Take care of our horses." I slung my shield and my helmet on the saddle and hefted my spear.

The headman said, "You will hunt in mail?"

I laughed, "I hunt men in mail. Should I show less respect to a wolf?" I turned to Llewellyn who held my standard. "You stay here with the horses. If more of the equites come, then have them follow us." He nodded, "Tadgh, use your nose!"

My scout scurried up the slope closely followed by my archers. My equites and I would struggle to keep up with them for we wore mail but I knew that the archers would not attack the wolves if we found them before I reached them. Gawan and Pelas walked close to me. The lower slopes were relatively gentle and the track was broad. It gave us the chance to look at the mountain. The wolves would not be close to the top. There was a tarn halfway up and beyond that there were no caves in which they could hide. They would be between us and the tarn. We also had a forest to negotiate. It ended well before the tarn but that too would be a treacherous place and one which the wolves might well use to ambush us.

I had rarely hunted wolves but those who had told me that they hunted like men. They worked together to bring down their prey and they cared not if that prey was a man. We were the wolf brethren and it was fitting that we should hunt the mighty beast. If the wolves were strong enough to take animals from farms, then they were bold and there were too many of them. The hunt was a good thing.

Soon the track became steeper and narrower. We approached trees and had to walk in single file. Our scout and archers began to mark the trail once we entered the forest. They were all expert hunters and they knew what to look for. The wolves might be careless this close to man but the closer we came to their home the more dangerous it would become. We twisted and turned through the trees. We had long since left any trail made by man. We were following animal tracks and trails.

Suddenly my archers appeared from behind some trees. I had no idea they were there.

"Warlord, they are close. Tadgh has crept ahead to spy them out. There is a cluster of rocks and we saw the shape of a wolf which was on guard. I fear they may know we are here."

"Then let us ready ourselves. Knock an arrow." I put my spear in two hands. All but the archers copied me. Pelas and Gawan were inexperienced. Osgar was only a little older than Gawan. I would be reliant upon my archers. The problem with that was that, while a spear could easily make a mortal strike, you had to be lucky for an arrow to do the same. A wolf's skull was hard!

Tadgh rushed down the slope and skittered to a halt. "Warlord I have found the den. It is in the rocks yonder but they know we are here. They come to hunt us."

Gawan said, "They will follow your trail here."

I looked at my brother in amazement. How did he know that? It did, however, give me an idea. "Then we make these trees our castle. Tadgh, you and the archers stand behind us. We will be a wall before you. Keep releasing arrows until they are dead or driven off." As they did so I took Saxon Slayer and jammed it into the earth so that I could get it in a hurry. I braced my spear against my foot and held it in two hands. I said quietly, "The danger comes if they get behind us. Pelas watch and let me know if they do."

And then we waited. It was nerve-wracking for we could all smell them but we could neither see nor hear them. I had heard that this was the time of year when they raised their young and the best chance to hunt them for they could not smell as well when the weather was cold. This would be a good test of that theory. I wondered if we had misjudged them until I caught a glimpse of an ear. It was less than thirty paces from us. There was not enough to see for an arrow to hit.

I heard a creak as Tadgh pulled back on his bow. I wondered what he had seen. There was a crack as he released his arrow. It went high. I heard a yelp as it landed. He had been clever. He had released blindly and his aim had been aided by the gods. He whispered to the archers. "On three all release an arrow into the air. Aim behind those rocks. That is where they are hiding." I heard the creak of bows and then Tadgh said, "One, two, three!"

The five arrows soared high and then they struck. We knew they had struck because the pack leapt from cover and headed for us. Had we had poorer archers then we might have been in trouble but they were all good bowmen and they quickly knocked another arrow and this time each took a target. It was our turn to be worried for there were just four of us and the wolves looked even larger and more numerous than I had expected. The arrows struck the animals but the wolves came on. It was tempting to hurl the spear but that would have been a waste. A huge male leapt at me. I raised the spear head slightly while still bracing it against my foot. I saw arrows protruding from its body but none were mortal. I chose my moment and thrust at his chest with my spear. I must have found his heart for there was a sudden eruption of blood and life left his eyes. The weight of his body and the slope pushed me down a little. Had I not braced myself I would have fallen beneath the carcass.

I had no time to congratulate myself for there were still more wolves. I took my sword and, holding it in two hands, brought it down on the neck of the wolf which was trying to get to Pelas. I had no spear before me and a female wolf leapt up at me. I stabbed at her. I struck the beast in the chest but missed the heart and I was knocked backwards. Her mouth opened wide for vicious teeth to fasten on my throat. I released my sword which was trapped beneath its body and put my mailed mitten into the gaping mouth. I pushed hard towards the throat hoping to make the wolf gag. It began to close its jaws on it and I felt pain such as I had never felt before. I rammed the fingers of my left hand into its eye and ripped it out. It yelped in pain and the grip on my arm lessened. I kept pushing at its head and pulling with my right hand. We rolled over and, as I did so I managed to take out my dagger and rip it across her throat.

Another wolf was in the act of leaping. I grabbed my sword and swung it sideways in the hope of making it flinch. The gods must have guided my hand for it tore across the side of the wolf's neck and half severed his head. The last few animals turned and ran for there were seven dead wolves. Three others limped off to their den. I slumped to the ground and took off my mail mitten. Gawan ran to my side. "Tadgh, you and the archers pursue the wolves! Pelas, get water. My brother is wounded."

"It is nothing. A bite that is all."

"A bite from a wolf! Let us look at it." He peeled back the mitten. The wolf's teeth had driven the mail into my hand causing lacerations but they had not pierced the flesh. The wolf's spirit would not take over my mind. When Gawan saw that the flesh had been punctured by mail and not the wolf's teeth he smiled and confirmed my thoughts. "You will not be turning into a wolf at any rate."

In the distance, we heard howls, snarls and then yelps.

"You do not believe that do you Gawan?"

"Myrddyn told me of shape shifters. Warriors who can become a beast. It is sometimes a bear and sometimes a wolf. We need a warlord who is a wolf warrior, not an actual wolf!"

My brother treated and bandaged my hand. My archers returned wiping their swords. Tadgh said, "We finished off the three who were wounded. They bought time for the others to escape. They were mothers and cubs. An old male led them. From their tracks, they were heading into the next valley. I think these folk are safe. The cubs will take time to grow; until then they are not a danger."

"Then when we return we will scour the land of these wolves and make it safe for our people. Put the dead beasts on spears. Their meat will feed the people and the skins will come in handy too."

I spurned Gawan's attempts to fashion me a sling and helped him to carry the largest male down the mountain. My shoulder was red and raw by the time we reached the village. There was a great celebration when we arrived. As the evening was coming on we stayed with the people. They were grateful as the presence of so many armed men made them secure. It was as we sat around their fire that I realised I needed to return to Rheged. I now knew that Myrddyn had sent me the dreams. I was meant to return to Rheged; it was *wyrd*.

We offered the villagers all of the wolf skins but the headman, Dargh, said that it was right that the largest two should be given to us for we had hunted them. I took one and gave it to my brother. The fur was black and there were small flecks of white and grey. It seemed like an animal version of me. When it was cured and cleaned it would make a fine cloak. The land of Rheged was cold.

We rode down the valley and over the col to the next valley. Here was where my uncle, Aelle, had lived. His fort by the river was burned for it had been made of wood. The Saxons had destroyed it. We had taken ships down the water when we had escaped the Northumbrians. We met groups of farmers who tended flocks on the slopes of the hills, fished in the rich water and grew crops by the rivers. I told all that we would be returning. What they wished to know and what I could not tell them was when that would be. We headed back up the valley of the small waters and returned to our camp by dark. It gave me time to wonder when King Cadwallon would say '*enough*'. I wondered if success over Edwin had changed him. Since the death of his wife, my sister, he appeared to have become a different king. Perhaps the death of my family had changed me too. It was hard to say. I was looking out. Others looking in would have a better idea.

By the time we left to return to Eoforwic, we had explored the whole of Rheged south of the river. We had hunted and killed the few bandits who remained but it seemed that the first band had been the only danger. There were no more men of Northumbria to hunt and with Edwin dead, I doubted that they would be a danger to the folk who lived there. All the headmen we spoke to were given weapons we had taken from their enemies. We told them how to make their homes stronger and I promised to return. It was hard to leave but I was still the vassal of King Cadwallon and I was sworn to obey him. So long as he lived I obeyed.

It was as we were passing Stanwyck that I asked Gawan what had been on my mind since we had hunted the wolves. "Have I changed Gawan?"

He looked at me, "Aye, brother, as we all change. We grow older and wiser."

"That is not what I mean and you know it for you read my thoughts."

He lowered his voice, "You mean have you changed as King Cadwallon has? Has your nature changed?" I nodded. "Perhaps King Cadwallon has become a shape shifter. He has changed and I know him not now. He has become greedier. The wolf hunts for food but the fox will hunt for pleasure and leave a carcass. You are a wolf but perhaps the King has become a fox."

"I asked about me and not our King."

Gawan's face became sad, "I get no pleasure from telling you this but you know I have the gift. I have it from my mother and Myrddyn nurtured it. I see into the King's heart. We began this war to stop King Edwin. We joined with King Penda to achieve that end but the Mercians returned home for they saw that we had done that. Why do we stay? We both know that his warriors have despoiled women and more. Answer me honestly, brother. Could you have stayed longer?"

I stared ahead at the walls of the city which loomed up across the vale. I said quietly, "You are right. Perhaps my father would have handled it differently. It may be that I am at fault."

"Our father would have handled it differently but that does not mean that you had done anything wrong. Our father was a father to the King. You are like a brother and that is different. In your heart, you know that. Remember Morcar!"

He was right. My father had been slain by my cousin, his nephew. I had to trust the gods and the spirits. They were guiding my destiny. I would follow the King and see where it led.

Chapter 3

"Warlord, Most excellent news. Edwin's cousin, Osric, has claimed Deira and he marches here to make war on us. He comes here to fight us! We need not stir. He will batter against our walls and when he has exhausted himself then we can destroy him and Deira will become ours."

"But my liege, we have horses within these walls. Let us meet him on the plain. There we can rout him."

He laughed. "And I thought that you were the strategos. Perhaps you are losing your powers, Warlord. If we let him spend his strength attacking these walls, then we have fewer men to fight and our victory would be guaranteed."

I saw his men nodding. This was their decision. I was about to continue arguing when I caught the subtlest of shakes of the head from Gawan. He had read my thoughts. I bowed, "Perhaps I am tired after our journey. I bow to your majesty's opinion."

"Good!"

Later when Gawan and I were alone in our quarters he said, "I had to stop you brother. You are right but had you argued then it would have driven a wedge between you and the King. That cannot happen."

"Why, what have you seen?"

"When we were in Rheged after I felt the presence of Myrddyn, I saw victory for the King but it does not bring joy for I have dreamed and seen the land between here and Ynys Môn. Carrion beasts are feasting on the dead; the army of King Cadwallon." He shook his head. "These Roman walls seem like a barrier. We are back here and my mind is a fog. I no longer think clearly."

Gawan was careful with his predictions. If he predicted thus then it would come to pass. The question remained, when?

I put those dark thoughts from my mind as we threw ourselves into preparations for war. Osric was coming from the north and the rich fertile lands of the valley of the Dunum. Our scouts reported that he had a large army. King Cadwallon was very confident for we had men who had rested all winter and who had not been beaten. Osric would be facing a successful army. In addition, the King of Deira had made the mistake of attacking a walled city.

King Cadwallon had his own scouts who were watching the approaching army. I sent Geraint to ascertain the numbers. I feared that they might not actually attack the city but cause chaos and mayhem in the lands about us. It was Gawan who used his other powers, his brain. Even though his connection with the spirit world was broken he could still think quicker than any man I knew. "Brother, he will not cause chaos for we are in his land. He marches here to rid the land of the invader and to enjoy the riches and the power which this city brings. King Cadwallon is correct. They will attack here. Like you, I think it is a mistake but attack he will. He will not harm the people but enlist them to fight for him."

My brother was the more thoughtful of us. He got that from his mother who had been something of a seer and sorceress. With the absence of Myrddyn, I was relying upon him more and more.

We would be fighting from the walls and that necessitated different strategies and weapons. I went with Pol, Gawan and the King to the porta principalis dextra, the northern gate. This would be the place where the men of Deira would attack. We stood above the gate. This was the heart of the old Roman fortress and the strongest of all of the gates. The river protected the flank to the southwest. If Osric had ships, then we might be in trouble but he would have had to approach from the southeast and navigate from the coast to do so. We ruled that out immediately.

There was a second gate less than three hundred paces to the northeast. That too was protected by a river, the Fosse. The attack, when it came would have to come across a thousand paces of our walls. We could easily man that section and stop any Saxons from climbing our walls.

I turned to the King. "Osric must be desperate if he is willing to risk all in such an attack."

The King said, quietly, "He is. We have had emissaries from King Eanfrith of Bernicia. He is willing to make peace if we allow him to have the land of Deira."

"He would be a vassal king?"

King Cadwallon nodded, "He is. It seems Aethelfrith's other sons are still taking refuge with King Raedwald of the East Angles. Eanfrith has taken upon himself to claim at least half of his father's throne."

It was Oswald, one of Aethelfrith's other sons, who was the real threat and so long as he was many miles away then his brother, Eanfrith, would try to establish himself as the legitimate King of Northumbria. It would be worth being a vassal king to achieve that end.

"Then we just have to hold Osric and his men?"

I shook my head, "No, Gawan. We can destroy them. We allow them to bleed on our walls and then when they are weakened we use our horsemen to drive them hence."

King Cadwallon did not look as though he approved, "Why risk our men? Our enemies will waste away."

"And while they waste away we are here far from your home. Who knows what mischief your enemies might get up to. When we visited Rheged there were Irish raiders there. If they visit your home while we are here, then it is our people who will suffer."

"You are right. We will end this quickly then. I leave the attack for you to plan." He smiled, "You are the Warlord."

"Of course, your majesty."

The scouts reported the enemy less than half a day away. The gates to the northwest and northeast were barred and the ditch filled with stakes covered with animal and human dung. Any who suffered a wound would find themselves having a long and painful death. There was little point having our equites upon the walls and I made sure my equites and those of King Cadwallon rested while they could. When they charged the enemy, they would need all of their strength. Instead, we used our archers, our squires and the many foot soldiers whom King Cadwallon had brought north to man the walls. The two walls were filled so that there was but the length of a forearm between each man. Each man had a shield, even the archers, and I was confident.

The last of the scouts returned and were sent downstream to enter by the southern gates. Until we decided to attack the gate would remain closed. The Saxons arrived piecemeal. They too had lightly armed scouts on ponies and they came to within bow range. We withheld from releasing. There was little point in wasting arrows on scouts. They would not be the ones who would be assaulting the walls.

Next came the Ceorls each led by their Gesith. There were many of these. They were small bands of men and they would all come from one town or village. The men had little or no armour. Some were lucky enough to have a helmet and only one or two had shields. The armour and weapons of their Gesith varied considerably. I saw one with a fine full hauberk, coif and full-face helmet. His men, too, were well-armed and armoured. The majority, however, had just a shield, a sword and a helmet. If they had armour, then it was a leather cuirass in the style of the Romans.

When we saw the hearthweru we knew that the King was coming. These were the bodyguard of the king. They each wore a hauberk of mail. Some had axes and all had a large round shield. Twenty of them came on foot and another twenty, along with the King and his standard, came on horses. Finally, we saw the fyrd. They were like a sea. They spread out behind the banners and hearthweru. None of them had either armour or a helmet. A few had a seax but all had a weapon of some description. They gave the numbers which Osric needed to attack. The ceorls would feel reassured by the presence of so many men. I knew it was an illusion. Better to have a few well-armed and well-trained men than a whole army of fyrdmen.

King Cadwallon was next to me. "I see neither siege engines nor rams."

Pol said, "I see ladders, Warlord!"

The King laughed scornfully, "If that is all that they have then they will never get out of the ditches!"

He was right but I worried that there might be some trick. I did not know this Osric. Aethelfrith's sons I knew. I had fought them before. I would judge later.

They ringed two sides of the city. Their fires burned in a large half-circle. Their men fished in the river and I saw others disappear to hunt. The animals they took would be those of Northumbrians. They would not hurt us. While the King celebrated the paucity of numbers and caroused until late, my men and I retired. We would celebrate when we won. Until then we would be like the Spartans. We would think of only one thing, war.

We rose before dawn. I went to the kitchens and ordered that cauldrons of water be boiled. Then I went to the walls. Some of our men were already on the walls having taken over as sentries. Pol, Gawan and I joined them as we watched the pinpricks of light which were the fires of the men of Deira.

"I am not impressed by this Osric, Warlord, I would have attacked at night."

"King Osric, Pol, unlike you, may not have enjoyed a visit to Constantinopolis where he could have read of different strategies and methods of scaling walls. Had he done so he might have had engines of war built."

Gawan nodded, "Of course, our father would probably have used cunning. We have a river running through the city. It would have been easy enough to use rafts to get men through during the night. Then they might have climbed into the city and opened a gate."

My younger brother was right. Although there were just four large gates there were other smaller ones. This Osric was no Alexander the Great. He was attacking from the most difficult side. He had, at least, prepared some large shields behind which his archers could shelter. I was not worried for Saxon archers were notoriously poor. A bigger danger was the men with axes. They could, if we allowed them, break down the huge gates. First, they had to breach the ditch for we had removed the wooden bridge over the ditch.

Dai had been King Cadfan's squire and he now commanded King Cadwallon's men. He walked over to join me. He looked at me, "When do we release our arrows Warlord?"

"When we see a target. There is little point in wasting arrows and, at the moment they are doing us no harm." I walked to the other side of the gate where Daffydd ap Miach stood. "Use your best archers to hit any of their bowmen. They are poor archers but they are the best they have got. When they are dead then our enemies will have to try the walls and then we can begin to slaughter them."

I carried my shield and held it close to me but none of us was troubled by the Saxon arrows. They were poorly made and fletched. Saxons made good swords but their arrow heads were carelessly produced. The bows they used were not as powerful as ours. Soon the bow men began to fall to the arrows of my archers. By mid-morning, the attack of the arrows had ended. I saw the King consult with his chiefs and, after a short time, the Ceorls, led by their Gesith moved forward behind the large shields. They carried their ladders. They did not worry me but the hearthweru wedge which followed did. Their armour and their shields would prevent our archers from harming them.

I turned to Dai. "Have your archers release their arrows. The Gesith are the ones who present the danger. If they fall then their Ceorls may well lose heart. Have the boiling water brought to this gate."

"What of the hearthweru?"

"They are armoured and the arrows will be wasted. Daffydd and my archers will strike any that are vulnerable."

The men of Deira had courage. Despite losing men they came forward. King Osric had decided not to attack both gates. He would see that there was little point. He needed to use all of his men to break down this main gate and hope his hearthweru would secure victory.

The men charged with bringing the cauldrons of boiling water laced with pig fat struggled up the stairs. The poles which ran through the rings at the sides stopped them from being burned. They placed them at regular intervals above the gate. We already had a flat piece of wood on a log so that they could be tipped over when the time was right. Two Gesith had been wounded and withdrew with their ceorls but another five had advanced to the ditch. When they laid down their protective boards to make an improvised bridge then more of them fell as King Cadwallon's archers found flesh.

The hearthweru came on behind and halted at the improvised bridges. The ceorls placed their ladders at the walls and the Gesith led the climb to the walls. It was harder for the archers to hit the climbing men and the squires began to hurl javelins at the climbing Saxons. It was then the hearthweru ran at the gate. They were a solid phalanx of men, well protected by shields, helmets and armour. They made it to the gate unharmed. I heard the axes as they began to hack at the wooden gate.

"Now!"

The two cauldrons in the centre of the gate were tipped and a moment or two later the remaining cauldrons followed. The combination of boiling water and pig fat cascaded over those at the gate. As they recoiled from the scalding mix the second flood struck them. The liquid found its way through their mail onto their skin and it burned. They could not rid themselves of the liquid and their flesh bubbled and burned. It blistered and it seared. My squires hurled rocks at them. It was too much even for hearthweru and they fled. The Gesith and their ceorls joined them and ran back to the safety of their own lines. Their first attack had failed.

I looked over the walls. Only one hearthweru had died but I saw twenty ceorls. Those who were not already dead would have succumbed to their wounds by nightfall. The men on the walls all cheered. It was not victory but it was first blood. We had not damaged their army overmuch but we had dampened their resolve.

I turned and shouted, "One man in two get food and rest until you hear the horn sound then relieve those on the walls."

"Aye, Warlord."

King Cadwallon said, "Are they not beaten yet, Warlord?"

"No, your majesty. We have hurt them and they have learned, to their cost, that we have archers. They will come tonight. In the dark, they can get closer before our archers can see them and they can attack on a broader front." I pointed to the bridge they had thrown over the ditch and the ladders lying on the ground. "They will use more of those wooden bridges and they will use more of their men. Tonight, we man the walls with all of our men and I will choose a band of equites. We will sortie forth when I judge the time right. We need to whittle down the hearthweru. The only way to do that is sword to sword."

I left Dai to command the walls. I was confident that they would need some time to lick their wounds. "Pol we will use my brother, Llenlleog, Lann Aelle, Kay, Bors and yourself from my equites. The rest can come from King Cadwallon."

"Why so few of our equites?"

"When King Cadwallon defeats the north and returns to his home he can train more equites. How will we replace any who fall?"

My words sank in. We were a dying breed. We had no sons now to follow us and the people of the west were farmers and not warriors. We could not stop the flood of Saxons; we could only stem it, albeit briefly. Ours would be the last flame of Rome burning in this northern land. As I went to prepare for battle I wondered where Myrddyn was. I needed his advice. My brother had skills but Myrddyn had been sent by the gods to save Britannia. I could not do it with Saxon Slayer alone.

I gathered the twenty-five equites we would use just before dusk. I gathered them at the gate. "We make a shield wall five men wide and five men deep. I will lead with four of my equites. Gawan will be in the rear rank in case I fall. Our aim is to kill as many hearthweru as we can. When I give the command to fall back then we do so." I looked at each of the nineteen equites Dai had selected. "We cannot carry back wounded men. I know that we are used to fighting on horseback but tonight we show these Saxons that even their best warriors are no match for us."

They banged their shields. I knew that the sound would carry to the Saxon camp and they would wonder what it betokened.

I joined the King and his leaders on the wall. "Majesty I will have to judge this well or we could lose the walls. We want the hearthweru and the ceorls to attack the walls this time. We have made them wary of the gate. I will lead the equites and attack the hearthweru who are between here and the river. If you think we are in danger of being surrounded, then have Llewellyn sound the horn three times."

"I will but why do you risk this attack? Surely we can let them bleed on our walls."

"We killed one of their best warriors, that is all. So long as the hearthweru remain undamaged then they will squat there like a toad. We destroy the hearthweru and then we destroy their army. Have most of our men sitting below the walls. Have just one man in six standing."

Gawan said, "Brother these are stone walls. If we build two fires here we can heat the water. It will be boiling when we pour it."

We had two cranes with which we had hauled stones up for us to throw down upon the attackers. This would save us having to haul boiling water from the kitchens. "Good, you are, indeed, like Myrddyn."

We soon had the fires built. They would be lit as soon as night came and the cauldrons and water readied for the attack I knew would come. Darkness fell and silence filled the air. That, in itself, was ominous. Osric should have had his men making their normal noise. He was gathering his men and preparing to attack. He would wait, I had no doubt until he thought we just had a few sentries. To encourage him I had torches burning on the walls. He would see how few there were. I envisaged him using his fyrd to crawl across the open ground towards the ditch. I peered into the darkness but could see nothing. They might even be at the ditch already. I was not wearing my helmet but I did have the wolf cloak about my shoulders. It hid my mail and made me harder to see. I would shed my skin before I attacked but, for the moment I was hidden from view.

Geraint and Tadgh were next to me. They were not only fine archers their scouting skills would come in handy. They both sniffed the air and, knocking an arrow Geraint pointed to the ditch. He could smell the Saxons. I nodded to Pelas and Llewellyn. They went along the wall tapping men on the shoulder to alert them. They prepared to stand. I left Osgar on the wall to keep me informed. Stones were already laid upon the two large wooden chutes which protruded from the walls. The water and oil were bubbling away. To the Saxons, the glow would have seemed like the braziers the sentries used to keep themselves warm.

I joined my men. We had axes and maces. The hearthweru would be so tightly packed and protected with mail and shield that a sword would not penetrate. We would use weapons which would smash bones and helmets. This was not a time for honour.

Osgar whistled down. I said, quietly, "They come."

I pictured them slithering across the ground. The fyrd, lightly armed and unencumbered, would come first followed by the hearthweru. The Gesith and the ceorls had been hurt the previous day. Osric would not risk them again in the front line. It was hard to wait unable to see the enemy. We had to trust to our men on the walls. Suddenly there was a roar as the fyrd crossed the bridges they had made over the ditch and the ladders slammed against the walls.

I heard Dai shout, "Now!" And there were screams as arrows struck flesh.

There was the sound of feet stamping across the bridge followed by the sound of axes slamming into the gate just two paces from our heads. It shivered and it shook. I yelled, "Water!" and a heartbeat later, "Stones!"

There was a series of screams and shouts as the hearthweru were doused in scalding oil and water and then a huge crash as the two mighty stones broke the bridge. Two squires lifted the bar and we pulled open the gates. The hearthweru were in disarray. Some were writhing on the ground. One had been crushed by a stone. I raised my mace and leapt at the nearest Saxon. I brought it down upon his head. It was my first blow and my pent-up anger was in the strike. It crushed the helmet and the top of his skull. Blood, bones and brains splattered the men next to him. Pol's mace smashed into the back of another hearthweru. I heard his spine as it cracked.

I quickly moved down the side of the wall. I was careful to avoid the ditch. One of the hearthweru who had escaped the deluge turned and rammed his spear at my middle. I brought my shield around and, stepping forward, swung my mace at his shield. I saw him recoil as my metal weapon, a gift from the Emperor of Rome, knocked him backwards. It was hard to pull back his spear for the wall to his right impeded him and I stepped forward again and hit his shield in the same place. I saw a crack appear in the wood and I knew from his face that I had broken his arm. The shield dropped a little. I stepped forward once more and this time feinted with my mace. He crouched and I swung my shield into his face. He lost his balance and tumbled into the spike filled ditch.

I saw ladders ahead of me. Warriors were being thrown from them. "Kay, Bors, with me!"

With my two warriors next to me, we made a human battering ram. We ran as fast as our armour would allow along the wall. Our weight was such that the ladders were knocked, one by one, into the ditch. Those who survived the fall were impaled upon stakes and spikes.

I heard a Saxon horn and the remnants of the attack tried to make their way back across the deadly ditch. I heard a cheer from the walls above and my name was chanted, "Warlord! Warlord! Warlord!"

We returned inside the walls despatching any wounded as we went. Their armour, treasure and weapons would be collected when daylight came. Then we would see the true extent of our victory!

Not all of the equites had survived the encounter. Two of King Cadwallon's men had fallen. As we had slain fifteen of our enemy it was considered a fair exchange. As dawn broke we saw that the ceorls and the fyrd's dead could be counted in dozens. Yet King Osric stayed north of the city determined, apparently, to gamble all on one victory.

We rested for the morning while the dead were cleared from our ditches. A pyre was built on the other side of the ditch and they were burned. The Saxons did not interfere. It was their dead whom we honoured. When I awoke King Cadwallon was in good humour. "We have beaten him back. What say we end this today? Attack his camp now while he licks his wounds?"

"A good idea, but the men who would lead the charge, the equites, need more rest. Let us make it in the morning."

He looked disappointed. "But why?"

"When we leave the city, we will have to lower the bridge over the ditch. They will see that and be prepared. If we put the bridges down while it is dark they will not see it. We leave silently before dawn and charge them when they are just waking. We can use two gates. If we use the equites and squires, then those on foot and the archers can follow us."

I think the fact that he could have a glorious charge convinced the King. "I will lead the charge from this gate, Warlord, you take your men from the north-eastern gate. That way we can employ a long line and drive them towards the river." He wanted the glory of leading the charge.

"A good plan, highness. Now I will prepare my men and our horses."

I sought out Daffydd. "I want our archers mounted and you will follow us in the charge. There is a piece of high ground to the east of their camp. They will have to pass it to escape. You and your archers can wait in ambush."

"Aye, Warlord."

"Pelas, you lead the squires."

"Me lord? You usually ask Llenlleog or Lann Aelle to lead them."

"That was in the days when we had twice the number that we have now. I need Llenlleog with the equites. This King Osric will not be easily defeated. If he did not have a backbone, he would have fled already. He will stay and he will fight. He gambles all on this battle. He will be King or he will be dead. I admire him for that."

We gathered behind the gate. It was open and the bridge had been placed over the ditch. I had impressed upon the King the need to make our attack together. A piecemeal attack would be a disaster. I watched the sky lighten in the east and I sent the messenger to the King. I put my heels into Star's side and led my men over the drawbridge. We could not help the noise that would be made by the hooves on the wood but the warning it gave our enemies would be minimal. I think we had the easier ride for none had fought on this piece of ground. I saw the King and his equites to our left. Llewellyn held the dragon banner. When we charged, its wail would strike fear into the hearts of our enemies.

King Cadwallon raised his sword. I unsheathed Saxon Slayer and did the same. As one the long line of armoured men rode forward towards the distant Saxon camp. Behind us was an even longer line of squires each of whom held three javelins. Following them was the great mass of Welshmen who fought on foot. I was confident that the equites would strike as one. We had fought side by side many times before. As we began to speed up the dragon began to wail and I heard the consternation in the Saxon camp. A sudden stab of light appeared from our right. Dawn was breaking and the red seemed ominously prophetic. The day was beginning in blood.

Their sentries saw the wall of horses and mail coming towards them and ran. These were the fyrd and with just a billhook for a weapon they stood no chance against mailed horsemen. There were brave ceorls who grabbed their shields, spears and helmets and tried to form a shield wall. They died well. I leaned forward to swing my sword like a scythe at harvest time. I sliced through spears and into the chests of warriors who, a short while ago, had been asleep. We swept them away and then I saw the hearthweru.

They had not been caught out. They had slept in their mail and they had a shield wall with King Osric and his standard in their midst. The last two days had whittled down their numbers but not their spirit. They were oathsworn and they would die as such. Pelas and the squires would pursue the Gesith and their ceorls. My archers would slaughter the fyrd. It was the line of equites, the best that we had, who would face the hearthweru, the best that the Saxons had. My equites rode closer to me than those of the King. It was just the way we trained. Pol's boot touched my left foot and Llewellyn my right. Our horses would not run into the shield wall they would turn. The secret was to turn the correct way at the same time. As one we swung to our right to allow us to use our shields as offensive weapons. We smashed them into the spears which were jabbed at us. The hearthweru would have been better to strike at our horses but they wanted us dead. A spear jabbed into my splint greaves and the spear was torn from the warrior's hand.

We continued around the end of the line and then, as I raised my sword, we wheeled to the left. The manoeuvre took the circle of mailed warriors by surprise. As a spear was thrust at me I grabbed it with my mailed mitten and pulled. The warrior should have let go but he did not and Saxon Slayer plunged into his throat. A shield wall is only effective if it is continuous. This had started with just one line of warriors. I had broken it and I thrust Star into the middle of that circle, trampling over the dead hearthweru. I swept my sword around to slice through the neck of the warrior who was trying to spear Llewellyn. Pol hacked through the helmet and skull of a third hearthweru and the whole of one side of the shield wall collapsed. We had height and we had swords.

The battle degenerated into a series of individual combats. I saw, on the other side, King Cadwallon fighting with King Osric.

It was fitting that the two of them should decide this battle for Deira. The warriors we fought knew that they were dead men walking and all died well. Most shed their spears to die, as a warrior should, with a sword in his hand. They lasted a few strokes only for we outnumbered them. When King Cadwallon used his longer sword and longer reach to take Osric's head it was all over and we had won. Deira was ours and its king was dead.

Chapter 4

The squires and the archers pursued the survivors until their horses were too tired to run. Geraint and his scouts established that no other army remained in Deira. King Cadwallon could not believe our victory.

"There is just Bernicia to defeat and then your father's dream shall become a reality. Northumbria will be Saxon no longer."

I knew that my father had hoped for such a thing but the people we had defeated were Saxons and they had Saxon families. Northumbria could never be Rheged again for there would be none with Rheged blood in their veins. The Angles had taken them all. I was in a dilemma. If I did not pursue the aims of King Cadwallon then I would be letting down my father. However, I knew that, if my father were still alive, he might have changed his ideas. On the other hand, a defeated Northumbria would make Rheged more secure.

I bowed, "It will indeed, King Cadwallon."

I left the King to celebrate with his men. It was right that he did so for it was a great victory. I made the excuse that I had to see to my men. It was not a lie. I went to find Gawan who was healing the injuries of those who had been wounded. I spoke with all the warriors who had been hurt. There were more than I would have liked. With but twenty equites and twenty squires then any loss would be felt.

Gawan followed me out, "You are troubled, brother." I nodded and waited. "You are right, father would not wish Northumbria to be part of Rheged once more. In the time of Morcant Bulc it was Bernicia. It was never Rheged and father was never one to conquer for the sake of conquest. Nor, I believe, was King Urien."

"And what of your vision? The King lives and prospers."

"And he is not yet back in Wrecsam. I have dreamed of an empty palace." He smiled. "I must confess I dream better when I am close to Wyddfa but my powers are growing."

"Then be as Myrddyn and advise me. What do I do?"

"It is not in either of our hands. *Wyrd* will decide what is to follow. You are Warlord and you must obey the King. You make sure that there is no threat to Rheged." He shook his head, sadly, "Neither of us has a family. The men we lead are now our family. We care for them."

My young brother was right. He might be much younger than I was but his wisdom had grown. In comparison, I felt like a dolt. With Saxon Slayer in my hand then I knew what to do. My judgement had, otherwise, sometimes let me down. I still wondered if I could have saved our father's life.

"Brother our father had to die. He was the sacrifice which gave us the victory today. He would not have had it any other way."

I had long since stopped being surprised when my brother read my mind. It was reassuring in a way. I could hide nothing from him and so long as he lived and rode by my side then there was a chance that the people of Rheged would survive.

It took some time for us to make sure that every Gesith submitted to the authority of the King. Some were not happy about having to do so but we made them swear. Some, like King Cadwallon himself, were now followers of the White Christ and they swore on the cross that their religion made much of. The ones who clung to the old ways swore by their gods. I felt that their oaths were more binding. To be fair to the men who called themselves Christians their oaths were kept just like those of the others but I had my prejudices.

Once the borders were secure I was summoned to King Cadwallon. There was just the King and Dai, who had been King Cadfan's squire and was now King Cadwallon's lieutenant, in the hall. I was asked to bring only Gawan. The King was seated at a table and a half-empty amphora of wine was upon it. He had drunk more heavily since his victory. Dai, in comparison, was as sharp-eyed as ever. The drink, however, did not seem to affect the King's speech or his mind.

"We have had a visit from an emissary from King Eanfrith of Bernicia. He is keen for an alliance and peace between us."

Dai nodded, "His army is small and weak. If we chose, then we could walk into Bernicia and take it."

"We could but would we be able to hold it, Dai son of Gruffyd? Mercia lies between this land and Gwynedd. How would we hold it?" I was still cautious. The men of Gwynedd seemed to have allowed the victory to give them delusions of grandeur.

The King said, "Perhaps we take Mercia too."

All three of us turned to look at the King to see if he was joking. His face told me he was not and I shook my head, "King Penda is a different prospect from Osric of Deira, King Cadwallon. We have fought alongside him and we both know that he is a good general with a powerful army. If he were an enemy then we might have to risk a war but he is a friend and his eyes look to his own enemy, Raedwald of the East Angles. You do not poke a wasp's nest. It cannot end well."

"Perhaps. However, one Saxon throne at a time. I wish you to travel to Din Guardi and meet with him. Discuss the terms for the alliance and then escort him here."

"You wish the treaty to be signed here?" He nodded, "Why not the Dunum? That is the boundary between Deira and Bernicia."

"I like this city. I am comfortable here. Besides, it is I who holds the upper hand. It will do him good to be humbled this way. He is a Christian and pride is a sin."

I did not say that King Cadwallon was also a Christian and his pride seemed to exceed that of Eanfrith. "When do I leave?"

"As soon as possible. I would have the peace made by harvest time. The land needs peace so that we can gather crops and animals for the winter."

I nodded. He was thinking like my old friend once more. The land had to be given time to heal. War damaged it, and with peace, it prospered. "I will take Gawan and nine of my equites. Some of my men were wounded and need time to heal. We will not need a large number, will we, my liege? We go for peace and not war."

"You do." He handed me a chain from which hung his symbol, the rearing dragon. "Take this as a sign that you come from me." He smiled. "You are known as well as I and I have no doubt that the sight of your shield and your banner will let all know that you are Warlord."

He was right, of course. I bowed and left to select my men. They were the equites who were closest to me. They were men like Pol and Kay, Bors and Osgar, Gryfflet and Llenlleog. We took ten squires and Pelas led them. Daffydd ap Miach was unhappy to be left behind. "Daffydd, we are a peace mission, I want you and your men to return to Rheged and ensure that none of the men of Deira has crept hence to make a petty kingdom of their own. When this peace is signed then we will return there and make Rheged a little of what it once was. Be back here in eight days' time."

We headed northeast and the crossing of the Dunum. I knew it well for it had been there where my father had first found Roman treasures: swords, nails, javelins. The Roman fort on the river seemed to be haunted by ghosts of our past. He had told me that an ancestor had once fought there, wielding Saxon Slayer and serving the Emperors of Rome. Each time I crossed that bridge I felt the spirits of the past calling to me.

It was almost a hundred and fifty miles to Din Guardi. Luckily it was summer and we could ride for many hours; even so, it would take three days of hard riding to reach that stronghold. Like the Roman fort on the Dunum, Din Guardi held memories. Myrddyn had somehow spirited my father into the castle where he had slain the treacherous Morcaunt Bulc. That King had betrayed King Urien and had him murdered. My father had abhorred such treacherous acts. He had always been, despite his low birth, an honourable man. I had never been there but my father and Myrddyn always said that there were no other fortresses which were as strong or as hard to take.

Our first camp was at the Dunum. The fort had long since been abandoned and yet the walls remained and gave shelter. King Eanfrith had promised us safe passage but that did not mean that we were not vigilant. It was a pleasant evening and while the squires prepared food I went with Pol and Gawan to the river. In winter the bridge was needed but in summer, and with no recent rain, it could be forded. I spied, in the middle of the river, a small island. Normally it would be beneath the waves. Perhaps the spirits guided my eyes I know not. I would have expected them to direct Gawan but it might have been that his thoughts were seeking Myrddyn. Whatever the reason I saw the evening sunlight glint from something on the island. I stood and began to stride through the shallow water.

Pol said, "Warlord?"

"I have seen something. It calls to me."

Gawan said, "Let him go, Pol. This is a holy place. Men have made sacrifices here to the god Icaunus. They have done so since before the time of the Romans. This is *wyrd*."

The sunlight dappled still on the water and the island. It seemed to be a beacon drawing me hence. I was slightly disappointed when I stepped onto the island for I had thought the glinting metal hinted at something bigger. I reached down and picked up a disc. As I touched it I felt a shiver run through me. I dipped it in the river and rubbed it. Upon it was a dragon. It was not the same dragon as that which I wore around my neck, the sign of Gwynedd, it was a dragon like that on my banner. It was Roman. There was a small hole in the top. As I held it I wondered if I should take it. This was a holy place. These were votive offerings. Would the gods be offended?

I shivered as I heard a voice in my head, it was Myrddyn, *'Take it, Warlord. This is wyrd.'*

Clutching it I waded back to my two companions. From Gawan's face, it was obvious to me that he had heard Myrddyn's words too. He nodded, "*Wyrd.*"

It was at times like this that I felt sorry for Pol. He looked blankly at us. "What? I do not understand. Have you not offended Icaunus by stealing from him?"

Gawan shook his head, "No, Pol, for Myrddyn says that this was meant to be. Let me see."

I held open my hand, "I think it is what the Romans called a phalera. It is a medal given to a Roman soldier for a great deed." I swept my hand at the fort. "As this is where one of our ancestors once lived and the place our father found a Roman treasure, I know that I was meant to find it. It is the second dragon I have been given in two days. It is important. It is a sign."

Gawan picked up the medal and clutched it. He closed his eyes. "This is smaller but it is more valuable and important than the one given by the King. You must guard this well, brother. It ties us to the past. The other ties us to a King who has been suborned by the thought of thrones."

Pol looked at Gawan. He had seen Gawan growing up. To Pol, he was still a youth. "You go too far, Gawan. King Cadwallon is our ruler."

"No Pol, Gawan is right. Since King Cadwallon became Christian he has changed. All of our victories seem to change him more. Can you honestly say that he is the same squire who fought alongside us all those years ago?"

I saw the doubt on his face but he was loyal. "He is a king and they must change."

"Did his father, King Cadfan, change?"

"No, but..." He stopped himself.

I smiled, "You were going to say that he had my father to guide and advise him."

"No, Warlord, I am sorry I meant..."

"We are old friends Pol and you cannot offend me. You are right. I am not my father nor can I ever hope to be. I try to be but I am aware of my own frailties and weaknesses. I lost my hold over Cadwallon when my sister died."

"You are different, brother, that is all. This is determined by the spirits. This is wyrd. We follow this path because it is determined for us. We might not like it but we cannot change it. What will be will be. And I have dreamed of dark and bloody times. The world will become bloodier before it is cleansed. Rheged will need the equites and their Warlord."

We stopped, once more, at this remote, deserted Roman fort which was close to this important Roman Road. I had been distracted all day. We were the wolf warriors and yet the sign of the dragon seemed to be fighting for my spirit. Was I the spirit of the wolf or the spirit of the dragon? I felt confused. Perhaps it was I who was changing.

That night as we ate dried meats and the last of our bread and cheese Gawan said, "You could be the spirit of both, Warlord, the wolf and the dragon."

I laughed so loudly that my equites turned and looked, "Go on, Gawan, my little brother who grows older and wiser each day, enlighten me."

The wolf is a pack animal. He hunts in a pack and he fights in a pack. That is you and your equites. He cares for the rest of the pack as you do for Rheged. The dragon, on the other hand, is a solitary creature. It hunts alone but it is all-powerful. When it wreaks vengeance then all is laid waste."

"That does not sound like me."

"Perhaps it is what you will become. I have told you of the dark days ahead. Rheged will need a leader who can defend it ruthlessly."

"That still does not sound like me. It may be that is King Cadwallon. He wears the dragon and he is changing. He has that streak of ruthlessness of which you speak."

Gawan allowed a silence to fill the camp and then he said, "And to whom did he give the dragon?" I said nothing. Was it symbolic, handing the dragon, the sign of his realm, to me? "I have told you that the King has a dark future. I have not dreamed your death."

"Meaning that you have dreamed the King's."

"I have told you I am no Myrddyn. I have seen something but it is not clear. I see through a vale of mist. What I do see is you in Rheged but I do not see King Cadwallon in Wrecsam."

Pol, who had been listening said, "Perhaps he rules here in Northumbria."

"Perhaps."

Gawan did not sound convinced and I reflected on his words as I slept. That night I dreamed. It had been some time since I had done so. It may have been the fort, the shrine in the river or perhaps the memory of my ancestor. Whatever the reason I dreamed. I daresay my head had been filled, each night, with dreams, but I had not remembered them. That night's dream was as vivid as the last battle I had fought.

I soared high in the sky and I looked down at the land beneath me. I flew west. When I reached Rheged I flew low over the water and people fled as I passed over them. As I looked in the waters I saw why; my reflection showed that I was a fierce dragon. I climbed high and settled upon the peak of Halvelyn. I saw hordes of warriors and they were spreading from the north. Others came across the waters in boats. There were as many as the birds which migrate each spring. I took flight and I powered my way toward them. I breathed and fire rushed from my mouth. My enemies were burned. They writhed on the ground and the ones who were untouched fled. I pursued them. They fled first to the island we call Manau and they tried to hide. Beating my powerful wings, I destroyed them but still, some fled and I followed them as they headed to Wyddfa. They reached the top and I swooped again. This time when I burned them they died.

I took flight and I circled. I saw a young woman alone on a headland south of the Holy Mountain. I flew towards her. She seemed not afraid of me and I landed. She was beautiful and when she spoke her voice was musical. It seemed to enchant me. She even knew my name. How could she see for I was a dragon yet?

"Mighty Warlord, your wing is damaged let me heal it with this potion."

She rubbed the salve on my wing and I felt at peace. All pain went and suddenly the young woman changed into a band of warriors with axes and swords. They fell upon me and I could not move. She had enchanted me. They began to hack and slash at me and suddenly I was Warlord once more. I had Saxon Slayer and although I was wounded I laid about me and slew many of the men who pursued me. I was sorely wounded and I fled up the mountain. If I could get to Wyddfa and Myrddyn's cave, then I would be healed. No matter how fast I ran the mountain was still out of reach. I turned and slew two warriors who chased me but there were still many more and I felt the life begin to leave my body.

I forced myself up the slope and saw, suddenly, a hole in the earth appear before me. Saxon Slayer could not fall into the hands of my enemies. I dropped the sword down the hole and, as I did so, I felt myself falling as though I was following it down into the depths of the earth. I tumbled and I fell. The bottom seemed endless. I saw the deep, dark pool looming up before me and then there was nothing.

"Brother!"

I opened my eyes and saw Gawan standing over me with concern written on his face. "I Dreamed."

"You dreamed your death." I nodded. "I saw it too. I am sorry."

"I was alone. Where were my men? Where were you? Why did not Myrddyn come to save me? Is he dead too? Is that why he could not come and save me?" I shook my head. "The sword was lost."

"It is there still, brother," I looked down and saw the sword still in its scabbard.

"I do not understand."

"Neither do I but we now know the future."

I shook my head, "I would prefer ignorance to this." I had a sudden insight. "Do you think father dreamed his own death?" Gawan nodded, "Then he is an even greater man than I knew for I know not if I can bear the burden."

"You can, brother, for you are Warlord."

Chapter 5

Din Guardi was the most imposing fortress I had ever seen. It stood on a rocky outcrop surrounded on three sides by the sea. I had heard that Dùn Èideann was as imposing but Din Guardi was powerful enough for me. If King Cadwallon chose war and not a diplomatic solution, then we would lose many men trying to take it. I was even more intrigued as to how my father and Myrddyn had managed to gain entry and kill Morcaunt Bulc. Perhaps the story of magic was true. I would not put it past Myrddyn. It made me miss the old man even more.

My thoughts returned to the present as we drew closer to its walls. If this was a trap, then we would all die. We were deep in Bernicia. We had passed many hill forts and seen bands of warriors but none had bothered us. Part of my mind briefly thought that this would be a good way for King Cadwallon to rid himself of me. I could not see why he might do that. The thought disappeared instantly. I had dreamed my death. I would die on a bare and rocky hillside south of Wyddfa.

A winding ramp led from the land up to the gates. I guessed that it might well be covered at high tide for the water was quite close to the base. Most of the walls were wooden but they had stone foundations and the gatehouse was made of stone, in the Roman style, with two small towers. The double gates opened and we rode into the lower yard of the fortress. King Eanfrith, he was obvious from the quality of his mail and his weapons, waited to greet me. He was surrounded by his hearthweru. There were twelve of them and they looked like powerful warriors. Each had a mail hauberk, full-face helmet and a mighty axe.

I dismounted and bowed, "King Eanfrith, I have come from my King to discuss the peace."

He smiled, "And I get to meet the mighty Warlord, the bane of my people who wields the sword of destiny, the one you call Saxon Slayer and which we call Blade of Doom." He clasped my arm. He must have seen my expression of surprise. "I am not like my brothers Oswald and Oswiu. When they fought with my father I was in Hibernia serving with the Uí Néill."

Saxon Throne

"They are fierce warriors."

"Aye they are and they have heard of you. Come let us go inside my hall for we have much to discuss." He gestured to my equites, "Bring in your warriors too. My hearthweru are keen to see their arms and armour." He laughed, "Normally we are too busy fighting for our lives to examine it too closely."

This was a peculiar experience. I found myself liking this Saxon. Could this truly be the end of the war? We could make peace with this man and I detected no deception. Gawan would be able to discern more. If we made peace, then Rheged would be safe. I would not need to fight enemies from the east. I spied hope in King Eanfrith's words and demeanour.

He had laid on a fine feast. They were so close to the sea that it was a feast of fish and seafood. It was one of the things I missed from Ynys Môn. Gawan and I flanked him. "I envy you two the closeness you enjoy. Even Oswiu and Oswald do not get on and they despise me. If they thought that I was brokering peace they would make war on me." He laughed, "They worship the White Christ but I serve the old ways as do my men."

Gawan smiled, "There can only be one Warlord. I am happy to be who I am. I do not desire to rule."

"It is good that you know who you are. You must be content."

I had not thought that. My family was dead but, suddenly, now that I knew my own destiny, I was content. The struggles of Rheged were almost at an end and we would have peace in the land. The land would prosper. Perhaps that was why Myrddyn had disappeared. His work was done.

King Eanfrith confided his fears in me, "Can I trust your King? I look in your eyes and feel that I can trust the two of you but King Cadwallon is a different matter."

"He is a good man and a good king. He fought blade to blade with King Osric bravely and did not stand and watch as many kings do. I have known him since he was a child. His heart is good."

He looked relieved. "Thank you, Warlord. It is known that your word is like the rock upon which my castle is built. It does not move and you can trust it. I trust you and your brother Gawan. This is the dawning of a new age! Tell me what does he propose?"

King Cadwallon had been a little vague but I had the principles in my head, "You are to rule Bernicia as a vassal king of Gwynedd. You will watch over Deira until King Cadwallon decides who should rule there."

"He will not let me combine the two kingdoms?"

"I think he fears Northumbria. Joined you are as powerful as Mercia." I shrugged, "I just speak the truth. We both know that Mercia and Northumbria are the two most powerful Saxon kingdoms."

"I like your honesty and you are right. This is better. I will not be tempted to go to war against King Cadwallon. We have enough enemies to the north and the west. The land needs some peace. We have fought for too long and the land suffers."

"You are right King Eanfrith, and my brother, the warlord, knows this. I hope that there will be peace."

The King smiled, "There will be peace tonight for my men are keen to talk with your, what do you call them? Equites?"

I nodded, "It is what the Romans called them. The word translates as knights."

"Are they like hearthweru?"

"A little; they have to train and serve an equite as a squire and must then provide their own mail, horse and sword. They swear to serve their lord." I pointed to Kay, Bors and Llenlleog. "Each of these leads their own equites and they all serve me and Rheged."

He put his arm around my shoulder, "Come, this will be a most instructive evening!"

It was a most excellent evening for our warriors could talk without blows. Ideas were exchanged and weapons examined. Stories were told and friendships made. We left some days later to return to Eoforwic. He bade farewell to his wife, a Pictish princess. She was with child and the King did not wish to risk her on the journey. The three-day journey south passed quickly. King Eanfrith had just brought his hearthweru. This was not a military expedition it was a mission of peace. He explained which lord lived where as we travelled south and I told him the tales of my father when he had lived close by. It was a pleasant journey. I sent a squire ahead to herald our arrival. It was not right that we should sneak into the city like beggars. This was a momentous day.

King Cadwallon had his equites arrayed in two lines to greet King Eanfrith. Their armour and helmets had been burnished and they gleamed and glinted in the afternoon sunlight. He stood on the steps of the Great Hall wearing his own crown and that of Deira. It was a powerful display of military might and authority. I wondered at that for it was a slight to King Eanfrith. He was not the king of Deira. The Saxon seemed not put out and they greeted each other like long lost brothers.

He seemed happy enough and he greeted us with a huge smile, "Come for we have a great feast and I say to all in this ancient city of Eoforwic that this day brings an understanding between Bernicia and Gwynedd. From this day forth we will be one."

I saw King Eanfrith frown at that and I wondered at the wisdom of such words. However, this was not the time for questions. I had no doubt that the next few days would see discussions and debate while a treaty was hammered out. It was a fine feast. King Cadwallon had his singer tell tales, not of the battles between Saxon and Briton but of heroic deeds from his own family. It allayed my fears that, perhaps, he had something else in mind for these talks. The next morning I was up early and Dai sought me out. "His majesty wishes to speak with you, Warlord. There is danger."

The King looked worried, "Warlord, Edgar, son of Osric, has raised an army. They are to the south of here in the old land of Elmet. He has taken Loidis the place they call Ladenses. I would have you take your men and eliminate this threat."

I looked into his eyes and I saw something but I could not discern what. Gawan was not with me and I wished he had been. He could have read the mind of the King. "Will my equites, squires and archers be enough?"

"It will be enough. He cannot have many men and there can be no hearthweru for we slew them all. He raises a rabble and they have cut the road south. We need that road for, when the peace is over we intend to travel home. Besides, I cannot send my men; it might offend King Eanfrith." He smiled, "You have done well to bring King Eanfrith into my hall. It will bring calm and stability to the land. God is pleased. King Eanfrith was

Christian once. Perhaps this is the peace that will make him one so again."

"I am not Christian either."

He laughed but it was an uneasy laugh, "Do not worry, Warlord. We have not given up on you. One day you will see the light."

I said nothing for he did not know me. How could I worship just one God for there were many? The world was a complicated place and each god was responsible for one part. It had to work in harmony. All had to be balanced.

I bowed, "I will go. We will try to be back to escort King Eanfrith home."

"Do not worry, Warlord. He will be here when you return. I guarantee that. We have much to discuss and there is no hurry."

Gawan was disturbed as we headed the twenty miles southwest to Loidis, the Roman name for Ladenses. "I like not this task brother. The King kept his thoughts from me. I am no Myrddyn and I could not read them but something hid them and I like not that. There was a fog between us."

"You fear we are in danger?"

"No, brother for we have dreamed your death already and it is many miles hence."

With Geraint and my scouts ranging far ahead, we rode confidently. Tadgh came hurtling back some ten miles from Loidis. "Warlord, we have come upon a band of Saxons. They are three miles up the road heading along the road with sheep and cattle. They have two men on horses."

"How many in the warband?"

"Perhaps thirty of them."

I turned to Pelas and Daffydd, "Take your men and deal with these Saxons. Ride ahead. I do not want them escaping."

"Aye, Warlord."

The lightly armed squires and archers could move much faster than us and twice as fast as the men on foot. We began to canter. It was an easy pace but a ground eating one. My squires and archers would not use the road. They would ride along the flanks so that they could form the trap into which we would drive them. For the squires, this would be a good test of the skills they had acquired.

Saxon Throne

This was not the flat land of the vale. There were hills as well as twists and turns, dips, rises and hollows. It prevented us from seeing them until we were less than half a Roman mile from them. They did not see us, at first, but they felt and heard the hooves on the road. Panic set in and they started to run faster down the road. The two with horses left their companions. My banner was well known and the sight of our helmets and shields would tell any who walked this land that the Warlord was abroad. They left their sheep and their cattle. We would collect them later. Flight was futile but to stand and fight would have resulted in their death anyway. They were so concerned with looking over their shoulders that they ran directly into my squires who were backed by my archers. Both horsemen were hit but one retained his saddle, even though wounded and rode towards the walled town we could see rising in the distance. It was not a large town, although in my father's day the King of Elmet had lived there. Its protection lay in a fast-flowing river. That too would bring its downfall for there was no bridge there. With just one gate in and out we could hold them safely within.

By the time, we reached Pelas my men were finishing off the wounded. "Well done, my squire. Have some of your squires fetch the sheep and the cattle, we go to the gates of the town."

"Aye lord." Pelas looked to me to have grown. He had led a charge and had not lost a man. He would remember this day when he became an equite and that day would not be long in coming.

We rode gently to the walls. We were in no hurry. The wounded Saxon made the gates and then they were slammed shut. I pointed to a spot two hundred paces from the gate. "Make camp there. I wish to lose no men taking this sty. We watch them starve. Daffydd, have your men stand watch. The squires can take over after dark."

I was so confident that they would not sally forth that I took off my mail. Pol asked, "What is the plan, Warlord?"

"We slaughter one of the cattle and a couple of sheep. We will eat well. We light the fires so that the smell drifts to the walls and in the morning I will give them an ultimatum."

Pol smiled, "This is my kind of warfare." He looked at the equites as they set up camp using the leather tents we used. "We are becoming smaller in number, Warlord."

"I know but I spy a kind of hope in Pelas and the squires. They do not make mistakes and they handled themselves well today."

"They were fighting men without mail who were little more than brigands. If they become equites, where do we get mail?" He pointed to his own mail. There were a couple of rings missing. "How do we repair our mail?"

"You are right to chastise me, Pol, I had not thought of these things."

"I would never dream of criticising you, Warlord but it is these small things which may come to hurt us."

He was right and I had to give thought to it.

The meat tasted good as we sat around the fires enjoying it; perhaps because it was the meat stolen from our enemies. The wind wafted the delicious aromas into the beleaguered town. For us, it was a pleasant evening. The days were long and we were far enough from the river not to be bothered by flies. My men chatted easily. When we had defeated Edgar and his men we would return to the King and I would beg permission to go to Rheged. Events had turned out well.

Gawan was the one to dampen my spirits. He read my mind and said, quietly, "I still see darkness ahead, brother."

"But you cannot know if that is tomorrow, next month, next year... it could be any time."

"True but we both know of hubris, do we not? Let us imagine that disaster is over the horizon and when it is not then our world is so much better."

"This is not like you, Gawan."

"And that should tell you how dark is the cloud in my mind."

I did not sleep well that night although I did not dream. My mind was filled with serpents and I saw treachery and betrayal everywhere. The next morning I dressed and, when the sun had warmed the earth, rode with Pol, Gawan and Llewellyn to the gates. Even though I knew that Saxons were the worst of archers I stayed more than a hundred paces from them. I waited until men had gathered on top of the wooden gatehouse. While we waited, I examined the ditch. It was not deep and I suspected that it was devoid of traps. The recent dry weather meant that it would be firm underfoot. It would not be an obstacle.

I looked up at the walls and shouted, "I am the Warlord of Rheged sent by King Cadwallon to punish Edgar the son of Osric. Your father was slain in battle and this is futile. You cannot win."

I saw a warrior with a full-face helmet. He raised his sword, "I am Edgar son of Osric and I claim what is rightfully mine!"

"You can claim it but can you capture it and can you hold it? I think not." I pointed to the river. "You cannot cross the river and this is the only way out. If you wish you can come forth and try single combat with me. Perhaps you might win."

He laughed and his laughter carried over to me, "You are the warlord with a sword which is magic. You have Myrddyn the wizard. I am no fool. We will stay within these walls and watch you bleed upon them." He dropped his hand and a handful of arrows sped from the walls. We took them easily on our shields.

"You are a brave young man but you are foolish."

I turned Star around and headed back to our lines.

Kay said, "When do we attack?"

"When they are hungry. Daffydd, have your men hunt. We will eat well while we are here. I want a close watch kept on the walls."

It was no hardship to camp by the walls. The weather was clement. We had meat and we had water. All that we lacked was a soft bed and some wine and it would have been Elysium. Five days after we had issued the ultimatum they signalled that they wished to speak with us.

I rode forward with Pol and Gawan, "You wish to surrender?"

"What are your terms?"

I ignored the lack of respect for my title. "Lay down your arms. The warriors will be taken to King Cadwallon for his judgement and your people will be free."

"Do you guarantee that we will be freed?"

"I guarantee nothing. That is the King's decision."

"Then I do not accept your terms. We have nothing to gain!"

"You have your lives for if we attack you then every warrior will be put to the sword and all those within taken into slavery.

Think about that. Tell your people my words. They have until sunset to surrender."

As I rode back Pol said, "Will they comply?"

I nodded, "I think that Edgar will seek to rid himself of mouths he cannot feed. It will be women and children who emerge but I do not like to make war on women and children. This is *wyrd*."

I saw Gawan nodding and smiling. It was foolish but I enjoyed winning the approval of my younger brother, he was a wizard and knew things I did not. If he approved, then the spirits did too.

They began leaving soon after we had reached our camp. "Kay, go and make sure there are no warriors amongst them."

"Aye Warlord."

I felt satisfaction that it was as I had predicted, they were women and children. None of the boys was older than ten summers. Edgar was keeping all those who could wield a weapon. I saw that they appeared reluctant to leave and they gathered in knots. I walked over. I spoke in Saxon. "You are free to leave. You can go."

One of the women, older than the rest, said in the old tongue, "And where would we go, Warlord? Our men have been kept within the walls. Edgar would not let them leave, even though they wished to."

She did not look Saxon. She looked to be of the old people. "You are from Elmet and you are not Saxon?"

"Aye Warlord. My husband Garth is the smith. He is Saxon but he is a good man. He does not like to work for Edgar. He was blinded in one eye for his opposition."

This changed things. I mounted Star so that they could see me. "I am the Warlord of Rheged. If you are of Elmet or Rheged and wish my protection, then stay." I took a breath and then added, "If you are Saxon and would accept me as lord then stay. If not, then take food and leave. May the Allfather be with you."

In the end, three women took their families east and the rest stayed. I held a war counsel with my men. "This changes things. We cannot wait for them to starve. It would be our own people who would suffer. We attack this night." I was gratified that they all nodded. We knew rough numbers from the refugees. It was a case of minimising our losses. "We kill only those with weapons who attack us. Edgar can make men stand on his walls and watch them fight but if we attack then our folk are less likely to fight. Pelas will lead the squires and I will lead the equites. Pelas attacks the wall to the left of the gate and we will take the right. Daffydd I want you and your archers to kill the sentries on the walls."

Pol nodded, "We use our shields to climb the walls?"

"We do. Our equites who have axes can break down the gate. I do not think they have seeded the ditch with traps. We will just have to be careful."

Gawan said, "We could make faggots and throw them in the ditch."

"That will help. Make them."

As soon as it was dark we gathered. Each equite and scout carried a faggot; a bundle of twigs and wood tied together. Even I carried a bundle. We moved quickly to the line of archers who waited close by the walls. We would be seen but not until we were less than forty paces from the wall and our archers would kill any they saw. It was a sharp-eyed sentry over the gate who spied us. He shouted just before an arrow plunged into his chest and hurled him to the ground. Our archers quickly cleared those sentries who made the mistake of standing upright. It enabled us to close with the ditch. We threw in our bundles and leapt across. Bors and Kay led those with the axes and soon there was a steady crack as they took it in turns to smash the door.

Inside I heard the shouts of alarm as they realised that they were being attacked. Two of my equites held a shield between them and I sprang on to it and they thrust me up to the top of the wall. I landed heavily but the gods smiled upon me for no one was near. I drew Saxon Slayer. The two sentries by me were both dead but I saw a band of warriors running from the warrior hall. I turned as first Pol and then Llenlleog landed behind me. With those two, I could take on the world.

We ran to the steps and descended. Halfway down I saw the Saxons gather and I leapt, with sword held out to land amongst them. My size and my weight meant I knocked them to the ground. Once again, I was favoured by the gods for my sword impaled one to the ground as I did so. As an axe came at me I blocked it with my shield and then swung sideways below it. My sword bit into the leg of a Saxon and carved it through to the bone. Pol, Lann Aelle and Llenlleog laid about them with their swords. Behind me, there was a crack and a cheer as the gate fell in and my equites, squires and archers flooded in. The men around the three of us were dead.

"We find Edgar and finish this."

"Aye Warlord!"

I shouted, "If you are not Saxon then lay down your weapons and you will be spared!" I said it in the old language. I saw men come from their huts, throw down their weapons and kneel in supplication. It was easier this way. I saw Edgar with his mail byrnie and a full-face helmet. They stood before the warrior hall. His hearthweru had no mail but they were the better-armed of the Saxons. They each had a shield, a spear and a helmet. There were twelve of them and they stood around their leader. He had chosen to die rather than live as a slave. I could understand the sentiment.

My equites had run to join me. We formed up into two lines and linked shields. The fifteen of us crashed into the knot of Saxons. They tried to hold us but they had not done this before. With our shields locked, we bowled them over. I stabbed at one, who fell at my feet, and my sword gave him a swift death. Edgar saw his chance and brought his sword over to strike at me even as I despatched the man on the ground. I twisted and brought my shield up. It was a good blow but I had suffered harder ones. I brought my sword around and it bit into his side. His mail was poorly made. I withdrew my bloody blade and punched with my shield. I struck his hand. He wore no mail mittens and I knew that it would have stung. I punched again, this time hitting his shoulder and he struggled to keep his feet. As he stumbled I brought my sword over my head and sliced down his middle, from his chest to his crotch. He twitched and shook as he bled to death. His hearthweru might not have been the best armed but they were brave and they died to a man around the body of their would-be king.

We had victory.

Chapter 6

All those who had surrendered and laid down their weapons were closely guarded while we searched for any of Edgar's warriors who were hiding. By the time dawn broke, we had them all. I spied a broad and muscular man with a bloody bandage covering one eye. "Are you Garth the smith?"

"Aye, Warlord, I am,"

"Your wife and family are safe with us but tell me, you are Saxon are you not?"

"I am Warlord."

"Then why did Edgar blind you?"

"Because I did not wish to fight you. There are others here, like me, who took the women of Elmet as our wives. In those days, I did fight your people. Since that time, we have lived peacefully here and I have come to know the ways of your people. We had been left alone. We had no king and Edwin left us to live as we chose. Even when his priests came to make us serve the White Christ he did not enforce his rule. Osric, Edgar's father, sent men to ask us to fight for him against King Cadwallon. Some went but most of us did not. War has passed over this land before now and left us alone."

Gawan nodded, "And when King Osric fell then his son came to punish you for not obeying his father."

"Aye, he did. Some of the elders were thrown, bound into the river."

I looked at the men before me. I had thought I would have an easy task. My plan had been simple, I would enslave the Saxons and then free the men of Elmet. I could see that was not as easy as I thought.

I spoke to all those gathered before me. "I will make you all an offer. I am going to Rheged in the west. It is a good land but there are few people. If you swear allegiance to me as lord, then I will take you there and I will protect you. I care not if you are Saxon or Briton."

They all shouted, "Aye!"

I held up my hand, "Garth, your wound speaks for your honour. Are all these men to be trusted or are there some of Edgar's men hiding amongst them?"

Even as he pointed two men holding concealed weapons leapt to get at me. Saxon Slayer was out but it was not needed as three arrows pierced each of the men who fell dead at my feet.

"Is that all of them?"

"It is, Warlord."

"Take everything you want from this place. We leave for Eoforwic as soon as it is all gathered. Use wagons and carts. Pol, have the town ready for burning. We will make sure that it is a stronghold no longer."

He asked, "Will not King Cadwallon wish us to give it to King Eanfrith? Is he not King of Northumbria now?"

I shook my head, "He is King of Bernicia and I think that King Cadwallon will allow him that but Deira and Elmet will be added to the jewels on King Cadwallon's crown. He has a kingdom but he would have an Empire."

The families came to help their men and, before noon, we were ready to travel. It was fortunate that it was still summer with long nights for the carts, wagons and walking children would slow us down. With the archers along the flanks and the squires at the rear, our long column was led by my equites as we headed back to Eoforwic.

Pol and Gawan flanked me while Lann Aelle and Llenlleog rode just behind us. "Did I do right then, brother?"

He nodded and pointed to the skies. A few light clouds fluttered against a blue background, "The Earth is content. This is *wyrd*. Remember that Lann Aelle's father was half Saxon. It is right that our blood becomes entwined. We need their skills."

Lann Aelle said, "Aye, cousin. I remember you telling me that we needed a smith. The world knows that the Saxons make the best swords. I think Gawan is right. This feels to me as though we have a chance to be reborn."

He hesitated and Gawan laughed, "Speak your thoughts cousin. My brother will not be offended."

"See, Lann Aelle, even your thoughts are not safe from our new Myrddyn."

"I was just going to say that I would like to build the town on the water. It would be the place where my father and Uncle Raibeart lived. I never knew it well but I have heard the stories of the waters which teemed with fish and the land which overflowed with game. I would build a home there."

Llenlleog said, "It is true, Warlord, this is *wyrd* for there are some comely young women there. Many of our equites have not yet had the chance to be a father. I see the hand of the Allfather in all of this."

And so, the last few miles to Eoforwic were filled with hope and optimism. The war was almost over and we had all survived. We had a people to lead again and the prospect of a new home. The air was filled with banter and laughter. There was joy right up until we saw the gates of Eoforwic. Gawan had the sharpest eyes and he saw something amiss. Birds flocked and swooped over the gates. Something must have disturbed them for, as they flew away, we saw thirteen heads adorning the gate. In my heart, I knew who they were but Gawan gave voice to the dreaded thought. "It is Eanfrith and his hearthweru. They have been executed."

Behind me, a babble of questions rose. "Silence. Until we find the reason for this I want no hasty actions. Lann Aelle we will camp our people to the north of the city. The camp which Osric made is a good place. It is now scoured of death."

"Why the north, cousin?"

"I intend to leave for Rheged in the morning and I do not want to have to negotiate the streets of Eoforwic. Pol you, my brother and Llenlleog will come with me while I speak with the King."

Bors asked, "Will that be enough Warlord?" He pointed to the heads which were now less than half a mile away.

I looked at Gawan who nodded, "I believe so. Lann Aelle, command in my absence."

I had to glance up at the head of King Eanfrith. I had given him my word that he would be safe and now he was dead. As we headed towards the bridge over the River Fosse I asked, "Did you see this?"

"I felt darkness when we left but I thought that was something to do with our task. I did not dream this outrage. Remember, brother, in Eoforwic my thoughts are clouded. When we went to find Edgar, I focussed my mind on that task and not on Eoforwic. I am sorry. This treachery was hidden from me."

I turned to look at my brother, "Treachery?"

He nodded, "I felt it as we passed beneath their heads. Their spirits remain yet. They will stay here until they are avenged. Myrddyn had a spell to protect from such spirits. I wish I had it now. I shall not sleep this night. I do not believe that the spirit of Eanfrith and his men will harm me but I would not blame them if they did."

"Then perhaps we join our people and camp beyond the city walls."

Gawan looked relieved, "That would be for the best and I will have men gather rosemary. It is too late in the season for wild garlic but what there is we shall gather. Myrddyn once told me that they can protect men from the dead."

We were viewed somewhat warily by the guards. I had no doubt that they all knew what had gone on and that I had given my word. I felt uncomfortable for I had fought alongside all of these men and now I knew them not. As the column carried on through the north-western gate, we turned to the Great Hall that King Cadwallon used. Dai met us at the steps. We dismounted.

He looked beyond us at the line of equites heading north, "Your men do not stay?"

"We have refugees from Loidis. There is no room for them here."

He seemed satisfied. "The King awaits you." He hesitated. "He asks if you will leave your sword."

I rounded on him. Dai had been a squire once and I had helped to train him. "Has King Cadwallon changed so much? Does he not trust me? I am Warlord. I carry Saxon Slayer and any man may have it if he can prise it from my dead fingers. Do you wish bloodshed, Dai ap Gruffyd? For if you do then you shall have it here. No one touches my sword!"

There were just four of us but each one of us had a reputation which no man would dare face lightly.

Dai held his hand up so that his men took their hands from their weapons, "No, Warlord for I do not have a death wish but I pray you to listen to the King."

I shook my head, "When have I ever acted hastily? I grow tired of the air and pestilence here. I yearn for Rheged. This is a sad day, Dai, for where there was trust and honour now there is treachery and dishonour."

"I protest, Warlord. I have not lost my honour."

I pointed to the south, "Then tell that to King Eanfrith who came here because he trusted me. I have no time for this. Take me to your King so that I may tell him the results of my last service for him!"

He looked at me, "My king?"

I nodded, "I am done with him. No matter what lies he tells me I will serve him no longer."

I strode through the doors and into the hall. King Cadwallon was seated on a throne which was raised upon a dais. He made no attempt to rise. I noticed a pair of priests hovering behind him, somewhat nervously. The King frowned. "I gave orders for no weapons!"

I strode forwards and saw that his guards had unsheathed their weapons. "Have you forgotten who I am, King Cadwallon? I am Warlord. I wield Saxon Slayer. I took the title Dux Britannicus from my father and I still have it. Do you think that if I wished you dead then these who are around you would afford you any protection?"

The priests disappeared and his guards stepped between us.

"Do you threaten the High King of Britannia?"

I laughed, "And who, in the name of the Allfather, made you High King?" I shook my head, "I do not threaten. I never have. If I wish something, then it is done." I pointed to the south. "I gave my word to King Eanfrith that he and his men would be safe and yet I see their heads adorning the gate. Why?"

"You question a king?"

"I thought I spoke with a friend whom I trained and who owes his success to me and my equites."

He gave a hollow laugh, "Your sixty men helped a little and that is all. You are getting old Warlord. I have learned, I admit, much from you but now I am the strategos." He pointed to the south. "You wonder why I slew Eanfrith? He would not acknowledge me as High King. Nor would he convert to Christianity. I had him and his men executed. I now control the whole of this land from the Wall to Mercia and Mercia had best watch out for I will rule this land as King Coel! Britannia will be great once more."

His delusions of grandeur did not interest me but the dead warriors did. "Did they die with swords in their hands?"

"Of course, not. They were bound and slaughtered. It is the punishment I will inflict on all Saxons until they acknowledge me as High King!"

Gawan said, quietly, "This city will know no peace until the dead are avenged. Their spirits will walk your walls and haunt your men's dreams."

"My priests tell them that is a lie."

I laughed, "And that is why they cower behind you!" I pointed a finger at him. "I will leave now, King Cadwallon. You have made me lose honour and I must make amends for that. I came here to tell you that I obeyed your request and Edgar is no more but I leave you now."

"You cannot! I rule this land!"

"You might have done once but no longer. You have lost that which made you a good king. The spirits and the land will no longer support you. You are now greedy and avaricious. Perhaps that is what this White Christ does to a man. I know not. This city might have changed you. You are not the young warrior I once fought alongside. You were married to our sister, now you cavort with whores and strumpets. Remember this, Cadwallon ap Cadfan, Rome was great and then they embraced the cross. The Roman Emperors had power but then they adopted a life of luxury and excess. This was Rome but it is Rome no longer. Ponder those words."

I turned.

"Stop him! I command it!"

Dai stepped before me. I just stared at him. His sword which was half out of his scabbard was slid back. He bowed and stepped away. The other guards saw him and emulated his actions.

"Stop him! I command it! Stop him!"

The King sounded like a truculent child. Something had changed him. Perhaps he had been taken over by a shape shifter. I would need to speak with Gawan. I flung open the doors and strode to my horse. I mounted and waited for the others, who had been watching my back, to join me. Dai came and said, quietly, "Watch your back, Warlord. The King has many who would seek the honour of slaying you in the night."

I nodded, "Dai, you are a good man and always have been. Leave him."

"I cannot, Warlord, I swore an oath."

"As did he. But he has forgotten his. If you ever do leave him then find me. I will be in Rheged and I welcome all such warriors." I looked around, "I say this to all true warriors who wish to fight for honour. The Land of Rheged welcomes all honourable men!"

Even as we turned to ride out I heard the murmur of conversations. King Cadwallon had miscalculated. His men now had doubts in their minds and a warrior who doubted was doomed to die.

"We must move quickly to Rheged. I no longer trust our old comrade. Gawan, how did you read him?"

"His heart is black now, brother. He is not the same man who left with us and King Penda to face Edwin. Something has turned him to a strange path. It happens with men. Did not his grandfather behave in a similar way?"

"Aye, Cadfan was hunted by his father and it was our father who saved him, defeated Cadfan's father and placed him on the throne."

Llenlleog said, "Perhaps he should have taken the throne for himself."

Gawan said, "You knew not my father. He served the sword and the land. He was ever guided by Myrddyn." He shook his head, "This may be my fault. Myrddyn knew how to control the King. I have failed."

"No brother, this is *wyrd*. Tomorrow I will send Geraint and half of our archers to scout out the way to Rheged. It will take us three days to reach it. Until we are behind walls I fear that King Cadwallon will be a danger to us."

"I think that he will hurry to Din Guardi and claim that crown too. We have time before he turns his gaze to us. We have breathing space and then we shall see what the land of Rheged can do to aid us."

Saxon Throne

When we reached the camp, I saw that Lann Aelle had not only erected tents he had reused the ditch which Osric had constructed and used the wagons and carts to form a circle. My cousin showed wisdom and caution. I gathered all of my equites, Pelas and Daffydd ap Miach. We told them what had happened. None of them wished to rejoin the King and that filled me with pride. We kept a good watch overnight as we wished no treachery to stop us from leaving. We left at dawn the next day. I rode at the rear with my equites. If Gawan was wrong, then the King would have to face me and Saxon Slayer.

It was a long day and we were exhausted but sixteen hours after leaving Eoforwic we reached the Dunum and the Roman fort. Our archers and scouts had prepared fires and hunted game. Our new people ate well.

"We will leave later tomorrow. We are safe here and it would not do to tire out the old and the young."

So it was that as we prepared to leave eight men rode in. There were too few for us to represent a danger and we waited as they crossed the old Roman bridge. It was five of King Cadwallon's equites and three archers.

"Warlord, we wish to serve you. We told Dai we were leaving. We did so with honour and we would serve you with honour too."

I took out Saxon Slayer, "Then swear an oath on this ancient sword. You all know that it will bind you to us."

Gruffyd ap David, the leader, nodded. "Aye Warlord. We follow not the White Christ."

My army was growing and, as we headed west and another twelve men joined us. Three more equites, four squires and five archers. They too swore an oath. I had decided to make my home Civitas Carvetiorum. It had been where King Urien and King Coel had held court. Prince Pasgen had briefly refortified it but our scouts told me that it lay abandoned and ruined. Raiders from the north, west and east had taken all that was of value. For the last ten miles, we followed both the river and the Roman Wall. The river was the Mother giving us protection whilst the Wall was a reminder that man could harness the land and use it. As we dropped from the high ground to the old Roman Fort protected by two rivers I looked at Gawan and we both smiled.

Saxon Throne

"We are home brother."
I nodded, "Aye and it is *wyrd*."

Part 2
Civitas Carvetiorum-Rheged

Chapter 7

Autumn would be upon us soon and all of us had to set to in order to make our walls secure and our homes dry. I left my equites to organise that while I went to visit the people who had followed us from Elmet. Garth had proved himself to be an excellent leader. He had organised his own folk. Along with his wife Seara, they were the heart of the people. I spoke with the two of them.

"My men are warriors. Your people are the farmers and the ones who produce that which keeps us alive." I waved my hand along the horizon. "This is good land and it has not been farmed for many years. They can take whatever land they like."

"How much land, lord?"

"Are they greedy men you have brought to me, Garth of Ladenses?"

"No lord."

"Then they will take what they need. Until more people join us then there is plenty for all. To the south is good farmland too and my cousin will take any who wishes there. But I need you to live here within my walls. I will pay you. There is a smithy here. It may need work. I suspect the bellows are broken and the anvil may need to be cleaned but your task is to make mail and weapons."

"What of ploughs and tools, lord?"

"You have sons. They can make those. When every squire has mail and a good sword then you can make tools but we are alone here at the edge of the world and we defend ourselves. Can you do this for me?"

He grinned, "Aye lord, I can. I will speak with the men and tell them what you say."

"There will be no crops and precious few animals until spring comes. They will, needs must live here over the winter but that will be no hardship for we will be both warm and safe. My brother is a wizard and he will dream our future."

Garth asked as he turned, "Warlord, what of Myrddyn?"

"He will return, one day but we know not when. He was ever thus. Myrddyn is not of this world. He comes and goes at no man's command. When the time is right and we need him then he will return."

Even as I said the words I was not convinced.

My men worked hard. We laid our mail to one side and Garth repaired those that needed it while we dug ditches and mortared stones back into place. All around us were enemies. My archers hunted and my scouts ranged far and wide. It was they who brought us our news. As the summer ended and the leaves began to dry they brought reports that Northumbria had been claimed by Eanfrith's brother, Oswald, who was building an army. King Cadwallon was laying waste to vast areas of Bernicia as he sought to establish his control. Crops lay unharvested in the fields and animals were abandoned as their owners died. The winter would be a harsh one for all.

Lann Aelle took four equites and went to the fort at the head of the water. When he returned, eight days later, he was happy. "We can rebuild it in the spring cousin."

Gawan said, "Then you will need women, farmers, people."

It was prophetic for, as the leaves started to fall a trickle of refugees and those seeking land and protection, came from the east. These were the ones who had had enough of war. Between Oswald and Cadwallon there was little to choose. Both took from those who could not defend it. They had heard of this land protected by the Warlord and they came with their sheep and goats. They carried their fowl and a few led their cattle. We made all welcome for Rheged was empty.

It might have been perfect but it was not. As the animals, which had been grazing on the hills were brought down and the berries and nuts collected my scouts reported sails off the coast close to Alavna. It was the pirates of Hibernia. They were not like wolves who hunted, they were like the foxes and the rats which preyed upon the weak. They came not knowing who lived in this land now.

Geraint and his scouts watched them from the hills above the estuary as they rowed their ships up the Ituna. We stopped our work and gathered our men. We did not wish to frighten them off. For if they came not knowing who was here we might defeat them. If they returned home for more warriors, then it might go hard with us. Their ships could be used and whatever they had upon them we could take. I wanted to destroy them. I wanted them to disappear so that their families at home would wonder what happened to them. In short, I wanted the pirates of Hibernia to fear the Warlord of Rheged. That would be our best defence.

Pelas and Daffydd divided their men into two equal parties. One, led by Daffydd, hid in the dunes by the mouth of the estuary. Pelas and the others were further upstream. Their task was to ensure that the three boats did not escape. My twenty-five equites waited in two long lines. To the enemy, when they eventually saw us, we would appear to be but twelve men. I intended to tempt them into an attack. The Irish were brave, wild and reckless fighters. They could run as swiftly as a horse and they feared no man. Some of them had two handed swords with which they could slice a horse's leg in two. They were not to be underestimated. They did not, however, wear mail and only the chiefs would wear a helmet. We were all better armed and trained. We each took a pair of javelins. They would break up the attack.

The Roman wall, at this point, was made of turf and acted as a barrier to a flooding river. It was three paces high and all that the enemy would see of us until they climbed onto its top, would be our standards. We stood just two hundred paces from the turf wall and waited. It was late afternoon when they finally arrived. We spied the masts of their ships. These were smaller than those used by the angles and the masts could not bear the weight of a lookout. That was fortunate. They would have no warning of us until they had left their boats. By then I hoped it would be too late.

All of the men I led had a great deal of experience. Those who had defected to us were excellent warriors. Their mail and their horses were not as good as my own but they would be more than adequate in dealing with these Hibernians.

One or two Irishmen stood on the turf wall. I saw them turn and wave to the others. If they disappeared, then we would have to follow for it would mean they had returned to their boats. We were the bait and we had to be patient and draw them on to us.

Saxon Throne

Even now my men would be creeping, unseen, closer to the ships. The longer they watched us the more chance we had of success. I guessed that three boats would have crews of between twenty and thirty. If they wanted slaves, then it would be nearer to twenty. As the rest of the warband appeared I saw that there looked to be about seventy men. A true estimate was hard for they milled about and pointed at us.

Two of the warriors ran towards us and lowered their breeks when they were sixty paces from us. Perhaps they thought to insult us. Kay said, "I could hit one with a javelin, Warlord!"

"I know but let them come from the wall. It will make our job easier."

Our inactivity was the final argument and the warband suddenly raced at us. My men knew exactly what to do once I gave the order. I waited until they were committed and were a hundred paces from us.

"Charge!" I knew they would not halt. These barbarians never did. They relied on raw courage. We were closing quickly. "Wheel and throw!"

I led one line and Llenlleog the other. I turned left and he turned right. As one, my line of equites turned to our left and each of us hurled our first javelin. Pol and I had read of this manoeuvre when we had studied in the east. It was a variation on a Cantabrian circle. We did not look to see where our missiles had struck. We rode around in a large circle. The Irish were in disarray for they did not know if we were fleeing or not. As we came around again we threw our second javelin. I could see that we had hit ten with our first javelins and slightly less with our second. We had, however, halted them.

I saw the first of my squires and archers as they reached the top of the turn wall.

"Fall back!"

Our plan was succeeding when disaster struck. One of the Irishmen, with a javelin protruding from his leg, managed to rip the javelin from it and he hurled it after us. Osgar was the last in the line. Had the javelin struck him he would have suffered no injury but it hit his horse in the rump. It skidded round and another warrior ran up to the horse which Osgar was trying to control and the pirate hacked its hind leg. The animal fell on its side with its hooves flailing. Osgar was trapped beneath his dying horse and the enemy fell upon him and hacked him to death.

I wheeled Star around and shouted, "Charge!"

My men needed no urging. Osgar had been an equite for a long time. They wanted vengeance. Drawing Saxon Slayer I led my men and we galloped at the barbarians. They were so intent upon butchering the already dead equite that the first two died while their backs were to us. We were committed now and we fell amongst them. Pelas and Daffydd raced to cut off their retreat. All orders were forgotten. We had a comrade to avenge. The pirates fought bravely and recklessly but there was no order to their fight. Each one wanted a glorious death and they received what they wished. They all joined Osgar in the Otherworld before his horse had stopped bleeding. Our enemies had suffered wounds as bad as Osgar for we were angry. For myself, I inflicted blows which reflected my anger with King Cadwallon and his murder of King Eanfrith. For the others, it was to avenge Osgar.

We took all that we could from the barbarian dead and made a pyre. They burned. We left Osgar where he lay and we put stones from the river upon him. Each warrior placed a stone and said farewell to our comrade and his horse We kept going until the mound was almost as high as a man. Then we cut and laid turf upon it. When the fire died down, in a couple of days, we would spread the ashes over the mound as a memorial to Osgar. He had died in Rheged. He was the first. He would not be the last.

We put the arms and treasures of the dead barbarians in the three boats and my squires sailed them up the river to anchor them within sight of our walls. Although their weapons were poor they could be melted down and Garth could turn them into mail, and arrow heads. Swords would need iron ore. As we rode through the gates I could not help looking at the mountains to the south. Wyddfa held many secrets: blue stones, gold and copper. Perhaps Halvelyn held similar secrets; who knew.

We feasted that night and sang songs of the past. Gawan sang of the death of the Warlord, our father, and Kay and Bors told tales of Osgar and his courage. For our new equites, it brought them closer to us. When we had finished singing and honouring the dead I sent for Pelas.

"Pelas, you have been my squire and served me well. You have led men and won battles for us. Today we lost an equite. Tonight, we gain another. Pelas, you are our newest equite. Take Osgar's spare horse until we can get two more for you." I gave him a gold coin. They were Roman treasure we had unearthed in Cymru. "Take this and on the morrow give it to Garth. Tell him he is to make you a suit of mail and make you a helmet. Then you must make your new shield."

All my equites banged their daggers on the table. It was not the round table we had had at the fort on the narrows but it would do. We knew we were all equals and none needed a table to tell them that.

The men of Elmet chose their own farms well and proved to be resourceful farmers. They had dried beans which they had kept from the summer crop. They planted them. It would ensure an early crop. My archers and squires rode the hills gathering stray sheep and cattle. There was little point in leaving them for the wolves. None lived between us and the two small tarns which lay before the long water. Lann Aelle had found eight families who still lived around the long water and when spring came he would build upon that community. We were small in number but, like an acorn, we would grow. I would also be a Warlord.

The men of Strathclyde had been our allies the generation before my father but now they were predators. There were many slaves who lived north of the wall. If King Cadwallon allowed us to live, then I would raid the land of Strathclyde and reclaim the animals and people who had been stolen from us.

And as the leaves fell and autumn brought its mists and damp we grew and we prospered. A steady trickle of both people and warriors joined us. Some came from as far away as Ynys Môn and Wyddfa. They were our people who had survived the plague and they brought us tales of the deaths of our families. Others came from Elmet, Deira and even Northumbria for there were people there who tired of war and longed for the protection my sword brought.

The first frosts of winter also saw the first marriages. Bors, Kay and Gruffyd all took girls of Elmet to be their brides. Others would follow. Gawan seemed happy that their union was bountiful for all three brides were with child. He saw it as a sign that our reign was bringing prosperity to the land. The first frost also brought disquieting news. King Cadwallon and King Oswald were both preparing for war. The spring might bring new growth but it could be snuffed out by sword and axe.

Gawan and I stood on the walls wrapped up in cloaks. He was the only one in whom I could confide my fears; he knew them already but speaking with him sometimes brought solutions. "We are not strong enough to fight either army, Gawan."

"I know but we may not have to. If they fight each other, then they may weaken so much that they cannot take us."

"That is not my fear. My fear is that one of them comes here first. They may decide to rid themselves of us."

"They would die trying to besiege us."

"No, Gawan, for we are a victim of our own success. The only way we can feed all the people we have here is to keep grazing our animals during the winter. They need the fields by the river. If we are besieged, we cannot do that nor can we fish the rivers and hunt in the forests. A siege would mean our death. We need to survive the winter and then build our forces up so that we can resist our foes."

A sudden breeze chilled me to the bone and I saw that Gawan had his eyes closed. He began to chant. I did not understand any of the words but I recognised the rhythm. It was an invocation of Myrddyn's. I waited until he had finished. It took some time. He looked exhausted. He gave me a wan smile, "I have asked the Mother to help us."

I nodded, "Then she is our best hope."

Just then the first snowflake of the winter fell upon me. It was followed by another until, within a short time, it was a blizzard. We hurried indoors as the storm raged. When we awoke, the next day, we saw a sea of white. Winter had come. Gawan's invocation had worked for the land from the Ituna to the Dunum was frozen. The high passes were closed and none could come west. We had to clear the snow from our fields to enable our animals to graze and those animals which were ready to lamb and calf we brought within our walls. Animals did die and those we ate. Others became ill and they died but not all. The wolves howled to the north but were silent to the south. The only hunters were Geraint and his scouts who braved the snow and the cold to keep us supplied. One of the Irish boats was used to go out into the estuary and fish. We ate. None of us was ever full but none died of starvation and we were warm. The forests and woods kept our fires well supplied. We had no Myrddyn but we had Gawan and his power had saved us. The earth was as one with us. We had been right and King Cadwallon wrong.

We still trained but we spent more time talking because we needed plans and strategies for the spring. Enemies would come. At Yule, that long dark time when the sun barely peered over the horizon we stayed within the hall which King Urien had built. It was packed with my equites, squires and archers. Outside might be cold enough to kill but within the walls of the hall, there was a warm fug.

I sat with Gawan, Lann Aelle, Pol and Llenlleog. We had only some of the wine made from the blackberry and the elderberry. It was raw but it was potent. It loosened tongues.

"What made Cadwallon change? We left Wrecsam and he was a good warrior. But the further north we travelled the more he changed."

Gawan smiled, "You have answered yourself Llenlleog. Wyddfa held sway over him. Perhaps Myrddyn too." He gave me a guilty look and I shook my head. "Once he left its control then the other side of him took over. Ask my brother. He could have ended the year controlling all the land between Mercia and the land of the Picts. All that he had to do was to back Eanfrith against Oswald and there would have been no Northumbrian army ready to battle him."

"Is that true, Warlord?"

"Yes, Lann Aelle. Eanfrith did not want to war against the men of Cymru. By his wife, he stood to inherit lands north of the wall and he did not want any of the Cadwallon's land. It was a foolish act. Cadwallon will pay for it. He sees himself as unbeatable. If he defeats Oswald, then he will take on King Penda and his Mercians. There he will meet his match."

"Can he beat Oswald?"

"He should, Pol. He has a bigger army and his equites are almost as good as ours. He has archers and Oswald has none. If I were to put gold on the outcome I would back Cadwallon but," I looked at Gawan, "my brother has dreamed a different outcome."

They all looked at him.

"I have seen a trail of dead and dying Welshmen leading all the way to the high passes. The magpies and chuffs feed well and the foxes grow fat."

Llenlleog shook his head, "If Saxons can defeat equites then we are lost."

Gawan said, "Were you not listening, Llenlleog? We are led by the Warlord. Listen to the wind and step outside, feel the snow. The Mother protects us from our enemies. When Spring comes, we will have a bounty of babies, and young animals. More men will flock to the dragon banner and we will grow stronger. So long as the Warlord wields Saxon Slayer then we will never be defeated."

I looked at him. I would not contradict him but we had both dreamed my death. The end would come. I would die alone and hunted. I knew not how. So long as my men rode with me then I was safe. I bore a terrible burden. I knew how I would die and could do nothing to prevent it.

I smiled, "So you should all do as Bors and Kay have done. Find women and instead of listening to my blather, make babies. Our way of life can only go on through our young. If the land is reborn then so are we."

Later when Gawan and I were alone he asked me, "And you brother? Will you take a woman again?"

I did not answer him because I knew not the answer.

Chapter 8

None of us could ever remember such a long and icy winter. I wondered how Dargh and his hardy folk by the long water beneath Halvelyn had fared. At least they would not have been bothered by wolves. They had been driven off by us. We had yet to visit the west of the land of Rheged but I did not relish the prospect of travelling there for I knew not what we would find. We had heard wolf packs all winter. Any who survived would be as tough as the animals who preyed there. And then, one morning the air felt less cold. A day later and the snow was not hard. I ventured out with a few of my equites and scouts. We took with us some of our salted and dried meat. Geraint led us south as far as the pass to the waters. We passed four farms where people had survived. The old had been taken and the ones who remained were thin and emaciated but they had survived. We only managed to reach the pass for we helped each farm to make a stew of the salted and dried meats. I had planned to travel further but there had been too many who needed our help.

As we returned I said to Geraint. "Tomorrow I wish you to ride as far as you can and find out who lives to the south of us. I will send my equites out with food to follow you. The earth has sheltered us from our enemies but, as in war, there are innocent casualties. We must save those that we can."

It suited my equites. After a winter indoors, it was good for us to ride. They, like me, were keen to help the people too. I had Daffydd and his archers travel north of the wall to hunt. Even as we had ridden back from our first mission of mercy, the snow had begun to thaw. When we left on the second day I saw our cattle and sheep had cleared the muddy snow to munch on the new grass which was peering through. It was a sign. The winter was over. Over the next six days, we traversed the land of Rheged, even as far as the southern coast. There, at the very tip of our land, the people had had the easiest time. The snow had left some days earlier than in the north. Geraint had discovered the people there and I had travelled to speak with the headman for they were the most populous village we had encountered.

It was a long ride and we were forced to ask for hospitality. The headman insisted, "Warlord, we have awaited your return for these many years. I am descended from the old ones. I am Pasgen son of Pasgen. My grandfather was King Urien's son."

I could not help glancing around at the mean and humble surroundings, "But you should be a prince."

He shook his head, "When my grandfather died my father brought us here. He hoped to take ship and join you close to Wyddfa but the storms raged and we had to spend a month here and then the winter came. We survived and my father thought it *wyrd*. We were meant to be here and to await your return. Save for the occasional raid by pirates we are safe here. This is our home now and we are happy. We have fish. The forests give us timber and the earth is fertile. We do not starve."

"I am back now. I will protect you from the pirates. Can you predict when they will come?"

He laughed, "Almost to the day, Warlord. They will come with the Spring tides. We have ditches and we have walls. We lose some animals but they soon tire of beating their swords against our walls. Our archers thin their ranks and they sail north for easier pickings. It is ever thus."

"Then this time we will have a surprise for them. Send a rider to me a week before the Spring tide and I will bring my equites. They will not have even one animal from this land."

When I returned to my home I spoke with Gawan and the others. "When I came here my eye was drawn to the east and Oswald, " I shrugged, "and perhaps, King Cadwallon. I can see now that I was wrong to do so. The danger to our people is also from the west."

Gawan said, "Do not forget the north. The villagers told us of slavers who prey from the north."

"You are right. Lann Aelle I would have you take the equites and archers who came from Cadwallon. Build your fort at the large water. There you will be half a day from Pasgen. When he sends to me I will join you and we will surprise these pirates."

He nodded, "And I will watch Alavna in the west and the slavers from the north. This year we hold what we have. Next year we take what we need."

I had Geraint and his scouts shift their attention, as the land warmed up, to the east. It took some time for the high passes to clear of snow. It had been a harsh winter.

Garth and his sons worked like Vulcan himself to turn out armour. Those squires who had the skills would be armoured as equites. I set Gawan the task of breeding bigger horses for them. Star had fathered many foals but now he was getting old and Gawan selected other horses who had the same traits as my war horse. I confess that I gave little thought to either the people of Elmet who had followed us or the families of Rheged. They would have to get on with their lives. They would be safe and when all danger was gone then I would do as Myrddyn would have done and make my people happy. Where was the wizard? I needed his wisdom.

The first emaciated refugees trickled over the high passes once all snow was gone. They brought tales of hunger and starvation; famine and disease. Neither King Cadwallon nor King Oswald would be able to field an army until high summer. Gawan and I thanked the gods and Mother Earth for their help. They had bought us time. The newcomers were cared for and nurtured. They would till the land on the farms where the winter had killed those who had once lived there. They were just grateful to be in a land which still had food. Our preparations had not been in vain.

The rider from Pasgen was expected for we knew roughly when it would be. Leaving six squires and ten archers I took the rest of my men south. Lann Aelle would already be closing with the village by the sea. It took all day for us to reach Lann Aelle and his men. He had established a camp in the forest some four miles from Pasgen's walls. This time the pirate ships were safely moored in the bay and beyond us but the pirates, according to Lann Aelle's scouts, were camped between the river and the walls of Pasgen's town.

"They have sent scouts out to search for farms and food." He pointed to the three bodies which were visible on the path. "These three were heading north."

"Then we send our archers and squires to capture or kill the rest."

"Capture, cousin?"

"Yes, Lann Aelle. I would know who commands these pirates for I would send them a message that I am returned. My men will rest and on the morrow, we will attack those on the shore. Daffydd, Geraint, have your men go in small groups and hunt the Irish scouts."

Although tired both men were warriors. Their scouts and archers would do as I asked.

Pol said, "You will not use the archers tomorrow for our attack?"

"No, we use our horses, our armour and our swords. They will not be expecting us. I doubt that they will worry when these three do not return. They will suspect they have found something to keep them occupied."

I sat with Gawan. "I will sleep, brother, and see if I can dream." He pointed south. "There is naught between here and Wyddfa. Perhaps Myrddyn can speak with me."

I watched as my little brother slept. He was growing in power but, even so, he was still desperate to emulate Myrddyn. The old wizard had been his mentor as my father had been to me. Both had been taken before we had become all that we could be. Gawan had the chance to become stronger. I now had no one who could teach me how to be a better leader. Would my people and my men pay for my mistakes with their lives?

Gawan's sleep was not a quiet one. I saw him toss and turn. He called out in his sleep and my sentries looked over, anxiously. I waved them away. As dawn broke, Gawan woke. Surprisingly he smiled, "Myrddyn lives! I know not where but he is alive." He laughed, "He is pleased with us both, brother." I could not help smiling for Gawan was like a puppy who was eager to please. "I saw armies in the east. There will be a battle. The Roman wall will see it again. It will be close to where our uncle lost his arm." I nodded. I remembered where that was. It was close to the Roman Cavalry fort. "I know not when, brother."

I smiled. That question had been in my head. "You have done well, little brother. Rest for I can see it has exhausted you."

"No, Warlord, for this day you will need my sword and men will need my skills as a healer."

We mounted. The archers and the scouts had left before dawn. There were just my equites and squires. We moved to the edge of the forest and watched the sun rise from the east. There was a little early morning mist. Once the sun rose it would burn away but it meant that visibility was more limited. The pirates had had guards and they were now building up the fires to heat food. The warriors rose to relieve themselves and use the waters of the river to wake them up. They were about to receive a rather ruder awakening. As we emerged from the trees my equites took their places alongside me. We moved steadily south. The squires would be the second rank. I hoped we would not need them. The mist began to clear.

We were a hundred paces from them when we were spotted. I heard the shout of alarm. I raised Saxon Slayer, "Charge!"

As soon as we began to trot the dragon standard began to wail as the air passed through it. The effect was always the same; it terrorised. Panic set in. Some tried to stand and fight. Those in the water called out to those on the boats to come for them. Had they stood and fought it would have been a better end but they were divided and we struck them in a solid line of horses and steel. They tried to hit my equites with their short swords and spears. Our mail and our splint greaves warded off their blows. I slashed my sword horizontally. It bit into the first warrior's bare chest. It cut him to the bone. I swung it over Star's head to slice through the skull of the warrior who was trying to spear Lann Aelle. My arm jarred with the blow. Pasgen and his people erupted from their walls, keen to take revenge upon these pirates. It did not take long to kill the ones who had been half asleep and woken to find equites in their midst.

I rode to the water's edge. Some had managed to swim out to the boats and clamber aboard. There were four boats; they were identical to the three we had captured. I took off my helmet and raised my sword, "I am the Warlord of Rheged! I have come home and I tell you that this land is now under my protection. If you come again then I will destroy you and I will visit the wrath of my sword, Saxon Slayer, upon your lands. I will slaughter every warrior and enslave every man woman and child. Heed my warning and find others upon which to prey."

One figure, at the rear of the last boat, raised his arm, "We hear you, Warlord."

The four ships sailed south. They would not reach home quickly for they had few to row. Their crews would have the chance to reflect upon my words.

Kay shouted, "Forty dead, Warlord! Forty and we lost not a man!"

"It is a start, Kay, and nothing more."

I dismounted and led Star to Pasgen. "Thank you, Warlord. We are thankful to you."

"I am back but use the weapons from these pirates to make yourselves stronger. I am a hard day's ride away."

Lann Aelle said, "But I am less than half a day. Pasgen, build a signal tower. I will build one on the high ground over the forest of flies. You can signal if you need assistance."

"I will do so, lord."

The tide was on its way out and we used it to dispose of the bodies. We hurled them in and the sea took them away. They would feed the fishes. The smell of burning human flesh was something the people of Pasgen's town would not appreciate. It was fitting that the sea consumed them. They came from the sea and they died by the sea.

It was late afternoon by the time all of my archers and scouts returned. They brought with them five wounded Irish scouts. Three would not live beyond the night but the other two would.

"Separate them!"

Gawan and I went to the most severely wounded of the pirates. He had a stomach wound. Gawan said, "Speak and I will end your pain and send you to the Allfather with a blade in your hand."

He nodded and spoke through gritted teeth, "Ask."

"Where are you from?"

"My ship came from the land of the Uí Néill. Ours is a poor land."

I nodded, "Such is life." I put his sword in his hand and Gawan slit his throat.

The others all told us similar stories. One ship had come from Dál Riata. I would have to give thought to them. I wanted all the raiders to know that they could no longer use Rheged as a larder.

We left for my home a day later having repaired the damage caused by the pirates. As we headed up the lake by the craggy mountain which brooded in the west Gawan said, "We should send Garth to see if there is iron in those hills."

"Garth needs to make mail and swords. But your suggestion is a good one. We will send others to find the precious ore. If it is there then we shall be invincible."

"Remember, brother, I see dark days ahead. It is as though we pass into a long tunnel. I cannot spy the end."

"There will be an end. Perhaps we will not see it but your son Arturus will and if not then his son." I patted Saxon Slayer. "This sword, from generations past, and this phalera," I held out the dragon medal, "tell us that. We are part of the story of this land. We are not the whole story. We build a future; I see that now."

"Perhaps that is why Myrddyn is not here. You needed to gain that wisdom, brother."

"That may be but I would still have Myrddyn at my side and he could help us both."

The days grew longer and warmer but we did not relax our vigilance. We knew that war was coming but we did not know when. We made more of our squires into equites. Squires were becoming rare and I saw no hope that we could replace them. The young men of Rheged worked in their fields or toiled in smiths. It was Gawan, inevitably, who saw a solution to our problem.

"Brother, we have three Irish ships out in the estuary. They fish and that is all."

"What else would we do with them?"

"I do not say this lightly. Let us send one to Ynys Môn. There may be some of our people there. Daffydd ap Gwynfor lived when we left. Perhaps he seeks a new home. We must see if there are those who followed us."

"Why should they return here?"

"Because, brother, you and father left Rheged because of the Saxons. They are here no longer. And because you are Warlord."

"And why should that make a difference?"

He laughed, "You are the only one who does not see that you have the power to draw men to your banner."

I smiled, I was not vain. "And who would captain this boat?"

"I would."

"You seek Myrddyn."

"I will not lie to you. I hope that Wyddfa helps me to send his spirit to aid us but I believe that there will be those who would serve us. Besides we need a way to send a message to my wife and son in Constantinopolis. If Daffydd ap Gwynfor is there then he can sail east. There are weapons we can buy there that will aid us here."

"It is a risk. I would not lose you."

"You will not."

"Whom would you take?"

"I would take Tadgh and some of the squires. We can pretend to be Irish."

I could see that he had thought this through. I had considered taking my equites to ride there but we could not afford to be without our swords for that length of time. "Very well but make sure you return. I have lost one wizard. I cannot afford to lose a second and, more importantly, my brother."

"I have not dreamed my death. I will return."

When he left, five days later, I found I missed him. Since our father's death and Myrddyn's disappearance, he had been a constant at my side. He was not a powerful warrior like Pol or Llenlleog but he was almost a part of me. I decided to use his absence to let other enemies know that I had returned. I knew that he would be away for at least six days and so I took ten equites and ten squires to ride north of the wall. Geraint came with me. I needed his ears and eyes not to mention his nose. We had had no sign of enemies and the frontier appeared peaceful. I knew that could be an illusion and we rode ready for anything.

We crossed the Ituna at a ford which was well to the east of my fort. There were forests up here as well as open areas where farmers had cleared the land for their animals. In the distance, I saw the smoke from one such farm. It was to the east and so I turned and headed west. I am not certain what we sought but in my mind, I wanted to get a picture of the land for I had never crossed the Ituna before. The land could tell me much about the people who lived here. Before the men of Dál Riata had come this had been the land of an ally. This had been the land of

Ridderch Hael. Some of his people, like Mungo, had come south with us. His grandchildren still lived on Ynys Môn. I wondered if Gawan would find them.

The men of Dál Riata were different to us and had a culture and a life which was different from ours. It would be reflected in the land. They like their cattle. Cattle raids were a common event in their homeland. Here we kept cattle for milk. It was sheep and goats which gave us our food. Cattle needed better grass than sheep and we soon saw where the incomers lived.

As we moved west we saw their cattle in the valley bottoms feeding on the rich grass there. It was not as rich as they had hoped. The ones we saw were thin and showed what a hard winter they had endured. Their herders saw us and drove them west away from danger. We did not hurry. We were not here to capture cattle.

A knot of riders galloped towards us. Two had helmets and all bore a shield but there were not enough of them to cause us worry. They halted and their leader shouted, "Who are you that dares to trespass on the land of Fiachnae mac Fergus?"

"I am the Warlord of Rheged and we mean no harm."

They looked at each other and I saw shields raised. Even my name put fear in their hearts.

"This is not Rheged."

"No, nor is it Hibernia whence you came."

I could see that I had perplexed them. "What is it you want, horseman?"

"Nothing save peace." He nodded and I saw their weapons lowered. "However, men from Dál Riata raided Rheged this year and last year. I am here to tell you that it will not happen again."

"It was not Fiachnae mac Fergus who did so."

"And yet this is his land. Tell your leader that I will punish any who raid Rheged. If he wishes peace and not to incur my wrath, then he should use his influence to stop others. If not then he, his people, and his cattle will suffer."

"You threaten our lord?"

I laughed, "Of course I do!" Shaking my head I added, "If he wishes peace then tell him to keep his allies north of the river. South is now Rheged."

I turned Star and led my men back to the ford. Kay laughed, "I think you have given them much to think there, Warlord."

"There is little point in politeness when you need a message delivered. There can be no doubt about our position. If the men of Dál Riata head south, then it is for war."

I felt much calmer as we crossed the Ituna. I never liked deceit. Now that I was Warlord then I could be honest. I spent the next two days with my equites and archers hunting. The young wild boar needed culling as did the deer. The fact that no one had hunted them for some time had created more than was good for the land. We ensured that we ate well and only the strong and the wily survived. We feasted and what the people did not eat we dried and salted. The Roman fort had many granaries and places to store food. We used them well. Who knew when times would be hard.

Gawan arrived home ten days after he had left. I had begun to worry. His boat was heavily laden and was followed by Daffydd ap Gwynfor in his larger merchantman. I walked to the shoreline to greet him. He dropped to his knee when he leapt ashore. I raised him to his feet. "My old friend you need not kneel!"

"Warlord, we did not know if you lived or died. We heard rumours of battles to the west and that King Cadwallon was Emperor. No one mentioned your name."

I looked beyond him to Gawan who shrugged. "I live but this is my new home."

Daffydd ap Gwynfor waved a hand at the young men and women who were coming ashore. "We have been waiting for such a summons. Since the King left and the plague came our island home has been a charnel house. People say that the gods have deserted us. The Saxons from Mercia threaten us as do the raiders from Manau and Hibernia." He lowered his head, "Some said you had deserted us too."

"This was always our home. Our time in Cymru was an interlude, no more. My father always intended to return and I judged the time to be right." He nodded, "Will you be my captain again?"

"Aye Warlord and gladly." He looked around. "This seems a green and verdant land but this is no place to land a ship. We need a stone jetty, Warlord!"

"Then you and my brother shall build one. Whatever you wish you shall have for today Rheged rises from the ashes."

Chapter 9

It took a month to build what Daffydd ap Gwynfor wanted. He required something solid to which he could tie his ship and then unload easily. While we did as he asked, he and his sons returned in two of our Irish ships to fetch back more of those who wish to leave our island home. The priests of King Cadwallon demanded a tithe for the church from each person on the island despite the fact that most adhered to the old ways. As Daffydd said to me, "We have no warriors to protect us. We would be better paying off the Irish not to raid us. Between the priests and the pirates, we are starving to death."

"And your trade with the east?"

"It has dried up. We are the last merchant ship for the rest have been captured or sunk."

"Then when we have more sailors you and my pirate ships will sail to Constantinopolis. We have a lot of gold and I would spend it there. We will make the merchants of the Empire trade with us once more."

Those were good days and they lasted until midsummer day. We had new squires whom we were training and archers who were becoming more skilled. We had them on the flat ground outside the fort training when I heard the alarm bell in the citadel sound. We grabbed our weapons as a rider galloped in. It was Iago ap Caerwen, one of Dai's most trusted warriors. He leapt from his horse and dropped to his knees.

"Warlord, Dai ap Gruffyd has sent me. King Cadwallon marches to make war on King Oswald. My lord begs you to come to his aid. He asks you to do this for times past and in memory of King Cadfan."

"Has the King asked for me?"

"No lord," he lowered his voice, "My lord begged me to plead for you to help the King. He knows not what he does. The King has changed, lord."

Then this plea came from Dai and not Cadwallon. That was disappointing. "Does Oswald outnumber him?"

"No lord but he has a fortified position north of the Roman Wall at Hagustaldes-ham. The King brings his host to destroy them." He looked at me and his eyes showed his fear. "My lord says that if you do not come then all will be lost. There are many of us who were unhappy when you left. If you return, then hope will follow. With you, we might win."

I looked across to Gawan. He smiled and nodded, "It is not for the King, brother. It is for the friendship we owe those who will die otherwise. We both know our father would have gone."

He was right. No matter how badly we had been treated we owed it to those who were with the King and those who remained at home to help him.

"Equites and squires, we ride. Daffydd ap Miach command until I return. Send word to my cousin what we do."

My captain of archers looked at me, "Will twenty equites and fifteen squires be enough, Warlord?"

"It will have to do for I will not strip my defences. The archers can defend my walls if danger comes while I go to help this foolish king. King Cadwallon has brought this upon himself. We have Rheged once more. We keep what we have. Come, Iago ap Caerwen, eat and we will give you a new horse. We ride to aid your master," I paused, "And the misguided King he follows."

I knew the place where the two sides would meet. As soon as Iago had told me of the route the King took then I knew. It was a strip of land north of the wall and hemmed in by crags and uneven ground to the north. The battle would have to take place in a narrow strip of land. It would take a clever general to win there. My father had fought there alongside King Urien when they defeated Aella. I had a bad feeling for King Urien had been outnumbered then and yet still emerged victorious. I am not certain what I would have done had not Dai asked for my help. One did not let down an old comrade.

It was over thirty miles to Hagustaldes-ham. We rode hard and I hoped we could reach there in a few hours for the Roman road was still a good one. As we rode Iago told me that King Oswald and his army were north of the wall which meant we had to cross it also. I knew it was a desolate part of the country and that our horses would not be in a good condition when they arrived but we were committed to this course of action.

Geraint and Tadgh rode ahead of us on their lighter ponies. They returned as we neared the cliffs close to the Rigg. It was a few Roman miles from Hagustaldes-ham.

"Warlord, the battle has started. King Cadwallon and his men are attacking the Saxons."

"And?"

Geraint shook his head. "It is a narrow front across which they fight Warlord. The axes of the hearthweru are slaughtering the horses of the equites."

"Is he not using his archers?"

"No lord."

"Then we do what we can. We attack the rear of the enemy lines. We are few in number. Hopefully, they will think that I bring a mighty host. Let us make up for our numbers with courage. Ride, equites of Rheged, and let us make this a day to remember a day when last debts were paid."

Once we left the road and crossed through the gap in the wall the ground did not suit our horses and we did not make good time. There were places we had to pick our way through. We heard the battle before we saw it. The men of Bernicia were not having it all their own way. We saw wounded men making their way west away from the battle. They fled when they saw our approach. I began to wonder if our sudden appearance might make the rest of the army panic.

The land rose before us and when we crested the rise we saw the battle before us. In the distance, I saw King Cadwallon's banner and before it the banners of Bernicia. Between us and our allies lay the whole of the Bernician army. We had had no time to prepare well for the fight and we just had our swords. They would have to do.

I waved my sword forward and we began to trot toward the Saxons. The ground was uneven, King Oswald had chosen it well. We would not be able to gallop. At best, we would be able to canter. Our woefully short line of twenty equites ploughed into the fyrd who were being urged forward by the Gesith. They stood no chance and we heard a collective wail as we struck them from behind. Hope sprung for I saw, ahead, the banner of King Cadwallon but, even as we struck the fyrd I saw it fall and then the Saxon line surged forward. We were too late and the men of Gwynedd had broken. The speed with which the bulk of the Saxons moved east told me that. The banner was gone. There would be no rallying point. We should have stopped then but honour and old friendships demanded that we at least try to rescue some of our friends.

Although the fyrd did not stand against us and fled I found that we could not ride as fast as we wished for the remainder of the fyrd were milling around in front of us. They were a human barrier. They were plundering the dead and oblivious to our arrival. The only way through them was with cold steel and we carved our way ruthlessly through them. The Northumbrians were chasing the fleeing men of Gwynedd. I could see horsemen in the distance and their backs were to us. They had broken.

The retreating horsemen were getting further from us. His hearthweru were in hot pursuit. And then we were through the fyrd and passing the last stand of King Cadwallon's oathsworn. They had stayed around the fallen standard to buy time for their king with their lives. Their horses lay butchered before them and the four or five who were left were beleaguered. Even as we approached I saw Dai ap Gruffyd as he was hacked down from behind by four hearthweru and the standard ripped from his dying hands. It was too much for my men and we tore into the warriors. The last of Dai's men fell before we could reach them. I leaned forward, as Star raised his front hooves, and I brought down my sword at the gap between the mail and the coif of the hearthweru who tried to face me. My equites gave no opportunities for the mailed warriors to escape. They were hacked, slashed and stabbed. They had slain our friends. Iago himself grabbed the standard and decapitated the Saxon who had been triumphantly holding the flag aloft. I skewered a warrior whose arms were filled with warrior bands. I struck so hard that the sword emerged from his front. I threw his body from my blade. He was the last. The rest of King Oswald's army was more than a mile away to the east. The men of Gwynedd were being slaughtered.

Handing my reins to Gawan I dismounted and knelt down by Dai. It was a mortal wound and I wondered that he lived still but he did for his eyes opened and he smiled. A tendril of blood seeped from his mouth. "You came. I knew you would. This is the end of the equites of Gwynedd, lord. I was the last."

"The King?"

He closed his eyes in pain and then opened them. "He is fled. Do not judge him, lord, the thrones changed him. Of late he would not take advice from me. Who was advising him I know not. Make Rheged safe, my lord. I go to join his father, King Cadfan. I should have died before this day. The glory days are behind us. Gwynedd is finished. You are the hope of the west. At least I have my sword in my hand, I..."

And then he died. The former squire of King Cadfan was faithful unto the end. His choice of a sword told me he died faithful to the old ways and I hoped that King Cadfan would welcome him in the Otherworld.

Gawan's hand shook my shoulder urgently, "Brother, we must go. We can do no more here!" I saw, far in the distance, to the east, the Northumbrians as they slaughtered the Welsh. They were too far now for us to reach. My brother was right. Even now a Saxon lord was rallying the fyrd. More than two hundred remained and we were but thirty. He was organising a shield wall. Others were rallying to his banner. We could fight them but what would be the point? We would be sacrificed for nothing. I mounted. Iago knelt still by his master. "Come, Iago ap Caerwen. Serve me. Your master would have wished it."

He nodded, "He wanted to join you but he remembered his oath to the King's father. He was faithful unto death." He held the standard. "And I will keep this as weregeld from my master and my brothers!"

We mounted and prepared to fight our way through the fyrd. Perhaps their leader knew it would be futile to stand in our way for he made a shield wall three shields high so that we would not be able to attack his men. We clattered past the wall of shields and spears. They hurled insults at us from the security of a wall of wood and iron. We rode west towards the setting sun. It seemed to me that the sun was setting not only in the west but in the west. King Cadwallon's brief dalliance with Empire had ended in disaster.

Our escape was not easy but my men had steel in their hearts. They had seen comrades with whom they had faced death, die.

They were in no mood for mercy and every Saxon foolish enough to stand, fell.

Once we had passed the last of the Saxons we continued west even though night had fallen. We knew the road and there were no enemies before us. We rode in silence. I was thinking of the times I had fought alongside Dai and also wondering how King Cadwallon would fare. His dream was over but I had no doubt that he would try to resurrect his ideas. However, with his equites gone, for I had seen their bodies, it was hard to see how. The moon had risen when we rode through my gates. Our horses would be of no use for at least two days. We had ridden them hard, almost to death. However, for Gawan and my captains, we would be as active as ants in the summer. We now had an enemy to the east. The Northumbrians were no longer a memory, they were a reality and we would have to fight them. Perhaps it might be next year but the day would dawn and we would need to be ready.

Over the next few days, stragglers from the disaster made their way to the west and my sanctuary. The first few had horses but the rest were lucky to arrive with their lives. In all, but a hundred men survived the disaster. We heard how King Cadwallon had finally fallen. He had been hacked to death at a place called Denis' Brook. It was east and south of Hagustaldes-ham. No one ever found his body. Many of those who caught him had been the brethren of Eanfrith. They exacted their revenge for the murder of the last King of Bernicia. Oswald had now declared himself King of Northumbria. At least one of the sons of Aethelfrith had reclaimed the throne that had been theirs. The golden years of Gwynedd were over. I could never go back now, even if I wished to, and those who had fled when Gawan had taken ship turned from a trickle to a flood. With no army to defend their borders the land around Wyddfa became anarchic as petty chiefs vied for power and King Penda encroached upon the land of his former ally. For us it was remote. It concerned us not for we had other matters to consider. We were alone.

The only hint of silver around the dark cloud which spread over us was that more of those who wished to leave Gwynedd, our people were able to do so. Out ships brought a steady flow of those fleeing what they knew would be a dark and dangerous battleground. Rheged might also become one but they were drawn to the Warlord and his equites. This was where we heard all of our news. Once the last of Cadwallon's survivors had reached us then the roads east were closed. Our land teemed with newcomers who settled on farms or in the town which was growing close to the fort. They brought with them their skills and they made Rheged stronger.

Daffydd ap Gwynfor became our lifeline. By the time of the moon before harvest the last of those who wished to join us had arrived and with them came some hope. As we spoke with those who had lived close by Wyddfa we heard of lights in the mountain. There were tales of my father appearing on Wyddfa's top and riding a dragon. Others reported seeing an old man in the forests; some said it was Myrddyn. None of the sightings was reliable but they were hints which gave my brother and me hope that Myrddyn might return one day. There were hints and rumours aplenty. Some said he had been seen in Gwynedd others that he had fled to our brethren across the sea in the land of the Bro Waroc'h. There were even sightings of him in the south of Rheged. They were all rumours but they gave us hope.

The land came to our aid once more. We had more mouths to feed but the harvest that year was good. It was better than good; none could ever remember such a high yield or such a plentiful number of young animals. It might have been only oats, barley and rye but it was heavy. The beans had also produced a glut that we could store for the winter. Out animals birthed healthy young and we determined to keep as many alive over winter as we could. With the fishermen who had come from Caer Gybi, we were now able to harvest the sea. The gods were doing all in their power to aid us.

For my part, I made my forts and our homes as strong as we could. I insisted that the newcomers live in villages. I ordered that each one have a ditch and a wall. I decreed that they farmed together. I had no king to consult and my brother concurred with all of my decisions. And to be fair to those who lived now in Rheged, they did as I had asked. I sent Pol with Daffydd ap Gwynfor to Constantinopolis. This was partly to assure Gwyneth and Arturus that we lived still but more importantly to begin to trade with the East. The copper we found in the mountains was more valuable in Constantinopolis and Pol would be able to buy, from them, that which we could not produce ourselves. Gawan and I knew that he would be away for months, perhaps half a year but the risk had to be taken.

As he sailed out of the estuary I wondered if I would ever see my oldest friend again. The world was now more dangerous than when we had been young. The seas were filled with pirates. Six of our archers and four squires travelled with him but it was a small enough force with which to repel any attackers.

Gawan saw my worry and he took me to ride north to the turf wall. "Brother, you keep all of your worries locked inside your head and that is not good. Share the burden."

I nodded, "I know, brother and I shall." We dismounted and stood on the ancient earth wall where we had massacred the first pirates and Osgar had fallen. His mound stood as a stark reminder of failure. "We have less than two hundred men who can fight."

"And that is more than twice as many as this time last year."

"But we now have twice as many enemies and no allies."

"And those enemies are all weaker than they were. We saw the dead Northumbrians. I know that King Cadwallon lost far more but the Saxons bled. We have time."

I smiled, "You make it sound easy."

"No, but I am a realist brother. Oswald has a long memory and his enemies were King Cadwallon and King Penda. You will be dismissed as an irritant in the west. The Saxons never yearned for this land, did they? They have barely scratched their name upon the stones. There were more people of Rheged when we came than Saxons. You brought more Saxons, those from Elmet than were here when we arrived."

"You do not see Oswald coming here then?"

"I do not see him coming yet but I am no Myrddyn and I do not see as far as the old man. Since we have left Eoforwic I see clearer but I am still learning how to use my powers. They have grown since we came here and I feel that there is more to come. When we dreamed your death that was the spirits both warning and reassuring you. So long as you stay here in the land of Rheged then you will not die. You only die when you can see Wyddfa's top."

That was both a hopeful and ominous thought.

"Next year then?"

"Before we are in danger? I think so. If the last of King Cadwallon's army has just reached us, then the Saxons will have the same problem. Will his people have gathered in the crops? I doubt it for most of those who farm the land fought and died at Hagustaldes-ham. The survivors will not be able to complete the task. We know Oswald to be many things but a fool is not one of them. He has a mind that he uses. He will only take us on when he believes he can win. King Cadwallon made mistakes. He had horsemen but he did not use them well. They were wasted. You will not make that mistake. King Oswald will have to come up with a cunning plan if he is to defeat you, brother."

I laughed, "You make me sound as good as our father."

He looked at me and said, in all seriousness, "You are better, brother, and that is why father was able to lay down his life so easily. Do you think he would have gone to the Otherworld if you had not been ready? We are all lucky to have you."

I nodded and looked east. "There is little point in keeping our army here, in one place. Lann Aelle now has ten equites with squires and archers in the centre of my land. I have too many here. We need some in the west, perhaps at Alavna and then some in the east, Brocavum. We must protect our borders. You are right about our horses. They are what keep us alive. We need to have our riders range far and wide. They will give a warning and can deal with any issues."

"Do you remember the Bro Waroc'h?" I nodded, "They are our distant kin and they have something which we cannot get here. They have better horses. We should send to their land and buy a breeding pair."

"We did that once and they died before we could see enough of their progeny."

He nodded, "Then we try again. We spend gold and that is all. If it will save lives and make us stronger then that is a better use than jewels upon our fingers."

"You are right and ever practical." We had much gold for we had taken it from the mines close to Wyddfa. We had taken much from the dead Saxon lords we had killed. We were rich. There were squires who had been responsible for keeping the chests safe when we travelled. Now that we had walls then it was secure beneath the secret stone in the citadel. "Who shall we send?"

"There is but one person, brother and you know who it should be. Me."

"If I let you go then, with Pol gone, I shall be alone. There must be others. Llenlleog? He is of the Bro Waroc'h."

"He can come with me but he is a man of the sword. He can protect me but I am the one who can read men's thoughts. Can Llenlleog detect treachery? No. The two of us shall go."

"And you think that taking my best equite outside of Pol makes me feel better?"

He laughed, "Then you must make the others as good as you."

He was right of course and time was of the essence. The winter storms would make the month-long journey impossible. Taking a small chest of our gold they sailed within two days of our decision. I say our for that was what it was. I was Warlord but Gawan was as much a part of me as my sword. Since we had come to Rheged I began to feel that we were one person and not two. I did not understand it but it did not make me uncomfortable.

After he had gone I gathered my equites. I told them of my plans. "Kay, I want you to go to Brocavum and fortify it. It will not take much. I charge you and the five equites I shall give you to keep the road east safe. Bors, I do the same with you. Alavna in the west suffers from pirate raids you and your five equites will watch there. With Lann Aelle in the centre and me in the north, we protect the heartland of Rheged. Our people will prosper and we will start to grow."

They banged their daggers on the table and chanted, "Warlord!"

I held up my hand, "I will keep Daffydd ap Miach and his archers here. Each of you needs to train suitable warriors to be archers and slingers. The farms which are close by your forts will give some of their produce to you and provide a fyrd in case of danger. I am the Warlord but you two shall be my lords of war in the west and the east."

"We will not let you down, Warlord."

"Every seven days I expect you to send a rider with a report of all that goes on in your lands. When my brother returns, we will discuss all that you tell us. My brother grows more powerful and, until Myrddyn returns to us, he is our guide to the spirits."

Pelas asked, "Will Myrddyn come? Is he not dead?"

"My brother says not and I believe him."

As my men prepared to do as I had asked I wondered if I had told the truth. Gawan believed that the old man was still alive but if so then why had he not returned? I missed the cave under Wyddfa where my father lay. When I visited there then I had more confidence. Yet, ironically the one place I could not go was the cave for when I did, then I would die. *Wyrd.*

Chapter 10

Civitas Carvetiorum felt empty with my twelve equites missing. We had ridden together for so many years that I was used to their comforting presence. I now relied even more on Llewellyn and Pelas. Iago had also stayed close by my side. I think he felt a little lost. He was the last equite of Gwynedd. He was still the guardian of the banner of Gwynedd. He was a link to the past when King Cadwallon had not gone down the dark road to glory.

I threw myself and my men into our new role. My squires rode each day to one of my other outposts while Daffydd and his archers both hunted and sought for the tracks of any enemies who might hide within my land. I took my handful of equites and we road north to the estuary and then along the Roman Road which ran alongside the wall. Once we went as far as the scene of the battle. We passed through the wall to the narrow piece of ground between the wall and the crag. It was filled with the bones of the dead. It was hard to tell which was Saxon and which was Welsh. We left them where they lay. What we did not see was evidence of a Saxon presence. None had tried to stay and farm. There were no Saxon merchants on the road. We were still safe from any invasion. I wondered how long it would last.

As we headed back, after crossing the Roman Bridge, we stayed to the north of the wall. Sometimes we do things and know not why. This was one such time but the steps of Star were guided by another. Gawan was not with me and it could not be him but someone did for we came upon the bodies of three Saxons. They were face down and had been hacked and slashed savagely. They were not warriors but looked to be refugees.

Pelas leapt to the ground. He put his hand on one of the bodies. "It is warm, Warlord, and the blood has not hardened." He stood and looked north. "There is blood in the grass there, Warlord. They wounded one of their attackers."

"We will follow, at least as far as the Tinea." There was a ford on the northern arm of the Tinea. It crossed the river where a small island rose from the waters. Over the years, the island had grown progressively smaller. Some day it would disappear but the ford would remain. I saw it in the distance and, on the other side of the boundary between my land and that of Alt Clut, I saw a warband. They were the warriors who ruled this land. Since my warning to their king, they had kept the peace. There were twenty of them and they had captives. We kept going and they watched us approach.

They were not afraid of us. I wondered at that. Even though there were but six of us we all wore armour and were obviously equites. As far as I could see only one had any mail and that was a mail corselet with no sleeves. He also had a round helmet. He would be the leader.

I stopped at the water's edge and allowed Star to drink. I took off my helmet and spoke to them. I pointed behind me; the route they had taken. "You have crossed over to the Rheged side of the river. I warned Fiachnae mac Fergus of the consequences."

The chief took off his helmet. "I am his cousin, Mungo mac Fergus. These are Saxons. We thought you would not care what happened to them."

"Then you are wrong. Perhaps I did not make myself clear. Your people stay north of this river and we will stay south. We want none of your land or your people. I will take these people back to my land for judgement."

There were eight captives altogether. An oldish woman, another who looked to be about my age, two who looked to have just become women and four children: two young boys and two slightly older girls. I knew what these raiders intended. They would sell them as slaves but first, they would have their pleasure with them. I would not let that happen.

"They are not worth fighting over, horseman. Certainly not worth dying for."

"And who says that we would die? I have fought your people many times and I have never lost. Can you say the same?"

"You would have to cross the river and that would break the peace. I do not think you wish to do that." He seemed to ponder for a moment and then he said, "I will tell you what I will do, I will fight you for them, on the island. On foot. If you win then you can have the Saxons. If I win I have your pretty armour, sword and horse."

"Just the two of us?"

"Of course, I need no help. It will be to the death, naturally."

"Naturally." I knew how his people fought. "You give your word that if I win I take the Saxons?"

"You have my word!"

I dismounted and took off my cloak. I handed my reins to Pelas. My squire looked a little worried. "He looks like a giant, lord."

"I know and he is much younger but I cannot walk away from a challenge. If I do it will encourage more. Watch for treachery."

I donned my helmet and hefted my shield. I drew Saxon Slayer and waded across the ford to the island. As I waited for Mungo mac Fergus to join me I noticed that the two older women held the others protectively in their arms. This was a clan. They were one family. What were they doing here on this frontier?

My opponent had also donned his helmet. I saw that he had a round shield and a hammer. I had seen longer but this one would deal a mighty blow if it struck me. I waited and tried to stay as relaxed as I could. I had many years' experience. He had brute strength. We would have to see which was more successful.

"I like your horse. It is big enough for me. Most are too small but I fear I will have to give your mail to my woman. It would not fit a real man."

He was trying to insult me and I ignored him. He was trying to distract me. He smiled, glanced over his shoulder and then launched himself at me. I had been expecting it and I stepped to the side. The problem with the island was that there was little room to manoeuvre. He had thought that gave him the advantage but I knew it did not. I could step inside his long reach. His hammer struck the sand. He was agile for he anticipated a blow and jumped to the side. I did not strike for I wanted to weigh him up and, hopefully, wear him out.

He frowned when I did not attack. He brought his hammer back, not over his head, but sideways and when he swung it was a horizontal strike. I could not get out of the way. I had nowhere to retreat. When it struck, my shield arm shivered with the shock. I had padding on the inside and that absorbed much of the blow but I would only be able to take a few hits like that. I stepped away from him and lifted my shield a little. I knew that I had surprised him. He had expected to have hurt me. He had made two strikes and I had seen the effort it had caused. The longer the fight went on the more he would tire.

When he saw that I was on the defensive he opened his left side a little to enable him to swing even harder. I had waited for just such a chance. As he swung I did the unexpected, I stepped in to him and stabbed at his middle. He was young and he was quick. He brought down his hammer to block my strike and it almost succeeded. He turned the tip but I wore mail on my hands and he did not. The edge of my sword slid over his hand and severed three fingers to the bone. Blood gushed.

He roared and hurled his shield at me. I was forced to duck behind my own and the shield clattered into it. He took the hammer in his left hand and laughed, "I can use both hands, you trickster!"

He was brave but the moment he shunned his shield he was lost. He swung his hammer wildly at my middle. With nowhere to go, I had to take the hit on my shield. He hit me so hard, even with his left hand, that I almost toppled over. He took heart and, despite the blood flowing from his right hand tried the same blow a second time. This time I did not risk being toppled I dropped to my knee and held my shield close to my shoulder. I took this blow with my body and it was Mungo mac Fergus who overbalanced. He began to fall forward. I stepped to the side. My sword darted out and I ripped across the back of his knee. I tore through the tendons. He fell to the ground and I stood over him. I put my foot on his left hand so that he could not rise and I held my sword to his throat.

"Go on then! End my life."

I slipped my shield around my back and took off my helmet. It told those who were watching that this was over. "You are a brave man. I give you your life." I pointed my sword at his men and shouted, "Bring the Saxons over and something to bind your chief's hand and leg else he will bleed to death." They hesitated, "Come, this is no trap. I give him his life. The Warlord of Rheged has spoken."

Mungo mac Fergus laughed, "No wonder you defeated me. You bear the sword that can never be beaten, the one you call

Saxon Slayer. I will take my life Warlord for few men fight you and live to tell the tale. I will have to learn to fight with but one good leg."

His men ran over, splashing through the water and driving the prisoners before them. The Saxons looked at me as they approached, "Go to my men. We will take you to safety."

He looked up at me, "I thank you for my life."

"Is this over? Will there be a blood feud?"

He shook his head, "I am a warrior. I issued the challenge and I live with the consequences." He gave me a wan smile, "Some of us do have honour."

"And courage. Farewell Mungo mac Fergus, I have rarely fought a braver man or a more honourable one."

When the Saxons were across I followed and mounted Star. I raised my sword in salute and headed back to the wall.

The Saxons walked between us. Pelas said, "How is your arm, Warlord? They were mighty blows."

"I think we shall have to repair the bath house. I need heat upon it."

He laughed, "I am surprised that you did not have a bone or two broken."

I looked down at the two older women. "And what is your tale? We saw your men."

"I am the sister of Garth the blacksmith. We were in the south of Deira when we heard that he had joined you in Rheged. My husband did not wish to serve Oswald. We were on our way to join my brother when we were attacked. Our men fought well but they were overwhelmed by the barbarians." She stared up at me and was not put off by my armour or my title. "Will you enslave us now?"

"No, for your brother is a free man as are all those who came from Ladenses."

"But we have no men. Who will watch out for us?"

"This is Rheged and we care for all besides there are many men who seek women." I pointed with my thumb behind me. "My equites need wives. I do not think you will be alone for long."

The old one, the woman who had yet to speak now spoke, "I am old. No one will want me."

I laughed, "I dare say, Gammer, that you have forgotten more than most of our women know. There will be tasks for you to complete. Do not worry. You will earn your roof. We do not discard the old when they are old. They have much to pass on to the young. You will be valued. Now we have far to go. If you wish you can ride behind me."

She shook her head, "No, Warlord. I will keep my feet firmly on the ground!"

That night we arrived back later than normal and Geraint and Tadgh came along the road leading to the wall looking for us. "We were worried, Warlord."

"We met our neighbours and I was delayed."

"Delayed?"

Pelas laughed, "Aye the Warlord defeated and maimed a giant from north of the wall. I do not think they will worry us again, at least not until he is healed."

Garth was delighted to see his sister and family. He dropped to his knees. "Thank you, Warlord. We have been taught to fear the Wolf and his warriors. The only people who should fear you are your enemies."

"And there are many of those. How goes the mail?"

"If we are to keep up with the demand, lord, then I will need to train my sons to make it too." He pointed to the two young boys who had joined us. "I can train them to make arrows and the heads for javelins. That will free up my sons and keep those two out of mischief."

Everything seemed to be working to a plan I could not see. It was *wyrd*.

Once the harvest was gathered the land began to change. Its colour went from green to yellow and thence to gold and brown. It was the gods painting the land and it never failed to impress me. It would soon be winter. The year had flown by and yet we survived intact. More than that, we prospered. There were marriages and many of the Saxon women who had joined us were with child. Our farms were now well defended and we prepared for another harsh winter should the gods decide to make it so. And then, the week after the last of the barley, rye and oats had been stored, Gawan and Llenlleog returned from the land of the Bro Waroc'h with our horses.

They had two stallions. One was chestnut and the other jet black. They were at least three hands taller than Star, our tallest mount, and four or five taller than the rest of our herd. We had tried this once before but the experiment had not succeeded. Gawan had learned much from the failures and was determined not to repeat them.

"Were you welcomed by your family, Llenlleog?"

"Not really Warlord. Only my brothers remain. The Allfather took the others. My brothers have not fared as well as I. Gawan offered them the chance to come and join me but they refused. They are obstinate."

Gawan said, "They are jealous! They saw that Llenlleog had become a great warrior with fine mail and they look the same as when we first met them all those years ago. We had to use all the gold for the two horses. They are much sought after. I think we will make sure that the breeding is successful this time. I will set the men to building a horse hall."

"Horse hall? You mean stables?"

"This will be grander than any stable you have ever seen brother. I think we failed last time because we did not treat these animals with enough respect. We will cosset them and treat them like kings. The mares they service will share their hall. I intend to succeed this time."

I nodded, it was a good idea. "And when you passed Wyddfa did you sense Myrddyn?"

He drew me to one side, "When we travelled south I did brother and the feeling was so strong that I almost took us inshore to find him." He shook his head, "I did not land and it was a mistake. When we returned, I felt nothing. He has gone."

"Dead?"

"No, brother, but he no longer lives by Wyddfa. He has moved and that means he could be anywhere."

"It was not a mistake, Gawan. Myrddyn will either come or not. His return, as was his disappearance, is out of our hands."

My equites and my squires were all involved in the building of the horse hall. There was no room for it within the stone walls of Civitas Carvetiorum and so we extended a ditch outside our walls and built a wooden wall around the site. Gawan had us dig deep and use the soil to make a rampart all the way around and he constructed the hall like a giant warrior hall. Because he had built it below the ground level it meant that its roof was not as high as it should have been I wondered why and then he showed me. "See we will use turf for the roof and that will keep in the heat but, more importantly, it ties it to the earth. It will be warm in the winter and cool in the summer. I have been thinking of this since we failed the last time. We did not think of Mother Earth. I want no stone in this hall."

"We will need to guard it."

"I have given thought to that too. We bring the sheep and cattle and put them within the ramparts. They will be protected from the worst of the winter weather and the herdsmen and shepherds can watch from the walls."

"You use our animals to protect our animals. *Wyrd.*"

He nodded, "I hope so and I hope that Myrddyn approves."

"He will, brother, he will."

While we were building it Gawan spoke to me of the wider world. Rheged was at the very edge of the known world. "I heard news of Oswald and Penda when we put in to Lundenwic. They are both set on a course for war. Oswald has moved his army close to the borders of Mercia. I fear that Gwynedd may be in danger. They have a new king, Cadafael."

I had never heard of him. "Where has he come from?"

"Men do not know. He just appeared with the remnants of the army which returned from Hagustaldes-ham. He has the support of King Penda and they are allies."

"So long as King Oswald is busy in the south then I care not for it gives us the opportunity to build up our forces. We will have to face him one day."

That night as I walked the walls of our new horse hall I wondered who this new Welsh king was. His army would no longer have the cutting edge that the equite had given it. He would have to rely on his archers. They were the best but they could not win battles. It was fortunate that he had an ally in King Penda. I wondered why King Oswald was risking so much by confronting King Penda. Edwin had been a good general but King Penda and I had outwitted him. I would be wary of taking him on myself.

As I headed for the gate I heard the two stallions snorting and stamping. That was good. We needed animals who had character. Star was one such beast but he was getting old. We would have almost a year to wait for the results of their work and longer before we could ride them. Perhaps we had been too rushed the first time we had tried this but we were now in Rheged and it would take an earthquake to shift us this time.

Daffydd ap Gwynfor made good time and his ship arrived at his jetty not long before Yule. Pol leapt ashore as soon as the hull touched. I allowed Gawan to be the first to greet Pol. He would want news of his family.

"Well?"

"Your wife pines for you but Arturus is excelling in his studies. The tutors of your son and those who train him for war cannot speak highly enough of him. He is now fluent in Greek and Latin. The Emperor himself has shown an interest in him and your wife and son now live in the Imperial Palace."

Gawan was not as excited as I thought he might be. "Did they not wish to come home?"

"Your wife did, old friend, but it would be unfair to drag your son away. I am not certain that he would have come. He has a good life there." He smiled, "Your brother and I were the same. That city gets into your blood and never leaves you. I was tempted to stay. Fear not it is just another year or two."

Gawan looked as despondent as I had ever seen, "Unless the Emperor offers him something in the Imperial Army."

I put my arm around my brother, "Then your wife will return. She only stays because of his age. Is that not right Pol?"

"Aye, it is." He turned as they began to unload their cargo. "We did well. The price of copper was high. Daffydd ap Gwynfor was asked for more and they wish slate and timber for they cannot get those. Both we have in abundance. And we have established links with merchants. Their ships will risk the seas to trade with us. We brought spices, lemons, helmets and some armour. We would have brought more but we were short of hold space." He smiled, "We have fine wine! I know it was not essential, lord but it is one of the few luxuries your equites yearn for. They deserve it."

"That they do! This will be a good Yule."

Part 3
Myrddyn

Chapter 11

Rheged 635

The land was precocious, as were the gods, and the snows did not come that year. If they did come, they were a flurry and a covering of white which disappeared with the dawn. The frosts made the land hard and then disappeared. And we heard no wolves. I had no doubt that our brothers were out hunting but they did not call to one another. We were able to ride each day. My men could visit the farms and ensure our people lived and no danger came. We even managed to send our ship to trade. Daffydd returned to Constantinopolis to take advantage of the shortages there. Who knew when enemies would threaten or the seas become more dangerous.

I also disliked the lack of knowledge. We decided that Daffydd would visit Lundenwic to trade and discover news. There he would pick up gossip, and news, as well as trading some of our items for even more gold. The spices he brought back were much sought after. So it was that he returned, just after the nights began to grow perceptibly shorter. He brought back mail, swords, spices, gold and news.

"Warlord, there is peace between King Penda and King Oswald. They are not allies but they fight no longer. King Penda has slain King Egric of the East Angles and King Sigebert. He now controls all but the West Saxons lord and King Oswald has returned north. I think he fears that Penda is too powerful at the moment. I suspect he plots and plans."

"Thank you, captain." Gawan had been listening. When we were alone I would ask him his views. "Tell me what do the traders and merchants of Lundenwic make of all this?"

"They are backing King Penda to become High King. His sister has married King Ceanwealh of the West Saxons. Only Oswald opposes him and they believe it is just a matter of time before King Penda defeats or subjugates him."

When Gawan and I were alone I asked his opinion. "Does this aid or hinder us? Should we embrace this or fear it?"

Gawan closed his eyes, "I have not dreamed our end but my thoughts have been troubled of late. There is something but I cannot put my finger on it. It is as though I look through a fog and I see shadows but I know not if they are a danger or an ally."

The spirit world was a strange place and I did not envy Gawan his visits there. When I had dreamed, I felt vulnerable; that was something I never experienced when I fought. "Then answer as a strategos and not a wizard."

"I fear that King Oswald will turn his eye to us. If he craves power, then Rheged may seem to be a plum to be picked. He fought and defeated Cadwallon. If I were Oswald I would think that perhaps equites were not the invincible force they were once were."

I nodded, "You may be right but King Oswald knows not the equites of Rheged if those are his thoughts. Cadwallon led badly and chose his battlefield unadvisedly."

"I know. I am merely trying to get into King Oswald's thoughts."

"Then we will build up our forces and prepare to meet him should he come west in the summer. His army has had half a year to recover and the winter has been kind. He will be stronger this year."

And so, we went on to a war footing. As we groomed our horses, oiled our mail and sharpened our swords I wondered how long I could continue to lead. I was getting no younger. In ten years or so I would be the same age as my father when he had been murdered. When I thought back to that time I recalled that he was not as powerful in battle. When would that happen to me? Would I know? As much as I appreciated and valued Gawan it was Myrddyn and his sage thoughts which I needed.

Just after the first new grass appeared my sentries reported armed men approaching our gates. The bell sounded and we went to our walls. It was not Saxons, it was Mungo mac Fergus and four other riders. They came without helmets and with open palms. They came to talk.

Pol, who had not met Mungo asked, "Is this a trap or a trick, Warlord?"

As I went down to my gate I shook my head, "They have sent someone I know. We fought last year. This warrior may not be of our people but he has honour as do his men."

When they dismounted, I saw that Mungo now had a long piece of metal strapped to the leg I had injured. His right hand was also in a metal mitten. He smiled as he limped towards me. "I recovered from our encounter Warlord. Perhaps I should thank you."

"Thank me?"

"Aye, since I had this fitted, " he smacked the piece of metal, "I cannot bow and I have to ride to war just as you do. There is always a bright lining to the darkest cloud."

I saw Pol smile. He saw before him a warrior; a kindred spirit.

"Come into my hall and we will have some wine. Then you can tell me why your cousin has sent you here."

Daffydd had brought some of the powerful red wine we liked so much and I poured a goblet for Mungo and myself. I saw his eyes widen in appreciation as he tasted it. "Gods but this is nectar. No wonder your men stay with you if they are served this brew!"

"We like it." I waited. He would speak when he was ready.

He began when he had drained his goblet and smacked his lips. I poured him a second as he spoke, "King Oswald of Northumbria makes war upon us. He has allied with the tribes and clans to the north of us and suborned them. He seeks to conquer Alt Clut if he can."

I nodded, "And what would your cousin have of me?"

"You come to the point and I like that. I told my cousin that he could trust your words. He asks that you become his ally but if that is a step too far then he begs you not to take advantage of the situation."

I sipped my own wine. "He does not want to have to guard the Ituna and the border."

"You have it. I hope you can fight at our side for with your horsemen we could send these Saxons hence."

I was silent. Where was Myrddyn? I looked at Gawan. He smiled and shrugged. He had no answer either. This would be my own decision. I closed my eyes and became acutely aware of the quiet in the hall. I heard the logs as they crackled. Suddenly a voice came into my head; it was my father's and I had heard the words before it had been something he often said, *'the enemy of my enemy is my friend'*.

I opened my eyes and saw Gawan smiling; he had heard the words too or perhaps he had put them in my head. With a wizard, one never knew.

"You have my word that we will not attack you. I will go further, we will make sure that your southern border is safe. No Saxon will attack thence but as for an alliance, I fear that I cannot commit to that yet. It does not mean we will not but we are still establishing our control over Rheged."

He took off his metal mitten and I saw that his right hand was now a claw. The scars still looked raw. He saw my look. "I cannot use a hammer but my blacksmith has made me a sword which fits into the mitten. I can fight. After watching how you used a sword I thought it best to learn such skills. Take my hand to confirm our words. I will take back your good tidings to my cousin."

I grasped his hand, careful not to squeeze. "You have my word as Warlord of Rheged."

After they had gone my equites pressed me for my reasons. Llenlleog asked, "We could take advantage of their weakness, lord and conquer the other side of the river."

It was Gawan who answered for me, "And what would that gain us? The land to the north of the river is not as good as the land to the south. There are no bridges and no fords. Any folk we had there would be in constant danger and we would waste men defending it." He smiled, "There is a reason the Romans built their wall where they did. Like my brother, I am happy to cling on to the land to the south of the wall."

Pol said, "You are right, Gawan. How do we keep the Saxons from the right flank of the men of Alt Clut then Warlord? Do we watch?"

"No, Pol, we cross the river and we patrol the northern banks. We know Oswald. He will send men in small groups to infiltrate and weaken. He will prod and he will poke looking for weaknesses. He showed at Heavenfield that he knows how to choose a battlefield. His cousin Edwin did not. But I will not leave Civitas Carvetiorum undefended. I will leave Pelas here with ten squires and ten archers. We leave on the morrow and travel to Brocavum. We will take Kay and some of his men too."

Llenlleog said, "I hope that there are few Saxons then for we take but a handful of men."

Pol shook his head, "We take equites, Llenlleog, and the sword of the Warlord, Saxon Slayer. We will win!"

As we prepared Gawan said, "You know that more than half of our equites are with Lann Aelle and Bors. They are not close to the river. We could use them."

"Aye we could but they are our reserve in case things go badly. I know that I am throwing the dice but I do not gamble everything. Besides I take eight squires with us. I would watch to see how they fare. Garth is already making more mail. We may have more equites sooner rather than later."

My small warband of twenty-four warriors left the next morning to ride to our northern outpost. I took Geraint and Tadgh with me. Once we had met with Kay they would seek out any danger. As we approached Brocavum I saw the two heads adorning the gates.

Pol said, "I see Kay has had trouble."

Llenlleog shook his head, "It may not be so. Perhaps someone disturbed his sleep. You know what a bad temper he has."

Kay met us in his yard. I pointed to the heads, "Trouble?"

"Saxon warriors. I think they were scouts. They were to the south of the wall. We have found tracks of others and so I left these here as a warning."

"Come, we must speak. Water and feed the horses we leave as soon as Kay is ready."

I told Kay of our meeting. "It makes sense, Warlord. We had seen signs of scouts during the winter but with no snow, it was harder to follow them. We kept watch."

"And have you seen anything of the men of Alt Clut?"

"No, Warlord. They have not tried to cross the wall."

Then they had kept their word. That was good. "We will make our base at Banna, on the wall. We have supplies on our spare horses."

We had not been here since we had rid the land of the Saxon warband. My father had had men stationed there briefly but it was exposed and vulnerable to attack. We reached there after dark and quickly made it habitable.

For the first three days, we saw nothing. With Geraint and Tadgh four miles ahead of us we rode up and down the wall. We saw no sign of Saxon infiltrators. We saw neither campfires nor tracks. Each night we returned to Banna. It was basic in its accommodation but it was secure. It could be held by a few warriors and yet provided a refuge for the farmers who lived close by. There were not many farmers yet. We were too close to enemies but if the peace held with Alt Clut then it might become populated once more.

On the fourth day, with a wild wind blowing from the east and the trees fighting it, Geraint and Tadgh galloped up. "Warlord, the Saxons. There is a large warband approaching the River Irthing."

I looked at the wild sky. Although it was hard to see the sun I knew that we had been riding for almost half a day. "How many?"

"I think there are a hundred."

"Have you seen their destination?"

"The river passes through some woods I think they will make for there. It is sheltered and cannot be seen from the wall." He looked east as though picturing them. "They will reach it not long before dusk."

"Then that is where we take them." It was four miles or so to the woods. It was just two miles north of Banna. It was a good thing we had been watching. I wondered if the fort was their ultimate destination. They would have known of it from Athelhere. I would worry about that later on. "Owain ap Daffydd, take your archers with Geraint. When the Saxons reach the river and begin to camp slay as many as you can then withdraw. Take no risks."

Garth was young but he would be the equal to his father eventually. He grinned, "Aye lord."

"Tadgh take us beyond the Saxons. We will take them in the rear."

"The fastest way would be along the road by the wall and then cross at the wall at the lone tree."

There were just twenty-one of us. Twelve equites, eight squires and one scout. We would be outnumbered by five to one. As we headed east along the road Llenlleog asked, "Do we try to destroy them?"

"If we can then, yes but I fear this will be too big a morsel for us. These are not the men of Alt Clut. They wear helmets and mail. They have good shields and their swords are the equal to ours. No, Llenlleog, our task is to stop them and send them home. Oswald will realise that he cannot use this way to attack Alt Clut."

We reached the lone tree which grew in a hollow in the wall. There was a gate through the wall for it was the site of a mile castle. The wind had not relented. It would disguise any noise we made when we approached them, our smell would be swept to the heavens. Tadgh led us north. The fells rolled gently north. I saw no farms. We were now in the land between Rheged and Alt Clut. It was too desolate for war. When Tadgh held up his hand I knew that he had found their trail. We headed west towards the Irthing and woods where my archers waited.

Although Garth commanded the archers they all deferred to Geraint. He had been trained by my father's famous scout, Aedh, and none was better at the task. He was also an expert in ambush and I knew that they had time enough to make the woods a death trap. Our task was to drive them toward that trap. I wanted to use our horses and our size to make them run for shelter.

We spied them when they were just a mile from the safety of the woods. We came up from a shallow hollow and when we reached the low ridge they were half a mile away. I raised my sword and Llewellyn unfurled the dragon banner. We trotted towards them. The wailing of the dragon seemed to be enhanced by the wind. It rose eerily behind us and the Saxons turned. When they saw us, whoever commanded took action and they began to run. We rode a little faster. I did not wish to risk a horse falling on the rough ground and we just gained on them steadily.

They ran at differing speeds and the eight who were at the rear were the slowest because they wore mail. The ones without armour sped towards the safety of the woods. A horse in a wood was not as dangerous as a horse in the open. I saw that the first men were less than two hundred paces from the woods. My archers would be a further half-mile away. I wanted them panicked and so I shouted, "Charge!"

We began to catch up to them as they became confused. One warrior tripped and fell. As he struggled to his feet Llenlleog swung his sword and struck him in the back of the head. His bloody red blade told the story. And then someone took charge. One of the Saxons realised that there was only a handful of us. As they closed with the edge of the woods one shouted, "Halt!" and twenty or so of them turned and made a shield wall. The rest ran on into the woods but twenty stood against us. They made a double rank with spears sticking out.

As soon as I saw what they intended I shouted, "Wheel, left and right!"

We had practised this manoeuvre before. As we swept around the side we smashed our swords against the shafts of the spears. They chopped the heads off enough of them to make the wall less intimidating for our horses. We wheeled around to hack some more and then we halted forty paces from them. They were well-trained; they did not flee but held their ground. Swords and axes appeared in the gaps where we had destroyed the spears. When our line was straight once more I prepared to charge again. In the woods, I heard, against the sound of the wind, the noise of Saxons being slain by hidden archers. The effect of the small number of archers was disproportionate.

"Tadgh, see if you can find flesh!"

"Aye, lord." Tadgh unslung his bow and knocked an arrow. He was an excellent archer. If the Saxons made a mistake, then he would exploit it.

"This time we get around their rear! Gawan you take the right!"

I led them off again. A charging band of horsemen would always force men on foot to seek solace with their fellows. They were too few to make a circle and we charged to make them think we would strike their shields. We did not. As we neared them I pulled Star's head to the left and swung my sword. It clattered and clanged from a blade which protruded from the double row of shields. My blow must have made a slight gap for I heard a cry as Kay hit one of the Saxons with his long sword. Panic ensued. I concentrated on rounding the rear of the line.

We were attacking those whose swords faced us and they had to spin around to face us. I leaned forward to hack across the neck of a warrior. He slumped to the ground in a bloody heap. Ahead of me, I saw Gawan as he led the rest of my warriors. I pulled my arm back to hit the next warrior when disaster struck. A Saxon leapt out and swung his axe two handed at Star's chest. It was a brave act for it cost him his life as my dying steed crashed into him, crushing all life as it fell upon him. I knew that I was going to fall and I put my right arm behind me. I did not want to fall on my sword. I flew over my dying mount's head and I tucked in my head. I managed to put my left arm and shield down. It cushioned the blow but knocked the wind from me.

I stared up at two Saxons who raised their swords to butcher the Warlord of Rheged. I could do nothing about it. I lay on my shield and tried to raise my right hand. It was trapped beneath something. The head of one of the Saxons flew over my own as Llenlleog took it and then a sword appeared through the chest of the second.

I struggled to my feet and saw the last five survivors from the shield wall run for the safety of the woods. One suddenly pitched forward with an arrow in his back. Gawan leapt from his horse and raised me to my feet. "I thought the spirits had deceived me, brother. I did not dream this."

"Thank you both, you saved my life." I knelt by Star. All life had gone from his eyes. "Farewell old friend. You were faithful to the end. Go now to the Otherworld. There my father will greet you."

The Saxons in the woods prevented any further goodbyes. I looked up at the squires, "Tend the horses and watch the banner. Equites follow me."

We headed into the woods. More than sixty Saxons still remained but ten of those with mail had been slain and I was confident that we would be able to do such damage to them that they would be forced to flee.

"We stay together. Do not let them pick us off one by one. Llewellyn, guard the rear."

Once in the woods, the sound of the wind diminished a little but, as it was coming from behind us it was hard to hear the noises from ahead. I had to have confidence in Garth and

Geraint. They had to keep drawing the Saxons deeper into the trees. I sensed a movement to my right and saw Gawan slice his sword sideways at a Saxon spearman who had leapt from the gloom. Iago, to my left, suddenly lunged forward and his blade came back bloody. The warriors we encountered were not heroes. These were the ones who hoped we would pass over them and then they could escape.

The trees became thicker and we moved more cautiously. It was a wise move for six Saxons burst from the gloom before us and ran at us. I easily took the blow from the slashing sword on my shield and instead of striking at his shield, I head-butted the warrior for he had no helmet. He fell at my feet and I skewered him. We stepped over their bodies and I heard shouts from ahead. The ground fell towards the river and the sky became lighter. I saw a huddle of arrow pierced bodies. Saxons were sheltering behind their shields as Garth and his archers hidden, even from us, continued to send arrow after arrow towards them. Their shields protected them but we were behind them.

"Now!"

We ran towards the men from Northumbria. The first six died without even knowing where we were. When the others saw us then chaos began. They ran in every direction. We slew all that remained and then there was just the sound of the last few Saxons dying.

Garth and Geraint led their horses and their men down to the river. "Pursue them!"

After making sure that all were dead we headed back to our horses. It took some time for we were going uphill and we were tired. When we reached our squires, I saw that we had not escaped without losses. Two of the squires lay dead while the others were gathered around the standard. Six Saxons also lay dead.

Dargh said, "I am sorry, my lord. They burst from the woods and were upon us before we saw them. Tadgh pursued them."

"You have done well. Ride to Civitas Carvetiorum. We need horses and a cart to carry back the mail and the weapons."

"Yes, lord."

"We will leave a message for the Saxons. Have the heads taken from the Saxons and placed on their spears here."

By the time our archers and scouts returned we had finished the grisly task. Forty-two Saxons had perished. Geraint told me that another sixteen had died as they fled east. The survivors would have to face the wrath of King Oswald. While we waited for our horses and the wagons we made a pyre of the dead Saxons and placed them over Star's body. He would take with him the dead we had slain. By the time Pelas and our horses arrived the pyre was well alight and the smoke rose high in the sky.

"Farewell Star. You were a war horse and you died in battle. All the glory of this victory is yours." I raised my sword and watched the smoke spiral to the sky. Perhaps it was my imagination but I swear I saw Star's spirit galloping towards the heavens.

"Gawan command the men while I return home. I must send to Lann Aelle. We were lucky today. Things could have gone ill for us. There is no danger from the big water. Until the threat from Oswald is finished I want him here."

"Aye brother."

"I will have you relieved in six days." I mounted the horse of one of the dead squires and headed west.

I returned with Pelas to Civitas Carvetiorum while my other men went to Banna. Our work was not finished yet but I needed a new horse and we had the treasure from the Saxons to examine.

Chapter 12

It was dark by the time I reached my home and I was weary. The death of Star brought me a stark reminder of my own mortality. I had much to do before I joined my father and my family. I spent the rest of the evening writing a letter to Lann Aelle. I asked him to leave enough men to guard his home but to bring the rest to the north. We would have need of them soon.

The next morning I went to Garth and we examined the mail and the weapons we had recovered. He held up the mail. "These byrnies are not as good as the ones I make, lord. I would not give them to an equite."

"Squires then?"

He shook his head, "Your squires will become equites one day. It would be a false economy to let them have these. If I might make a suggestion, lord?"

"Of course."

"Many of the farmers who came here are warriors who took up farming. I was a warrior too. Keep the byrnies here for the men who defend your walls. It is the same with the helmets and the swords. The swords are of good quality. It will make this a harder place to take."

"You think we will need to fight soon?"

"Lord those who have taken refuge here have done so because they see that war is coming. It is no secret that King Oswald and his brother Oswiu hate you. He is a spiteful man. He hated Edwin and Osric too. Many who come here choose the dangers here because they know with you there will be an end to it. If they had stayed in Bernicia or Deira then war would ever have been their bedfellow." He threw one of the damaged mail shirts onto a pile to be melted down. "Besides this country is better than Bernicia. I can see why you fight for it. We know that war is coming but we have a better chance of peace here, with you than in other parts of this land."

"And the mail for the equites?"

"Do not worry, lord. We now have iron from the hills to the south and Pybba who came recently is in the forest. He makes charcoal. With charcoal and iron, we can make much better metal." He smiled, "It is *wyrd*. We needed better iron and the means to make it appears. The gods favour you, lord."

Lann Aelle arrived four days later. He had eight equites and eight archers with him. I told him what had happened, "I will send some mail shirts down to your fort and swords too. All those who live in this land must be prepared to fight for it."

"And they will cousin. They are good people who come here." He smiled, "And the women too. I have taken a Saxon woman and she is with child already."

I was genuinely pleased for him. "Then you and your men start to make the new equites. When Arturus returns from Constantinopolis he will have good men to fight beneath his banner."

We headed the next day to relieve Gawan and the others. The news was all good. No more Saxons had dared to come.

Gawan said, "I will ride with you, brother. I need to do more of my share of fighting and besides, I fear for your life if I am not close by."

"You are a good equite Gawan but..."

"It is my powers you need, brother, and not my sword. Besides, I would spend more time with our cousin here. We are the last of the blood of our family."

We took Lann Aelle towards the Irthing. Although it was in the land of Alt Clut I did not think that our presence would be a problem. I was keen to have my scouts search for any signs that the Saxons were close. It also gave me a chance to ride my spare horse, Copper. I had only acquired him when we had left Gwynedd. Then he had been a young horse but the grass of Rheged suited him. His golden coat now shone and he had a mane which was almost white. He was as different from Star as it was possible to get.

We saw no signs of Saxon warriors but we did see riders. We took no chances and we drew our weapons and went into a defensive formation. As they were horsemen I doubted that they were our enemies but it paid to be vigilant.

I relaxed when I saw it was Mungo mac Fergus and four of his oathsworn. "Warlord, I am pleased to have met you. I was coming for help because..." he nudged his horse closer to mine and I saw that he was distraught, "Warlord, Saxons have taken my sister and my mother and others as hostages. We fought a battle seven days since and we were soundly beaten. This Oswald makes war in a new way. While we fought with the King in the far north of our land a band of thirty Saxons attacked our home. They killed the guards and took my family."

I nodded, "Seven days or so since a second warband came along the wall. They might have been aiming to do something similar. We routed them at Irthing."

Gawan asked, "Where did they take them, Din Guardi?"

He shook his head, "That was what we thought. We lost their trail in the forests but we captured a Saxon. He had the war shits and they had left him. Before he died he told us that they had taken them to the burn of the Otter."

I frowned, "I do not know it."

"The land between here and Din Guardi is full of fells, moors and small valleys. There is a stream which teems with otters. Close by is an old stronghold of the people who lived here before the Romans. Oswald has made a wooden tower there. He holds my family there."

"Is Oswald with them?"

"No Warlord. He is heading for my cousin's castle far to the north. He sent a message that if I tried to help my cousin my family would die."

Gawan said, "He is treacherous. They may die anyway."

"I may be crippled but I will not let down either my king or my family." His eyes pleaded. "I need help, Warlord."

I did not owe this man anything and yet I could not, in all conscience, walk away. I had crippled him. Part of me also thought that this was a good way to hit back at King Oswald. If this place was deep in his own land, then he would think that he was safe. I looked at Gawan. He had been in my mind when I had been thinking. He nodded.

"Lann Aelle you and your men stay and watch at Banna. Send a rider to Civitas. I want Geraint, Tadgh, Iago, Llenlleog, Pelas as well as Owain ap Daffydd and six archers. I want spare horses and supplies."

Lann Aelle threw a suspicious look at Mungo. "Is this well done, cousin?"

"It is *wyrd,* I know that. I cannot run from my destiny. I was asked for help. When did my father ever refuse to help any who asked for it?"

He nodded, "You are right. May the Allfather be with you."

As they rode off leaving Gawan, Llewellyn and myself with Mungo and his men Mungo said, "I owe you all now, Warlord. No matter what happens in the future I am your ally."

"How many more men do you have?"

"This is all that remains. The rest died defending my home."

There was little I could say to him. Instead, I put my mind to our task. "How far is it to this river?"

"A half a day's travel but the land over which we must travel is both wooded and wild."

"And how many men guard them?"

He looked a little lost, "I am not certain of the exact number but there are less than there were. We attempted to take them. I would say no more than fifteen remain but they are hearthweru and there may be others at the hall."

"And is it just your sister and your mother who are held?"

He shook his head, "They took my two daughters and two servants."

I knew the answer before I asked it. "And your wife?"

"She died when they tried to take them. Her fingers bore the flesh of those she fought. She was a woman with spirit. I shall not find another like her."

When my men arrived with four spare horses they said nothing. Geraint had been with me when we had hunted Morgause and Morcar, my father's killers. He would find these Saxons. I told them what we sought. I asked, "Geraint, Tadgh, do you know this place?"

Geraint looked at Mungo, "Lord, is it halfway between here and Din Guardi?"

"It is."

"Then we know it. We should ride, Warlord. It is a half-day journey but we can reach there before dawn if we leave now and rest the horses once or twice."

My scouts knew their business and I nodded. "We are in your hands until we find them."

Darkness fell soon after we had headed north and east. We rode close together so that we would not lose touch with one another. Owain ap Daffydd rode at the rear of our line. We were well protected. We also rode in silence. Sound travelled was one reason but all of us were lost in our thoughts. I daresay my men thought that I was foolish to help a man to whom I owed nothing. I was thinking of how the destinies of Oswald and myself were entwined. It had been he who had fought the witch Morgause and she had enchanted my nephew. He had killed my father. I had killed the only obstacles to Oswald's accession to the throne; Edwin and Osric. There was a reason why I was hunting these men but I did not know it. It was just *wyrd*.

Geraint and Tadgh knew horses and we stopped twice to rest them. Not only did we have to rescue the hostages we had to escape and for that, we needed fresh horses. The four my men had brought would be needed for the family of Mungo mac Fergus.

In the late hours of the night, I noticed that the trees had thinned and we rode, occasionally, through scrub and moorland. Geraint had been right to travel through the night. We would not be seen this way. When Geraint held up his hand and disappeared then I knew that we were close. I knew not how he knew such things. We dismounted while we waited. I knew that I wished to speak with both Mungo and Gawan but it was night and sound travelled. The winds had died and silence, save for animals, was all around us.

I saw the first hint of dawn as Geraint and Tadgh reappeared. He came close and used sign language to tell me what he had seen. The hall was less than a mile away. He had counted six sentries. There was a wall and a ditch. I nodded and remounted. I rode next to Geraint as he led us to the hall. Dawn did not break quickly. The day promised to be overcast. It meant that it was still almost dark when we reached the woods which were two hundred or so paces from the hall. We dismounted and hobbled our mounts. I saw a stream and, behind the bank, the hall.

I waved forward Owain ap Daffydd. I pointed at the wall and mimed for them to take out the sentries. He nodded and he and his archers ran to the walls, followed by Tadgh and Geraint. We watched as they moved like shadows over the ground. I knew where they were and I saw them but I doubted that the sentries would. They disappeared from sight when they dropped into the stream. I saw them again when they climbed the bank of the Otter Burn. Patience was now needed. There were nine bowmen and but four sentries. Owain would wait until he could guarantee to kill all of them. I drew my sword in anticipation of success.

I did not see the arrows fly but I saw the Saxons fall. One made a thump as he hit the ground. I raised my sword and we ran forward. Mungo was soon left behind. He could barely walk, let alone run. My archers and scouts had left the bank and were already at the wall when we crossed the stream. Inside the walled hall, I heard noises. It was not an alarm but probably the sentries' relief had been disturbed by the sound of the crashing body. My archers had boosted two of their number up the ramparts. They would open the gate. We crossed the ditch. It had no traps within it and it was not a Roman Punic ditch. It just kept the hall dry.

As we neared the wall I heard the commotion inside when my two archers were spotted. Owain was boosted as we reached the gate and I heard his bow string twang as he protected his archers, running to open the gate. As the gate began to open I heard a cry from inside. We pushed and entered the Saxon refuge. One of my archers lay with an arrow in his leg. His fellow, Aed, was tending to him.

There was now enough light to see and, as we spread out into a half-circle, I saw the Saxons as they ran from the hall. Three bodies lay on the ground between us. Owain rarely missed. Other archers were aiming at the will o' the-wisp that was Owain and the warriors from within were racing towards us. There were eighteen of them. The light was now bright enough to show us that.

"Archers behind us and cover us." There were not enough of us for a wedge and so I just shouted, "At them! Saxon Slayer!"

Until Mungo and his four warriors arrived to help us we would be six against eighteen. Even as we ran to meet them one of them was slain by an arrow. A second tripped and fell as he misjudged the bodies lying before him. Although we were not in a wedge formation we had fought enough times together to naturally form a tight group. Llenlleog anchored the right for he was the best swordsman we had.

Saxon Throne

The Saxons had grabbed spears. That suited me. They were intended to keep us at distance. Gawan deflected the spear which came for my head and I stabbed forward with Saxon Slayer. It struck him in his mail. It was better mail than most Saxons wore but my blow was hard and it knocked him to the ground. His fall forced the ones around him to move and as I stepped over him I was able to stab him through his open mouth. My men were outnumbered but we had done this so many times that the Saxons were like novices by comparison. Iago had vengeance on his mind. These were the men who had slain his master and he was like a wild beast as he recklessly hacked and slashed at all before him.

Pelas and Llewellyn had stood at my back more times than I cared to remember and each time a spear came at my sword side they struck it down. And then I heard a roar of anger as Mungo and his oathsworn threw themselves into the fray. They came at the Saxon right. Fighting for both family and honour they were like wild animals who did not care what wounds they suffered. None had mail and two fell to blows which our armour would have prevented but their heroic charge not only broke the will of the Saxons it enabled us to break through the heart of them and make our way to the hall.

The sun had risen now. As my archers finished off those we had not slain I saw the door of the hall open and the last three Saxons emerged with two women held before two of them and two children held before the third. They had seaxes at their throats.

"Hold! Or these die!"

They spoke Saxon and I held up my hand, "Mungo! They threaten your family."

"I will rip out their hearts if they hurt them!"

I shouted, "You cannot win, Saxon. If you kill them then this man will make your death painful." I sheathed my sword. I wanted him to relax and I was readying my right hand. I raised my right hand. "I am the Warlord of Rheged and I swear that if you let them go then we will give you free passage back to Din Guardi!"

The speaker laughed, "We are hearthweru of King Oswald. We will die with honour."

I dropped my arm and nine arrows sped towards the Saxons. All three had their faces pierced by at least two arrows. Mungo and his two remaining warriors hurried to their family. My archers did not miss.

"Llenlleog, search the hall. Geraint and Tadgh, have the archers fetch the horses." I did not intend to stay any longer than we had to. The frequent rest we had given our horses meant we could travel back as soon as the hostages were secured. I went over to Mungo who held his family in his huge arms. "We cannot stay long, Mungo."

He nodded, "They have four horses of their own."

That meant we had more horses to carry back the hostages and the weapons and armour. "Good for they wore good mail."

The woman I took to be Mungo's sister spoke. "The leader was Aelle. He was the cousin of Oswald's sister. He was a Gesith."

"Get your family to the horses. We do not have time to give the honour we should to your oathsworn."

He pointed to the hall. We will put them in there and burn the hall down. It will be a fitting memorial to them and it will tell Oswald that this is not over. He owes me weregeld for my losses. This is a blood feud now."

Mungo mac Fergus might have been crippled but he still had a presence. He would not forget.

It took half of the morning to finish. The hall was well alight and the hostages mounted as we left to head back to the wall. We had decided not to risk going anywhere near Oswald's war bands. Mungo had a hill fort far to the west. He deemed it safe from Oswald. We agreed to escort him. The extra horses were laden with mail and weapons. The Saxons had been rich and carried both coins and jewels about them. We took them as payment.

Geraint and Tadgh led and Mungo followed with his family. His last two oathsworn were close behind. I rode at the back with Llenlleog and Gawan.

"That was well done, brother."

I cocked an eyebrow, "The spirits approve?"

"More than that, brother, I heard Myrddyn's voice in my head and he approved too."

"Does that mean he is in the spirit world and he is dead?"

"I do not think so. I am not as skilled as Myrddyn. I cannot always discriminate between the thoughts of those who are alive and the spirits of those who are dead."

"Our father never comes to you?"

"No, but my mother does. They are content in the Otherworld."

It was too far to ride all the way to the refuge of Mungo mac Fergus and so we halted at Banna. Kay and his equites would give us protection and I sent the squires back to my fort with the booty. As we ate, Mungo's sister, Ailsa, told us of their treatment and of the death of Mungo's wife. He said little but I saw him becoming angry.

When she had finished, he said, "Men do not make war on women." He looked at me. "You would never attack any who were not warriors but this Oswald makes war in a way which is not noble."

I said nothing for I knew that Mungo's people had enslaved many of those who had lived in Rheged. I think what he meant was the senseless killing which made the land weak and gained nothing for those who waged war that way.

"If your King cannot defeat King Oswald then you may find yourself at peace with your enemy. Have you thought about that?"

"If my cousin makes peace I will fight on. I will send for men from Dál Riata." He smiled, "You have given me inspiration, Warlord. You came back to Rheged with a handful of men. My cousin and his general poured scorn on your numbers and yet you have shown that you can hold what you have if you use determined men. That is what I will do to protect my land."

His mother said, "My son, do not make war on our people."

"That is not in my hands. I believe my cousin will fight on. If he does, then I will stand at his side."

We reached Mungo's refuge the next day. It was well made on a high piece of land and surrounded on three sides by the sea. "Oswald will struggle to take this rock."

"This is our heartland, Warlord. The seas here are always warm and we rarely get snow. You have a good land but compared to this it is a wasteland. That is why we fight on for Oswald cannot capture this."

"And it is a good castle. The gods must have smiled on you when they gave you this land."

We headed home having been rewarded with a small chest of silver. When I attempted to refuse it, he became angry saying I impugned his honour. It was a character flaw in Mungo. His pride would kill him one day but I could not help liking the man. We had come close to killing each other and now we were friends, tied by a bond of blood. *Wyrd.*

Chapter 13

We kept Lann Aelle with us for a month while we saw how the situation in Alt Clut developed. A new message came from Mungo. With most of the land of Alt Clut in Northumbrian hands, King Oswald had decided to end his offensive. There was a truce and the men of Bernicia headed home. The land the men of Alt Clut had lost was now Saxon. King Oswald established warlords along the new border. Mungo's messenger left me in no doubt that Mungo was not happy about the situation and for him, the war was not over. Once the crops had been planted and summer came then there would be those amongst King Oswald's Gesiths who would seek war. Men like Mungo would also not settle until they had recovered what they had lost.

For us, it meant we could withdraw our men to their homes. Kay and Lann Aelle could continue training new squires, archers and equites. Our ships still plied their trade with the Bro Waroc'h and Gawan watched the mares grow. He was determined not to make the same mistakes he had the first time we had bred. It had been an expensive failure. This time he would learn from our errors.

I rarely asked for much for myself but I pressed him to have the baths repaired. Pol and I had grown used to them when we had lived in the east and, after many days' labour by Gawan and the slaves, the baths at the fort were ready. Unlike Constantinopolis we had a readymade supply of fuel for the fire. It enabled us to keep the water heated all year round. There were so many trees that we would never exhaust them in our lifetime.

The first time we used the baths was a good day. We anticipated the pleasure from the moment we woke. We watched the smoke from the fire, heating the water, rise in spirals and we were ready to use them the moment the temperature of the caldarium was right. The three of us, Pol, Gawan and myself indulged ourselves. We spent the whole day in my only luxury. We were in the tepidarium longer than we had ever done so before. I wished to feel cleansed. It also afforded us the opportunity to talk. Pol was almost a third brother and we shared all of our thoughts.

The single part which was not as satisfactory as it might have been was the slaves who oiled us and used strigil. They were clumsy. Gawan smiled when Pol complained, "They have never done this before. I will teach them. Perhaps we might even pay them to make them more careful. What say you, brother?"

Despite the rough treatment, I was happy and I nodded sleepily. "Whatever you wish brother, although I would have thought it would be easier to buy some more suitable slaves when you send Daffydd to trade there once more."

He laughed, "And I thought I was supposed to be the one who could think. You are right, brother."

After we had finished in the frigidarium we sat on the wooden benches and drank wine. "This is not a bad life Warlord. I thought I would miss the life in Gwynedd but I do not. Here we are not dependent upon a king whom we have to serve."

"You are right Pol but I wonder how long the peace will last."

"What do you mean, Gawan?"

"King Oswald and his men will not take kindly to our interference. He hates my brother as we well know. He will turn his attention to us one day."

I frowned, I had put thoughts of war from my head but now that my brother had put them there I would not be able to let them lie.

"He has two ways to come. He travels over the high passes from the east and finds Kay blocking his path or he comes through the land of Alt Clut. It is the latter I fear. Despite the good intentions of Mungo and his cousin they are no match for the Saxons. I think we use the two Irish boats we captured as ships of war. We can use them to patrol the river as far as the ford. Manned by archers and slingers they could stop a crossing, at least long enough for the equites to reach them. We have two which are just gathering weed for they are too big for fishing." I turned to Pol, "Find an archer who can command the boats."

"It takes them away from other duties."

"True but Owain and his father have trained more archers. Not all are good horsemen but they could be boat archers for us."

And so, the baths paid for themselves by giving us ideas. As the grass and the crops grew I went with Llewellyn and my new squire, Agramaine son of Kay. He was young and lacked many skills but he was keen. More importantly, he had inherited his father's bulk. He would be a big man. He had been spared the plague which had taken his mother for he had been one of the grooms who had cared for the horses when we had campaigned with King Penda and King Cadwallon. The time spent with the army had prepared him well. Now Llewellyn and I needed to make him skilled enough to be an equite. I also wanted to get to know Copper. He would have to be my horse until we had bred bigger ones. I liked him but I had been used to Star. When I had been younger, changing a horse would have been exciting. Now it was like all change, unwelcome.

We rode west first. Bors at Alavna lived a lonely existence. Perched on the coast he had little contact with the rest of my equites. When I visited him in his newly built castle he seemed happy enough. Like, many of my equites he had taken a local woman. I think the fact that we had lost so many of our friends made life more precious. Certainly, he did not feel the need to leave.

"I like it here Warlord. It feels safer than Gwynedd. I know the Hibernians are close but I have a better idea now how to protect us." He patted the walls. "They have good stone here and I have built it to be strong."

Even as I walked along his walls I saw the future. "Then I will have Daffydd use Alavna to bring in our goods. It is not far from Civitas Carvetiorum. This is a better port for him to use. You will need to have your men catch as many wild ponies and horses as they can. Some of the goods which come in will be for Lann Aelle and some for me."

"Aye, we can do that." He grinned at the sight of Agramaine. He and Kay were very close. "And it is good to see this young fellow a squire. He will need a mighty horse."

Llewellyn laughed, "And more mail than anyone else!"

Agramaine was an agreeable youth and he took the banter in good part. We enjoyed a pleasant evening in Bors castle. I felt happier when we left. Bors came with us as we headed south. He left us at the deserted ruin that had been Hardknott. It was a desolate place but I could see why the Romans had built it. No one could travel through the pass without being subject to the scrutiny of the garrison. If the day dawned when we had spare men, then I would rebuild it. There was a quicker way which passed through the valley of the tarns but I wanted to see the parts of my land which I did not normally visit. I also wished to visit Pasgen to see how his work progressed.

We stopped and spoke with every farmer we met. There were no towns and no villages. Farmers eked out a living as best they could and their farms were all within sight of each other. I would have preferred them to be gathered together with a ditch but framers liked their own space. They were totally self-reliant. All of them had a ditch running around and a wooden wall. The walls were not to keep out men but their animals in and wild animals out. Dead crows and magpies were hung from the fences as a warning to other carrion. Many I knew had been here since the time of King Urien. Some of the old men remembered my father and I was touched by the regard in which they held him. His name still meant something. I promised them that I had returned to stay and I had no intention of leaving.

As we headed for Pasgen's port I noticed that the forests grew thicker and the farms were fewer. That explained why Pasgen and his people were so isolated despite being on the coast and also told me why it was only the pirates who bothered them. We could barely find a trail. Had it not been for the sun dipping to our right we might have gone around in circles. As it was we reached Pasgen's walls as the sun made the western skies bright red with a promise of fine weather.

Pasgen's isolation was confirmed when I found that we had more news of the outside world than he did. We were feted by his leading families for they had all become more prosperous since my arrival. No longer did pirates take half of their produce. There were fewer bandits roaming in the forests and life was good. I did not take the credit. It was the earth which was doing this. The power of the people of Rheged made Rheged more powerful and more fruitful. It was what the people of the White Christ did not understand. Man had to work in harmony with the earth.

Rather than heading due east, I rode north. The long water with the high mountain had always fascinated me. The mountain looked like a face. When I had been growing up and travelling with my father I had been a little afraid of it. Now Garth of Elmet mined it for iron and copper; it was the life blood of our land yet few folk lived there. I determined to find out why as I headed north.

We passed just three farms. The first was farmed by Nib. He was of Rheged stock and his family had lived there for six generations. He had a farm by the end of the water and he lived by fishing, hunting and by tilling a small patch of land. He could offer no explanation as to why more did not live in this valley.

Torver the Bowman lived halfway along the valley and he had served as a young man with my Uncle Raibeart. He had suffered a wound to his leg and never left the valley. He lived there with his family. His son was married to Nib's daughter. It was the way of the valley. He did offer an explanation. "Warlord this land is not good for crops. It has shallow soil and steep sides. It is filled with rocks which break even the finest plough. It runs northwest and the mountain shades the valley, save for the water for most of the afternoon. I am like Nib. I hunt and I fish. We are lucky enough to have a small flock of sheep. We make fine cheese but my flock grazes all the way between Nib and the head of the valley where Gurth the shepherd lives. His sheep graze the land close to the tarns. If there were more farms, then someone would starve."

Gurth, the last farmer, lived alone. His wife had died years earlier and his two sons had been taken by wolves. He was old and I could not see him surviving another winter. I felt sorry for him. "Why not move closer to Torver the Bowman. He seems a kind man. You could join your flocks."

"Thank you, Warlord. But I like my own company. I can sit and look down the long water and remember my family and the old days. You are like your father, you care about people. Prince Pasgen now, he never spoke to us save to tell us he had taken a sheep or two." He sniffed, "Sometimes he wouldn't even do that, we would just find the head after his men had butchered it but your father, well, he was interested. He knew farms and he knew animals." He smiled, "I shall see him soon enough when I go to the Otherworld. I have lived long enough."

We bade him farewell. Men came and went but the valley remained. As we headed northwest to take the road to Lann Aelle I wondered if that was what Myrddyn had done. Was he like Gurth and tired of life? He was old and perhaps he had had enough of the world. My father always told me that their destinies were entwined. When my father was murdered, it might have been a sign that his life was also over.

We met no one else again until we came to the bridge over the Brathay. We were so close to Lann Aelle's hall that we were all looking forward to a fine meal and a comfortable bed. The small farm which was there also provided assistance for those who needed help with goods when the Brathay was in spate. I had met the farmer and his wife once before. The woman came out with some ale when she saw our approach. I took some coins from my purse and gave them to her.

"You have a fine farm here, mistress. Do you have many bandits around here?"

"Not bandits lord but wolves have plagued us in the past. Not lately though. It has been quiet since you and the young lord at the Roman Fort returned." She appeared to be enjoying the chance to talk. "Mind you there are many incomers now. Between here and the bog water are now four farms. Time was there was just us and old Gurth. Why I have heard of folk living in the caves of the Lough Rigg."

I felt the hairs on the back of my neck prickle and I wondered why I had not brought Gawan. "There is a cave there?"

"Aye Warlord but it is said to be haunted by a witch. My husband saw lights there seven days ago when he fetched in a sick lamb. Proper frightened he was. Nothing good comes of living in caves! Nasty damp places."

"Mistress, tell your husband to put his mind at rest. My men and I will visit there now and see what haunts this cave."

Her face fell, "Warlord, you are a hero, a brave man but do not put yourself in harm's way. We leave the fell things of the cave alone and they will not bother us."

"I am not afraid for I have the sword, Saxon Slayer."

"Take care Warlord; now that you have returned we would not lose you."

We handed back the beakers and headed towards the Rigg. "Is this a wise decision Warlord? Should we not wait for Gawan?"

Llewellyn laughed, "You will learn, Agramaine, that the Warlord fears nothing. This is just a story spread by gossips. Lights in the skies could be hunters cooking their catch. We will be safe so long as the Warlord rides with us."

I hoped he was right for there was something vaguely disturbing about this report. There were many wizards and witches and not all of them had my best interests at heart. We had thought that Morgause was a force for good and yet she had bewitched Morcar and turned him towards a dark and deadly road. I know that I should have sent for Gawan. If you sought a wizard or a witch, then you had best take your own with you. However, something drew me there. It was partly that I knew this was not my death. I would die in the dark but not this dark.

It was only when we rode through the forest up the narrow trail from the river that I realised that this could mean the death of Agramaine or Llewellyn. I reined in. "You two ride behind me."

"Why Warlord?"

"Because I command it, Llewellyn!"

They obeyed and we twisted up to the high crag and rigg. Trees grew above the mouth of the cave and in the fading light, it looked for all the world like hair on a woman. Was there a witch within? Once that thought was in my head then the rocks which rose before me at the mouth of the cave looked like teeth. Was I becoming bewitched and leading my two men into a trap? I urged Copper on. Even my horse seemed reluctant to close with the gaping maw of the cave.

There was a large flat area before the cave and a pool. The sun was setting to the west and while there was no sunset there was an eerie light playing on the water. Copper stopped. He would go no further. He was afraid. I dismounted and handed my reins to Agramaine.

"Watch the horses." I drew Saxon Slayer and began to walk towards the entrance.

Llewellyn said, "Do you want me with you, Warlord?" He sounded nervous.

"It is your decision. I will not command you."

I heard him say, "Here, Agramaine, hold my reins too. We cannot let the Warlord go alone."

As I neared the entrance I saw a faint glow emanating from within. The gossips were right. Someone did live here. I watched where I placed my feet and made sure that I did not step in a puddle. I wanted no splashes. As I turned, for there was a bend in the cave, I saw that there was a fire burning in the far end and it illuminated a huge chamber. I could have fitted twenty halls, one above the other, in the space above my head. There was another glinting pool of water inside the cave off to one side, and then I suddenly spied a figure. He had his back to me and he was hunched before the fire. I walked slowly towards him. With my left hand, I gestured for Llewellyn to go to my left.

I was within ten paces when the figure spoke, "It has taken you long enough to find me, Hogan Lann! I thought for a while that I would have to come to find you!"

"Myrddyn! You have returned!"

He turned and I saw a skeleton of a man. He looked to have aged by fifty years since the last time I had seen him.

He nodded, "Yes I have returned but it will not be for long. You and your brother will need me in the short time I have left."

Chapter 14

I turned and saw Llewellyn's face. It was as if he had seen a ghost. When Llewellyn saw the wizard, he dropped to his knees. "Have I died, lord? Is this the Otherworld?"

I smiled, "No, Llewellyn. Fetch Agramaine and the horses within. We sleep here tonight." I looked at Myrddyn. He looked frail, almost transparent. "Have you food? Have you eaten?"

He pointed a bony finger, "There is some fish I caught in the water."

My new squire led in Copper. "Agramaine, prepare the fish and cook them on the fire. I have much to ask Myrddyn."

Agramaine's eyes widened, "It is Myrddyn?"

I realised that he had never met the wizard. When we had left Gwynedd, the old man had been a recluse. Myrddyn gave me a questioning look, "Kay's son."

"Yes boy, I have returned and make sure the fish is not burned. I cannot abide burned fish!" As Agramaine hurried to the pool of water where the fish were laid he said quietly, "Tell me he is not as slow as his father."

"Kay is not slow... No, Agramaine is quick-witted. Come, you procrastinate. We have sought you these many months. Gawan has needed you. Where have you been?"

"I have sent messages to Gawan when I could but he needed this time to grow. He is more powerful now, is he not?"

"He is."

"And that is because I was not here and he had to learn things for himself but I have seen the future and dreamed my death. Gawan needs me or he will die and you need my hand to guide you. At least for a short while." I must have looked disappointed, for he smiled. "You have done well. You have done better than I could have hoped and all the decisions you have made have been the right ones but there is danger ahead. You are not prepared for what is to come. That is why I have been sent back."

Llewellyn had unsaddled the horses and hobbled them. They drank in the pool. He took out grain and prepared their feed. Myrddyn chuckled, "Horses that drink from that pool are

Saxon Throne

enchanted." I looked over as though I would see a change in them. "You will see nothing but they will become different beasts."

He winced and drank something from a small leather flask.

"You are hurt?"

"I am old. I was old when first you knew me. Now then ask your questions while the fool's son burns the fish."

"I have but one question; why did you disappear? Cadwallon is dead. Had you been there to guide him then you might have stopped it."

"Have you learned nothing from me? It was *wyrd* that Cadwallon and his men died. I could have done nothing about it. But what was the result?"

"Gwynedd is weaker and Oswald rules. He is more powerful than ever."

He shook his head, "He is not as powerful as Edwin was and his time on this earth is short. I have almost more time than he does! No, Hogan Lann, you returned to Rheged. That was meant to be. You have done as the spirits and your father intended, you are making Rheged into a fortress and you are melding together the best of both peoples. It is *wyrd*. It is a dream your father and I had since the time of King Urien. It could not happen while Prince Pasgen lived."

"But..."

"What you have done only you could have achieved. You brought the old peoples, those from Rheged, Elmet, Deira and Bernicia and you have married them to those Saxons who follow the old ways. Saxons flock to your banner. Men from Strathclyde seek to follow you. You have forged the alliance with Alt Clut. That would have been an impossible dream with either Prince Pasgen or King Cadwallon. They had to die." He paused, "As did your father. And soon I will join them both."

I could smell the fish cooking and I laughed, "You prevaricate, old man. You have not yet answered my question. Agramaine, is the fish ready?"

He looked over, "My lord I am fearful. If I get this wrong, then the wizard will turn me into a toad!"

I saw the twinkle in Myrddyn's eye reappear. It was something with which I had grown up. He winked at me,

"Perhaps just a frog. Bring it over boy! The taste will be the test."

Agramaine brought the fish over. Llewellyn had washed four flat slates and he brought them over. I smiled as Agramaine sat almost behind me for protection from this wizard. Myrddyn put down his slate and took out a small wooden box. He opened it and said, "Here, boy, fetch your fish."

Agramaine was terrified but he obeyed. Myrddyn took something from the box and sprinkled it on the fish. Agramaine said, fearfully, "Is that a potion, lord?"

Myrddyn chuckled, "No, it is salt from Ynys Môn. It is as precious as gold and will make your fish taste sweeter."

Even Llewellyn laughed. We ate. I saw that Myrddyn picked at his food and ate slowly, chewing most carefully. Having said that he picked it clean to the bone. He nodded, "Not bad. You are a better cook than your father, boy. I hope you are half as good a warrior and now, Hogan Lann, before I tell you my tale, have you wine?"

"You know very well that I have, Myrddyn, for you have read my thoughts since the day I was born."

He laughed, "And before, Hogan Lann!"

"Fetch the wine, Llewellyn." My standard-bearer brought over the leather skin.

Myrddyn unstoppered it and drank sparingly. He smacked his lips. "I should have spent my last years in Constantinopolis. There it is warm and I can drink this all day." He handed the flask to me and I drank. "I was duped, Hogan Lann. Morgause deceived me for she was a powerful witch. She brought me as close to death as any and did for your father. I wondered how and so I returned, after we buried your father, to the cave. I spent many months seeking answers from the spirit world. Perhaps too long. When I discovered the answer then it was almost too late. Morgause was one of three sisters. They were descended from an ancient line of witches. Each was a powerful spæwīfe. I did not know at the time just how powerful."

"They live yet?"

"Who is telling this story, you or me?"

"Sorry, master."

"The fact that Morgause had fooled me should have warned me but I was arrogant. It was not a plague or a pestilence which killed your families in Gwynedd, it was the sisters, Morwenna and Morgana. While I wrestled with the spirits in your father's tomb they insinuated themselves into your wife's circle and your families were poisoned. It was their revenge on you for killing their sister."

"Where are they now?"

He shook his head impatiently and I became quiet once more. "It was Brother Oswald who told me all." He looked reflective. "He was a priest of the White Christ and yet I liked him. He was clinging on to life when I found him. He told me how the two witches had arrived. They claimed that their village had been laid waste by Oswiu and his men. Myfanwy was always kind and she took them in. They proved to be fine cooks and that was how they poisoned your families. They were clever. They chose the feast of Eostre when Myfanwy invited all the families of your men to the Great Hall. Father Oswald was the only man but he ate sparingly. It was also the time the Christians call Easter when the White Christ went to the Otherworld. Oswald only ate the bread. It took longer for him to die."

I nodded, "He knew who had done it for they were the only ones who did not die."

"You are right. Oswald was laid low but still conscious and he heard them speak as they took the jewels and crowns from the women. They spoke each other's names. He lived long enough to tell me and then he died. It was I who spread the tale of the plague. I did not want the witches to know that I knew who they were. I have spent the time since then seeking them. They are like serpents. They crawl and hide in dark places. They change their skins and they are careful. They almost caught me once. I had an acolyte, Aiden. He died for me."

"Aiden? I do not remember him?"

"No, I picked him up on my travels. He was an orphan but he had as sharp a mind as any. He died so that I might live. I must have grown careless or perhaps my powers weaken. They managed to find us and they poisoned the hare which Aiden was preparing. I was lucky that he was hungrier than I and he ate a fatal portion. I was ill and weak." He smiled apologetically, "It is why I eat more slowly. I have not eliminated all the effects of the poison."

"And where are they now?"

"That is why I travelled here. They have always been the servants of Oswald. It was he who put Morgause up to the murder of your father and, they hoped, me. I followed them to his court when he was close to Mercia. As soon as they joined him and he headed north I came to find you. Now, do you see how he was able to defeat King Cadwallon with fewer, inferior warriors?"

"No, how?"

"They came to Eoforwic and they used potions and spells to change King Cadwallon. Did you not wonder at the change in him after you defeated King Edwin?"

"Aye, but I thought that was our victory alone."

"You misjudged your old friend. In those last years, he was not himself. The draughts they gave him changed him. They must have been close to him for they used their words and their charms too."

I suddenly had a picture of the two women who had been constant companions in Eoforwic, "I saw them! They were almost like twins!"

"They were. Did you not see a resemblance to Morgause?"

"I did not then but I do now. How was I so blind?"

"They were both powerful witches. Together they are more powerful than I. I feared for your brother. His mother must have watched out for him. Had you not gone to Rheged to hunt then..."

"So that was *wyrd*?"

He nodded, "It was. And now they are with him at Din Guardi. They advise him and they direct his course. I am not strong enough to defeat them on my own. I need Gawan." He nodded towards my sword. "And this is the day of Saxon Slayer."

"My sword? Why?"

"One who wielded that sword killed the ancestor of these witches. A curse was laid on it. Until the spawn of the witch is killed then the curse remains."

"And when the curse is lifted?"

"Then the work of the sword is done. The time of the Warlord will be over." He looked at me sadly. "You know this, Hogan Lann, for you have dreamed your death. You have seen the sword thrown into the dark hole in the earth. You saw it splash into the subterranean pool. It always had an affinity to water. You will return it there until it is needed again and then you will die."

I might try to avoid my death by staying in Rheged but it was only putting off what was meant to be. One day, when the world was purged of the sisters and Oswald, I would go to Wyddfa and die.

Wyrd.

Chapter 15

We left at first light for Lann Aelle's stronghold. We needed another horse for Agramaine who had given his to Myrddyn.

"How did you get here, Wizard?"

"Why I walked, of course! I spoke with people as I travelled and got to know their thoughts. It was illuminating. I paid my way by healing and giving potions. It is not the first time I have done this. When first I served your father, I trod the same road. Only the people have changed. The earth was still familiar beneath my feet."

Now that Agramaine had overcome his fears of the wizard he bombarded him with questions. We had just crossed the Brathay again and Myrddyn had answered what seemed like a thousand questions when Myrddyn said, "I did this with you Hogan Lann and then your brother Gawan. It seems I am to be pestered until my dying day."

"Enough Agramaine, there will be time for questions. Myrddyn will be staying at Civitas Carvetiorum."

"I am sorry, lord, but it is like walking with a legend. The stories I have heard... how he flew with the warlord and slew a king. How he appeared in the midst of a Saxon host and healed their King."

I looked at Myrddyn who looked smugly at me and shrugged. I smiled, "And they are all true."

We received a rapturous reception from Lann Aelle and his equites. It was as though my father had been reborn. Their only disappointment was that we turned around and left as soon as we had another horse. Lann Aelle shouted, as we headed back towards the Scar of Nab, "I will visit Myrddyn. I have much to ask of you."

"It is my lot to answer questions. Who answers mine?"

We were a few miles from home when I saw horsemen approaching. It was Gawan with some of my equites. He had a huge grin on his face. Myrddyn chuckled. "His powers are growing. I tried to conceal my presence from him but I failed.

We will need these skills soon." I looked at him for enlightenment but he gave me one of his enigmatic smiles.

Gawan was euphoric. I had not seen him as happy in years. "I sensed you master! I felt you some days ago. It was faint at first but then grew stronger."

"That was the proximity of your brother. You have much to do, Gawan."

We continued to head home, "I have become a much better warrior already."

"Forget that skill. Why even those lumps Kay and Bors can wield a sword as well as any. You are unique. You can use your mind as a weapon. I told the Warlord that my time is limited. I must teach you all that I know before it is too late."

"Too late?"

Myrddyn waved an irritated hand, "I will not waste my words here. You will have to wait until I am indoors with a warm fire and some of your brother's wine. Then, and only then, will I speak."

I laughed, "It is as though he has never been away, is it not? But I for one am relieved that we have him back, grumpy or not."

Even those who had never met the old man were drawn to my streets as word spread of our arrival. Everyone, Saxon and Briton alike had heard his name and the stories of his powers. He was either something to frighten the children with or he was hope for the future. He actually smiled as he rode through my gates. He could put on an act when he needed to.

"You have united the peoples, that is no mean feat, Hogan Lann. Your father would be proud of you."

"And you Myrddyn, what of you? Are you proud?"

He looked at me as though I had spoken in a foreign language. "You are what you are, Hogan Lann. I am pleased that you are still alive and sorry that I could not save your family but you are not of my loins so why should I have pride in your achievements?"

As I dismounted I said, "Could it be that you have helped to form me? You are the potter and I am the pot."

"Ah, I see. You ask am I pleased with what I have produced? Then the answer is yes! I have done a good job and that deserves a large goblet of wine!"

I sighed. I should have known that I could never win an argument with him. It was like a battle of wills. He held Saxon Slayer and I had a stick! There was no contest. We ensured that he had a fine chamber with a brazier. The old felt the cold more than we did. Once we had unpacked his few belongings we joined him in the hall. He was as close to the fire as he could get without actually being in it. Gawan and I dismissed the others, except for Pol and we sat close to him. We looked at him expectantly.

He sighed, "I have already told this to Hogan Lann. I suppose you want me to repeat it?"

I smiled, "I can make sure that it is the same story, wizard."

A twinkle appeared in his eye, "You are sharp these days, Hogan Lann." He told the story and not one word differed.

Gawan looked relieved when he had finished. "I thought I was losing my powers when I could not see what was in King Cadwallon's mind."

Pol said, "And I think I know the two witches. They were the ones who shared the King's bed. Now that I come to think of it they had a similar look to them. But their hair was different."

"A different colour?"

"Aye Myrddyn."

"They would use plants to make the colour change. They are like skin changers. They are both powerful witches. They hid themselves from Aileen and, for a time, from me. I have had to spend long days and nights in the cave with the spirits. I travelled far and wide to learn the skills which we will need to defeat them. You will be worked as hard as you have ever been." He looked at me. "I want the west tower emptying of everything. Gawan and I will be there until he is ready. I need a servant to be outside the door both day and night."

"Very well and when do you start?"

"We begin at dawn after we have tested your sword, Warlord."

"My sword?"

"Morcar used poison which he had from the witch. He used it on the sword and it was out of our hands for a while. It needs purification and cleansing. Had I not been stuck down by the witch we would have done it at Wyddfa." He smiled, "It was not by chance that you returned here. We have somewhere we can use and it is close by."

He said no more save that there were to be just the four of us and none of us was to wear mail. The only weapon which would be allowed was Saxon Slayer.

I was intrigued but I obeyed. We gathered in my hall and waited for Myrddyn. He said not a word and we followed him. He left by the west gate. I wondered where he was going. He stopped by the old fish pond. It had always been there. We never fished it. We had the river and the sea. Our horses sometimes used it as a drinking hole. I had been told that the Roman garrison used it to keep fish for the table of the commander of the fort.

When we reached it Myrddyn said, "Send your guards away. We shall not need them." That done he asked, "What do you know of this sword?"

"Our father found it buried close to the Roman fort on the Dunum. It was ancient and came from the time before the Romans."

Myrddyn nodded, "Did he tell you the story of the water? This water?"

There was something nagging in the back of my mind but it was like mist; I could not hold on to it. "I confess, no."

"When your father served King Urien he had a dream and he and his brothers came alone here. He threw the sword away and then found it."

"Now I remember. When he told me, I could not believe he did such a foolish thing. What if he had not found it again?"

"I was not here with him then but I would have approved. And I am going to ask you to do the same thing. I want you to throw the sword away."

"But why would I do that? The Saxons fear it. My enemies fear it. It inspires my men! I will not risk it!"

"Then you do not trust the sword. If you trust not the sword, then it will let you down."

Gawan said, "Remember your dream, brother."

"But why the test, Myrddyn? The sword is not harmed."

"And how do you know? If it is harmed, then we will not find it. If Rheged is doomed, then we will not find it. If its work here is done, we will not find it. When you find it then it will be whole and there will be hope."

I sighed and held the sword in my two hands, "Very well." I prepared to throw it.

"No, Hogan Lann. Turn around and close your eyes. Throw it over your back." He turned, "Pol and Gawan turn your backs also. Your father did this. He trusted the sword. You must do the same."

I turned. I held Saxon Slayer by the hilt and closed my eyes. I quietly intoned, "Saxon Slayer do not desert me." I threw it high over my back. It seemed an age before I heard a splash.

I was about to turn when Myrddyn's voice said, "Stand still until I say otherwise."

The wait was interminable. I could barely contain myself. I have no idea how long I stood with my eyes closed waiting for the command to turn. When Myrddyn spoke, he was next to me and I jumped.

"Now you can turn."

There were ripples on the water but I could not see their centre. "Now what?"

"Go and find your sword."

"What if the water is too deep?"

"The last time I heard such a petty whining tone from you Hogan Lann you had only recently finished being weaned. You are Warlord! Behave as such!"

I turned and began to wade into the water. I had no idea where it was. I reached down and found weed and mud. I reached again and found the same. This was hopeless. I turned. "Where do I start?"

Myrddyn had sat on the ground and his eyes were closed.

I waded deeper. The water was up to my waist. I kept reaching down and finding nothing. Something brushed against my leg and I shivered. It was a fish. They had my sword and I did not! I had lost Saxon Slayer. A foolish old man who had lost his mind had persuaded me to do something foolish. A sudden thought came to me; perhaps he had been bewitched. Perhaps he was now in the service of the witches.

I turned and looked at my men. Gawan was smiling and shaking his head. Myrddyn's eyes were closed but he spoke, "If I was in the service of the witches why would I have told you of their existence?"

Now I felt the fool and I returned to my task. I seemed to have covered the whole of the pool and still I had not found it. "This is hopeless! I have lost the sword! Rheged is lost."

Myrddyn stood and I saw that he had a disappointed look on his face. He snapped at me. "Do you wish me to come and find it? Perhaps I should wield the sword! You are looking for the sword. Empty your mind and let the sword find you. Close your eyes and lie back in the water. Free your mind from all thoughts of the sword. Picture... picture your father."

I had nothing else to lose. I lay back in the water, expecting, at any moment to sink beneath its black and murky waters but I did not. Where was that sword? I began to sink a little and then I saw my father. It was not a vision of when he had been mortally wounded it was when I had followed him into battle and he had raised the sword to signal victory. I smiled at the memory. I had followed the sword through many such victories. I had held it too, many times when we had vanquished our foes.

And then I saw a woman. She was not a woman I had ever seen before but she was striking and she held the sword. I saw her walk across the water. That was impossible! Behind her marched a grizzled Roman horseman who scowled at me as he approached. I was not certain anymore if I was still on the water. I had lost all sense of time and place. Was this a dream? Had Myrddyn enchanted me?

Then the woman, I guessed she was a Queen for she wore a coronet and a torc around her neck, leaned forward and said softly and seductively, 'Save my land. The sword that was lost has been found. Take it!"

I did not know what she meant but I felt something brush against my leg again.

The warrior, who had a scarred and grizzled face snapped, "Are you a warrior or are you a mouse!"

I put my hand around and moved it through the water and this time when I reached down my fingers found the hilt of the sword. As I raised my arm my feet sank into the silt and the muddy ooze. The water was up to my knees and Pol and Gawan had looks of awe on their faces. In my hand, I held the sword. The magic had worked.

Myrddyn just said, "The sword is healed. The Warlord can go to war once more."

Chapter 16

Gawan was whisked away by Myrddyn into the west tower and I did not get the chance to ask him anything. Pol kept shaking his head, "If I had not seen that I would not have believed it. A mist came over the water. Did you know that?"

"I saw a woman come towards me; a queen I think and a Roman warrior. I held the sword Pol and I do not believe what just happened but one thing is clear. The sword is as magical and mystical as we believe. I begin to hope that we can defeat King Oswald."

"Except that we now have two witches to eliminate first. Not to mention the fact that we do not have enough warriors. We could field an army of less than one hundred at the moment."

"Then we use our minds. I want you to go to King Penda and seek an alliance." The experience had sharpened my mind.

"You want him to fight King Oswald for you?"

"No, for he would not do it. I first seek to be allied with him as the ruler of Rheged. It is in his interest to defeat Oswald. Then I would have you visit Gwynedd. Find out who rules there and if they will join an alliance against Oswald."

"They will have few men and no leaders."

"Nonetheless they will have warriors and there may be warriors who will fight alongside them. Mention that Myrddyn is still alive and lives here in the north. It might aid our cause. Finally travel to Powys and seek their King."

"Powys and Gwynedd are at war."

"They were at war, who knows how the land lies now? This is about thrones and kings, Pol. If Northumbria grows powerful then it threatens Mercia, East Anglia and Wessex. If this embassy fails, then I will visit the East Angles."

"And what of Alt Clut?"

We are almost in an alliance with them. I will visit with Mungo. His cousin has made peace but we may be able to shore up our northern border."

Pol took just two squires with him. He was the most experienced of my equites. Leaving instructions for servants to wait hand and foot on Myrddyn I left with Llenlleog, Pelas, Iago and Llewellyn. We took Agramaine and three squires as well as Owain ap Daffydd and some archers. We went not for war but we would go prepared to defend ourselves. I took a helmet for Mungo. Garth had made one in the same style as mine. It covered half of the face and had a mail aventail to protect the neck. I would have taken armour but he would have refused to wear it. It was not the way of his people.

Despite the fact that we had aided Mungo I was still wary as we crossed the river. I had Geraint and Tadgh as scouts. This was new land to them but they knew their trade. Aedh had taught them both well. Soon they would need to find others to take over from them. None of us was getting younger. Myrddyn had aged so much that it had frightened me too. When we reached Mungo's stronghold, two days later I felt a sense of relief. We had arrived without a death amongst us.

We were greeted as heroes. His family must have told all of our rescue for we were cheered not as those who had crippled their chief but as heroes who had saved their land.

"Warlord, this is a pleasant surprise."

"Which is a polite way of asking me why I am here."

"Of course not. I told you that you were always welcome."

"First, I bring you a gift. It is a helmet. Your thick skull needs protection."

"It is a fine helmet. I thank you."

"And to tell you that Myrddyn has returned. He lives now in my castle."

"And that is the best of news! We have hope if the wizard fights against Oswald."

"However, it is not all good news for I have learned that King Oswald, despite being a Christian, has two witches who use their power for him. Then it is good that our wizard has returned."

"Come to my hall for I can see that you bring news of the greatest import."

We were seated in his hall and enjoying a honeyed ale. "Tell me of your cousin. Does he plan to fight Oswald or is he happy for peace?"

"He is not happy about peace but he cannot raise an army yet to take on the might of Northumbria. Their priests say we fear to attack because their One God protects them. The truth is my cousin's best men all died."

"Then I will tell you that I intend to travel east and harass King Oswald. I have beaten his father and I have beaten him before now. I tell you this for it may bring trouble for you. I will not be precious about the land I cross. I may have to travel the roads we took to the Otter's Burn. I would not do so without telling you."

He grinned, "You have honour! I give you permission to use my land. More than that I will offer you my guides. They are men who lived in the land which is now ruled by Oswald. They know back ways and hidden paths. They all wish to continue the fight. Their leader is Angus mac Angus. There are ten of them and they live in the woods north of the Ituna. When you leave, we will visit with them."

There was no hurry to leave. It was better for our alliance to have firm foundations. Mungo's warriors were keen to talk to Llenlleog and the equites. As warriors, we looked like no one else. They fought half-naked sometimes. It was not always bravado which made them do so, they did not have good smiths. The Saxons did have. They were particularly intrigued by our swords which were both longer and stronger than their own. Our swords had tips which meant we could stab. Theirs were just finely made iron bars. My recent experience with Saxon Slayer had made me loath to risk others touching it but my equites were happy for the oathsworn of Mungo to hold and swing their weapons.

I watched with the chief as the two sets of warriors exchanged views. "Our helmets and our swords come from those we kill. Recently we have not won and I fear it is the fault of our weapons."

"It is like a circle, Mungo, you cannot win because you have poor weapons. You have inferior weapons because you cannot win. I have seen your men fight and they are brave but I have also seen their swords bend when struck by a Saxon one. A bent sword is just an unbalanced metal bar. They are also shorter swords than those the Saxons use. They can be effective but to do so you need to get in close and fighting, as you do, individually, that is almost impossible."

"You are saying we cannot win."

I smiled, "No, I am saying you cannot win in open battle. Not, at least, until you have better swords, shields and some helmets. Use the land and use ambush. You have told me already that your men know this land. That knowledge can defeat an enemy. Make the Saxons fear to leave the walls of their burghs."

"This makes sense but I fear that some of my warriors still wish the glory of a combat seen by others."

I pointed to his maimed hand, "Much as you did when first you saw me." He nodded and, self consciously covered his crippled claw with his left hand. "You have learned. Teach them."

We left two days later and headed northeast towards the thick woods and high lands of the disputed border. The Saxons thought they had defeated all the warriors who lived there but Mungo led us to a clearing in a forest where we dismounted and waited.

We were there for some time. The horses drank from the small burn which ran through it and the men ate some of their rations. We were patient. Geraint nodded at me when he knew that the men of the wood were coming. Had they been enemies then we would have been prepared.

Angus mac Angus could have been the twin of Mungo. He was a huge bear of a man. He even wore a wolf skin over his back. His long hair was tied in four pig tails and was limed. I had not seen the like for a while. In Constantinopolis I had read how the warriors of Britannia had done this when they fought the legions. In his hand, he held a war axe and there were three seaxes in his belt. He was barefoot. His men, who appeared like wraiths from the trees, looked to be variations of him. Most held spears in their hands. They were not what I was expecting.

He was wary as he approached us. He gave a deferential half bow to Mungo but kept his eye on me. "Angus mac Angus this is a friend. This is the Warlord. You can trust him."

Angus did not smile but he nodded, "I will trust him when I know him, chief. Why do I need him as a friend?"

"Because he can help to get your lands back for you and to avenge those of your men who fell when the Saxons came."

He nodded and pointed to one of his men. "We do well enough."

The man took a Saxon head from the sack.

I smiled, "The Saxons are like fleas on a dog. Just taking one or two heads will not get rid of them."

"And how can you and a handful of men on horses help us?"

"Firstly, there are more than the warriors you see here. We did not come to fight, yet. We came to talk. Secondly, we use cunning to defeat them. Tell me, Angus, do they have a burgh close by?" He looked as though he had not heard the word before. "A walled fort behind which they hide when you are close."

He nodded, "Aye some way the other side of the forest. It used to be the place of the clan Brus but they were slain in battle. It was called the Walls of Brus for the clan thought that their wooden ramparts would protect them."

"Then we draw them from their hall and we trap them here." I pointed to his wolf skin, "Much as you did with the wolf."

He took it from his shoulders and held it up. I saw scars running down his chest. "We do not trap wolves! We go into their dens and we fight them as warriors!"

His warriors banged their spears on the ground and cheered.

I waited for their cheers to subside. "And they scarred you and killed some of your men?"

He nodded, "My son died bravely."

I nodded to Geraint and my horse. "Had you ambushed the wolves then you would still have the wolf skin and your son would be alive." Geraint threw me my wolf skin. The wolf had been larger than the one Angus had killed. "I too have fought a wolf and killed it with my sword. My men did too. The difference is that we live and your son is dead."

For the first time, he seemed more at ease, "And you can teach us how to ambush the Saxons?"

"More than that we can fight alongside you so that it is their hearths which are empty after the fight and not yours. Between us, we can take this burgh. And then we find another. If you fight with me then this is the beginning of the end of the Saxons in Alt Clut."

His eyes narrowed, "And why should a Roman like you help us? You hunted us!"

"True for then we were enemies but now we are allies. As for why, let us just say that I fight King Oswald. He threatens my land and my life too." I could see that he was still undecided, "And another reason that I know we will win is Myrddyn. The wizard has returned and will be at our side when we need him."

That grabbed their attention, "The wizard lives? We heard that he died."

"No, he has been speaking with the spirits and now he knows how to defeat the Saxons."

Angus came over and held out a tree trunk of an arm. "Then we will fight at your side!"

Later that day we left the clearing and headed home. Geraint would be able to find their meeting place. We would return when we had made our preparations. The equites of Rheged were going to war. We were cautious as we travelled home for the land was controlled by Oswald. Angus and his men, however, made them travel in large groups. We saw their sign and we avoided them. When I chose to attack, I wanted it to be in the heart of their land and to come as a complete surprise.

My men told me that Gawan and Myrddyn had not stirred from their tower since I had left. I would give the old man all the time that he needed. I was just grateful that he had returned. I sent for Lann Aelle and Kay. I would need most of their equites.

I sat with Daffydd ap Miach and we drank some wine. Daffydd was the same age as me. Our fathers had fought together and we had continued that tradition. He was a barrel of a man but pulling a war bow for more than twenty years took its toll and I had come to a decision.

"Daffydd I will not be asking you to come to war with me and to lead the archers." He nodded. "I need you here." I waved a hand around the old Roman fort. "I want you to command the garrison of this fort."

"Garrison? If you take the archers and the equites I will have no garrison, lord."

"You will but it is one which you must train. It is the men who work here; Garth and his smiths. Aed son of Owain, the baker, and Iago son of Gruffyd the groom. There are the men we use in the boats on the river. They are all men and they know how to use weapons. They just need to use them better than they do. They will never need to fight outside the walls. You can teach them to use bows well. You know how to deter an attacker with hot oil, pig fat and sand. You know how to make ditches killing fields. Will you do it?"

He looked at me, as a friend and not a warlord. "And who will lead my archers?"

"There is only one man who can do that, Owain ap Daffydd. Does he meet with your approval?" His son's name made him nod.

I saw the smile break upon his face, "He is a little young but with a bit of advice, I think he would be the best man to lead my archers. I will watch your castle, Warlord, and I thank you for this confidence."

My equites arrived over the next two days. I still did not see Myrddyn or Gawan. I was not worried; they would emerge when they had finished. Lann Aelle and Kay were eager to go to war. Kay grumbled, "I like not this sitting behind my walls and just watching. My sword arm aches for bodies to hew."

Lann Aelle said, "But is it wise to stir up the Saxons?"

"Myrddyn has already told me that they are keen to hurt us still. Remember what he said about the witches? They killed our families. If for nothing else, we make war until we end the threat of them."

"You are right cousin. And do not misunderstand me. Like Kay, I am eager to make these Saxons fear us but we are still short of men."

"That is why I now have Daffydd as commander of my garrison. I will take every warrior from within my walls."

We sipped the wine and Kay said, "And how is the boy? Is he satisfactory?

Kay was gruff but he was a good father. "He is as good as Lann Aelle was for my father, I can speak no higher of him than that."

Kay beamed, "Then I am happy."

We spent the afternoon discussing how we would supply our men and where we would be operating. My servants told me that the food was ready and we were about to sit down when

Myrddyn and Gawan appeared. I was shocked by Myrddyn. He appeared to have shrunk even more. If his eyes had not been as sharp as ever I might have worried.

"Are you finished?"

"No, brother. I have a long way to go but Myrddyn says we need a break."

The old wizard nodded, "He is like a lump of clay. When first you work it then it is both hard and not pliable. The more you work at it the easier it becomes. He is pliable now. My hands will find it easier."

Lann Aelle and I laughed, "Well, brother, how does it feel to be compared to a lump of clay?"

"Believe me, he has called me much worse over the last days."

Myrddyn had to suffer Lann Aelle's questions as we ate. Surprisingly he did not seem to mind for he had the appetite of a bird and he answered and did not eat. He drank well enough.

"You do not like the food, Myrddyn?"

"I find it hard to eat much these days. The poison the witch gave me should have killed me. It did not but it did something within me." He shrugged, "I do not need much food."

I looked over at Gawan. He gave me a sad smile. When his training had finished then he would tell me. Myrddyn suddenly gave me a sharp look. I looked away guiltily. Then he said, "And what have you been up to Hogan Lann?"

"I have Pol making an alliance with Penda and the men of Powys and Gwynedd."

"And you have spoken with the men of Alt Clut."

"If you know what I have done then why are you asking me these questions?"

He smiled, enigmatically, "So that you will be used to answering questions as I am. Besides Gawan has not read all of your thoughts yet. He is exhausted from our work. Tell him."

I shook my head, "We are going to raid the Walls of Brus. It is an isolated burgh and the clan who live close by are keen to raid. When we have destroyed them, we will seek another target. I hope, by then, that we will have an answer from King Penda."

Gawan nodded approvingly and Myrddyn said, "You have learned from your father, Warlord. He began to make alliances as King Urien did."

"Will it be well?"

"Do you really want to know? I know that when you dreamed your death it upset you." Myrddyn's sharp eyes seemed to pierce me. I knew that he read my mind. Could he read my heart too?

"It came as a shock, that is all."

"Then I will say that you will defeat King Oswald but Rheged's time is short." I looked into Myrddyn's eyes and saw just steel.

The faces of Kay and Lann Aelle fell. Kay burst out, "Then is this all in vain?"

"It is never in vain. We are part of the land and the land changes. The rivers do not follow the same course they shift over the years and they move. Mountains sometimes tumble. Trees grow and trees die. It is part of a greater plan. We play a small role." He asked, "Would you stop the fight?"

Kay was stumped, "No, for what would be the point. I just do not like to lose."

"We thought we had lost Rheged when Prince Pasgen fled. The Warlord has shown that we can get it back. We will lose it again... some day but you have children and they will have children. You must tell them the stories of the Warlord. The dream must be kept alive. One day we will win but we will not be here to see it."

Kay shook his head, "He has grown even more difficult to understand since he came back but I shall keep fighting. It is in my blood and Agramaine shall tell his children of what we all did. *Wyrd.*"

Myrddyn laughed, "Now you understand, Kay."

Chapter 17

My two leaders brought their equites to my fort eight days later. Owain ap Daffydd was honoured to have been chosen to lead his father's archers. I saw the resolution on his face. He would do all that he could to maintain his father and grandfather's high standards. To many people, the fifty men I led would seem like a small force. It was not the largest army I had ever led but they were all the best that we had. The twenty equites were better than a hundred hearthweru or oathsworn. The fifteen archers could not be bettered. The ten squires would all be equites soon and the five who led our baggage train were all handy men with a sword. I wanted a fast-moving column which could strike, and if threatened, withdraw.

Geraint led us unerringly to the clearing. We dismounted, took off our saddles and waited. A short while later Angus mac Angus and his men appeared. They came so quietly that only Geraint and Tadgh knew of their presence.

The chieftain looked at the men I had brought, "There are more men than I thought you would bring. You must be serious."

"We are. Should we camp here or have you somewhere else in mind?"

"This is as good a place as any. The Walls of Brus are not far to the east." He scratched his beard, "Tell me, Warlord, how do you plan to take this stronghold?"

"Through cunning. Tomorrow my archers and my scouts will go with you and ambush their hunters."

"How do you know they will hunt tomorrow?"

"I am guessing that the farms in this area do not keep many sheep or cattle."

"You are right."

"If they can get it then Saxons eat meat. I would hazard a guess that they hunt every day. While you do that, I will take my equites and we will capture every Saxon farmer and their families from the farms which surround the burgh. We will bring them here first and when they are all collected my squires will take them to Mungo."

"Why?"

"The Saxons took many of your folk as slaves did they not?"

"Aye, Warlord many families were enslaved."

"Then we exchange one set of slaves for another. The strength of your people lies in the families themselves. If they are returned to you then it will make you stronger. However, I suspect that such an exchange will not take place until we have destroyed the burgh. That will take a few days. I need you to tell me where the farms are so that by the end of tomorrow we will have set the Gesith or Thegn in the burgh an interesting problem. Then we wait until he makes a mistake."

"You can be sure he will do such a thing?"

"I will force him to make mistakes. We will sit astride the road to his burgh and stop supplies from getting in. That will also prevent messages getting out too."

"You wage war in a different way to the one I am used to. I will watch and learn."

We discovered that there were eight farms within a mile or two of the burgh. They had been farmed by the men of Alt Clut and so we had an idea of their layout. We rode in to each one quickly and with men coming from all directions. Of the eight farmers three fought us and were slain but the rest were all driven, with their animals, to the clearing. We had struck so quickly that they had no chance to even think of escaping and we tied ropes about their necks and ankles. Agramaine and the squires herded the captives to Mungo where he could use them as hostages.

When Angus and my archers returned, they were in high spirits. They had found and ambushed eight hunters. All had died. Their weapons were given to Angus. I sent Lann Aelle and Kay with their equites to the western side of the burgh along with eight archers. I had five equites and the rest of the archers with me. That night I explained what we would do. I had to be careful to explain it well; my men knew my methods while Angus did not.

I intended to taunt the Saxons into fighting me. "I will go with one mounted archer, Owain ap Daffydd, and my standard-bearer, Llewellyn. I will demand the surrender of the burgh. They will probably do one of two things. They will either do nothing and laugh at me or, more likely, they will send a rider east to Din Guardi to tell their king that I am here. King Oswald will want to catch me if he can. The riders he sends will be taken by my cousin. I will do this each day until whoever commands in the burgh decides to rid himself of me and my insults. He will come to get me and I will lead him into the forests where the rest of you will ambush them."

Angus was, quite rightly, sceptical. "Can you be sure they will do this?"

"I am a tempting target for our enemies. I shall be the bait."

The three of us rode the next morning to view these wooden Walls of Brus. The Saxons had cleared the ground from all around the walls. It was scrubby land anyway and the nearest cover was almost a thousand paces away in the forest where Angus mac Angus and my equites waited. I halted a hundred and fifty paces from the gates and, while I waited I examined it critically. It was poorly made. The walls were not high enough and the ditch was of little use save to keep the water from getting inside. They had no tower within. I could have taken it easily but I might have lost warriors. I could not afford that. I needed to use my mind instead.

Owain said, "Someone comes, Warlord." He pointed at the gate. I saw two men with helmets.

"Now it begins. Prepare an arrow." I took out my sword and raised it. I had to shout for my voice to carry. "I am the Warlord of Rheged and this is Saxon Slayer. I am here to tell you to surrender to me. This is not Bernicia!"

At first, they said nothing, at least not to me. They were too far away for me to hear much. I saw them speaking with each other. There was a discussion and they pointed and jabbed their fingers. Eventually, one man shouted, "I see three men on horses! We were the ones who slew the King of the Welsh. We do not fear you, Warlord! Go before we add your head to the ones we took at Heavenfield!"

I turned to Garth, "Now!"

He released an arrow. It flew in the air. I watched as they followed its progress. Suddenly one of the men put up a shield and took the arrow as it was about to strike one of those with a helmet.

I shouted, "Now do you fear me?"

In answer, half a dozen arrows were released from the walls. Only one came close and that landed on the earth ten paces from us. I shouted, "You have until this time tomorrow to surrender or I will become angry!"

We rode slowly away. I wanted them to know I was not afraid. Llewellyn asked, "Why should they do anything, lord? There are only three of us."

"That is why they will do something. They know me and they will suspect a trap. Their leader will send men to fetch help. They know me. They will expect us to have more than three men but they do not know that Lann Aelle and Kay wait for them."

We returned the next day but I just took Llewellyn. Their response was the same. When I returned to the clearing a rider came from Lann Aelle to tell us that they had slain six messengers who had tried to reach King Oswald. The plan was working. The same day Agramaine and the squires returned. I now had the men I needed for the next phase. On the third day, I went alone. I shouted, "I tire of this. Tomorrow I will come and take your miserable walls and rid myself of this annoyance."

When I returned to the clearing I gathered them around me. "Tomorrow they will try to take me. I will lead them here. I want them ambushed."

Angus said, "They will suspect a trap. They will not enter the woods."

"I know which is why you, Angus, and your men will not be in the woods. You will stand before them. Owain will have my archers and Llewellyn will have my equites. They will ride around the Saxons and attack them from the rear. That, they will not expect. Tadgh, you will ride tonight and have Lann Aelle close with the burgh. When he is certain that the Saxons have followed me, he is to storm the Saxon burgh."

"Aye Warlord."

"Agramaine you and the squires will also go with Llewellyn. Tomorrow we will see just how much you have learned."

"I would rather be by your side, Warlord."

"I know but this is something I learned from Myrddyn. When he does a magic trick, he makes you watch one hand while he uses the other to perform the trick. I want their attention on me."

168

I rode as dangerously close as I could to the walls when I approached the burgh. I was not reckless and my shield was ready for any arrow which came my way. I now saw the faces of those on the walls. There were just three of them and none wore mail. I could see that they looked drawn. It had been some days since they had been able to hunt and they were hungry.

"Have you an answer? Do you surrender?"

Their answer almost took me by surprise. The gates opened and warriors rushed at me. I whipped Copper's head around as I drew my sword. A spear was hurled at me and it clattered into my shield. Even as I turned I saw that there were over thirty of them. Glancing over my shoulder I saw that they were less than forty paces from Copper's rump. Had I wished I could have escaped them but I wanted them to follow. Since Copper had drunk from the enchanted pool in the cave he had been a different horse and he had a power in his legs which astounded even me. I kept Copper at the speed the men were travelling. Ahead of me, I saw that Angus mac Angus had done as I asked and the ten men of Alt Clut waited thirty paces from the trees. I began to move away from the Saxons. When I reached Angus, I stopped and wheeled Copper around.

The Saxon leader held up his hand and halted his men. He shouted, "Do you think that Athelhere of Din Guardi will fall into this trap, Warlord? We will not follow you into the trees where your archers will slaughter us."

I dismounted and, slapping Copper's rump sent him into the woods. I turned and stood next to Angus mac Angus. "We are going nowhere. I see before me but thirty Saxons. Angus here and I could deal with that!"

Seeing the Warlord dismounted must have goaded them into action for they ran at us. They were forty paces from us when those at the rear heard the thunder of hooves as my equites and squires galloped towards them. Owain ap Daffydd and his archers rose from the scrub and knocking arrows began to pour arrows onto those at the rear. The Saxons stopped.

"Charge!"

I led Angus and his men to hurl ourselves at the stunned Saxons. The sudden appearance of my men had caught them by surprise. Angus and his men had no armour and they reached the

Saxons first. All the pent-up fury of men who had been chased from their land was in their hands that day. They seemed oblivious to the weapons of the Saxons. Angus mac Angus was so full of wild abandon that he failed to see the Saxon leader who raised his sword to slash into his back. I just managed to bring Saxon Slayer down hard upon the Saxon's shield. It was a powerful strike and the warrior had to put his sword arm to his right to regain his balance.

He turned to me and spat out, "You are ever the trickster! I shall kill you now, for you are not on your horse."

"I do not need a horse to kill a worthless warrior such as you!"

He swung his sword in a wide arc in an attempt to knock me over. I braced my left leg and leaned into my padded shield. I took the blow and then darted my right hand forward. The strike took him by surprise and he did not bring his shield around quickly enough. My sword rasped against his mail. Sparks flew and I saw his tunic beneath. As I withdrew my sword for another blow I hit his sword hand with my shield. He took a step back and it allowed me to feint at his damaged mail. This time he brought his shield around quickly; he had anticipated the blow. I, however, changed the angle of the strike and went for his neck. His mail shirt was not a good one and there was a gap. He had adorned himself with polished stones on a leather thong. The beads he wore offered no protection and Saxon Slayer slashed across his throat. Bright blood flooded from the wound and I saw the life leave his eyes. As he fell I saw the rest of Angus' warriors all watching me. He was the last to die. We had won. I took Saxon Slayer and removed his head. I took his cloak from his shoulders and wrapped the skull in it.

I whistled and Copper came from the edge of the woods where he had been grazing. "Go and see if Lann Aelle needs help." My equites and squires galloped off. As I mounted I said to Owain, "See to the wounds of our friends and take what you can from the dead. Come to the burgh when you are done."

The Walls of Brus had fallen. As I entered the open gates I saw Lann Aelle gathering the prisoners who remained. He had taken his helmet off and he grinned when I approached. "I have never had such an easy victory. There were only four warriors who could fight and the rest surrendered. They were starving, cousin."

"Good. Llewellyn and Agramaine come with me. Kay, take charge here. Lann Aelle, bring your men. Geraint and Tadgh, we ride to the next Saxon town. We have a message to deliver to King Oswald."

We were now riding in Saxon land. This was Bernicia. I did not know exactly where the next settlement would be but I headed down the valley for the Saxons used burghs on hill tops to control the remote valleys. I knew that the Otter Burn was to our south and as we crested a rise I saw a hill fort in the distance. Looking at the sky I worked out that we would have just enough time to reach the fort, deliver our message and then return to the Walls of Brus before dark.

This was a well-made fort. It nestled on a bluff above a twisting river. This would require a siege and war engines to take it. I did not need to try to take it. The land told our enemies that we were approaching. As the road rose and fell so we would be seen from a distance. There were a couple of farms nearby and the farmers rushed their families into the fort as we approached. The walls were manned and we halted close enough to shout.

"I am the Warlord of Rheged and I have a message for King Oswald!"

A bearded warrior with a full-face helmet came to the top of the gatehouse and shouted, "I am Ealdorman Oethelwold. I will send your words, Warlord although you show no respect to me by bringing armed men into my land."

I nodded and removed my helmet. "As the men of Northumbria are constantly raiding my land I do not worry about such considerations. I came here because I have destroyed the men who guarded the Walls of Brus and I have captured the farmers and their families. If your king wishes it, I will exchange your Saxons for the men of Alt Clut he enslaved."

There was a murmur from the walls and then Ealdorman Oethelwold said, "I do not believe you, Warlord. It was a strong garrison and they would have told me had you been raiding. Do not try to trick me. Now that your wizard is dead you are losing your powers."

That was interesting. It told me that the witches were still serving King Oswald. "Firstly, I never lie, even to a Saxon, and second this is no trick." I untied the cloak from my saddle and threw the skull onto the ground before me. "This is your Gesith. I slew him with Saxon Slayer."

His face showed that he recognised him. "Ida was my cousin. I shall remember this. Very well I will send the message to my king. Where will you be? The Roman fort?"

"I will wait at the Walls of Brus. Your king has one month. If he has not sent me word, then I sell the slaves to the Hibernians. They seem to like Saxon women."

"One month then."

We turned and headed west. "They will come to attack the Walls of Brus."

"Of course. And they will march down this road. We look for places where Geraint and Tadgh can watch and we prepare the burgh. I will send to Mungo. I am certain he will wish to send men to hold the fort."

"You seem more confident cousin."

I told him of the sword and the vision. "I am not destined to die in Rheged and certainly not in Bernicia. Besides with Myrddyn back, I believe, despite his gloomy prognostications, that we will win. He has told me that Oswald will die. Perhaps it will be if he attacks me at the Walls of Brus."

"Perhaps."

The land rose and fell sharply. There were forests and woods which would aid us but the slopes were too steep for horsemen. We could use archers for the roads would be equally difficult for mailed Saxon warriors. There was a deep-sided, wooded valley to the north of the Walls of Brus. That would protect the forest from attacks there. It seemed to me that they would come either along the Otter Burn or the river valley which led from their own stronghold. Either way, they would have to descend and travel along the north bank of the Tinea and that was a steep-sided valley too. The task was one for Owain ap Daffydd and my scouts. They would warn us and slow them down.

Angus mac Angus was already improving the defences when we arrived. The heads of the Saxons were arrayed before the fort on spears. He grinned, "A little warning to the Saxons of what they can expect."

I told him what we had done. "I will send a rider to Mungo. He will need to reinforce you."

"There are many more of the folk who farmed here. They will return."

I was intrigued, "How will they know?"

He looked, surprisingly, a little shame faced. "Our families live in the forest still. I confess I did not totally trust you, Warlord. I am sorry. I will bring them in and send one of the boys with the message. We have ponies."

"I understand the mistrust. Do not worry for we have a common enemy. Who knows, one day we might be enemies again."

"You are wise. We might. So, you think they will come?"

"They were kin to the Ealdorman. He will come. Oh, I do not doubt that he will send a message to King Oswald but he will try to retake it himself first. He will seek the glory of being the one to cow the warlord of Rheged. We will slow him down and weaken him before he gets here but I will have to keep my horsemen out where they can do more harm. My squires will fight within your walls. You need food. Have your men lay in supplies."

"We will. There is a well and the Saxons did not damage it. When our families come then we will make it strong once more."

"Are you certain you want your families here? Are they not safer in the forest?"

"We fled once. No more!"

He was determined. I told my archers and my scouts what I wanted. "We will see to it, lord."

Tadgh brought the news that the Saxons were coming two days later. "The Ealdorman is bringing a warband. His hearthweru have mail, of sorts. It is made of pieces of metal sewn onto leather. The rest do not. There are a hundred of them. They will be here by noon. Owain is already slowing them down. When the Saxons try to close with them they use our horses and retreat. One, the Ealdorman, and three others are mounted."

"Good. Keep harassing them." I shouted, "Equites! Mount your horses. Angus, they come!"

"Good, then we will give them a warm welcome."

With my squires and the families who had joined us we had almost forty armed men on the walls. Some only had slings but they would hold the enemy at bay long enough for us to do our worst. I led my nineteen equites and positioned them on the high ground to the north of the fort. There was a narrow burn which ran behind us. It would not hamper us for we could easily cross it but it might slow down men who were not expecting it.

We waited in two lines. It disguised our numbers and gave us two opportunities to attack them. When they came, it was in a slowly moving wedge of shields. My archers had taught them to defend themselves. The dour horseman led the host. When they saw us above them they halted. I saw them debate. What did he do about these horsemen who would attack his men if they just attacked the walls?

King Cadwallon's death and the disaster at Heavenfield had taken away the fear of equites. I saw the hearthweru who had axes forming up in the centre of the wedge and then they came towards us. The four Saxon horsemen followed at the rear of the wedge. Their shields protected them from any arrow attack from the fort and they must have thought that they would do as King Oswald had done and hack our horses to death.

King Cadwallon had been duped by Morgana and Morwenna. I had no doubt now that he had listened to their words and taken them as replacements for Myrddyn. It explained why he had shunned both Gawan and myself. They must have persuaded him to choose a narrow battlefield where he could not manoeuvre. We could. They came up the slope. I was impressed that they kept their formation. It mattered not. I had no intention of waiting for them.

"On my command, we go around the wedge and attack the Ealdorman and his riders. Then we attack the rear of the wedge. Listen for my orders. When I shout 'fall back' then head for the burn!"

"Aye Warlord."

"Now!"

We moved so quickly that the wedge did not even break stride. A Saxon voice yelled, "Shields!" They thought we would be foolish enough to attack them head-on. When we galloped around them they must have wondered at my plan. I saw the four horsemen draw their swords. The Ealdorman was no fool. Saxons do not fight on horses and they dismounted before we could reach them and threw themselves into the protection of the shield wall. It was no longer a wedge. The rear ranks had turned around and presented spears but the fact that they had opened ranks to admit the Ealdorman and his men meant that Pelas and Llenlleog were able to hack and slash at the two who were slow to reform. The two unfortunate Saxon ceorls fell and then the wall of shields came up.

"Reform behind me." I reined Copper in forty paces from the Saxons who were busy shuffling into a circle. I could see that with the men whittled down by my archers there remained some eighty-odd warriors.

"What do we do, Warlord?"

"We wait, Lann Aelle. They cannot move and soon they will need water. They will be thirsty. The burn will beckon them. We wait for someone to weaken. Pelas and Llewellyn, capture those horses and take them to the fort. The Ealdorman will now realise that he is afoot. It may encourage him to talk."

An hour later and the Saxons remained in their circle. I knew that the shields and the spears would be heavy. We had no such worries. I rode closer to them. "So Ealdorman, did you come with such a large escort to tell me that King Oswald has agreed to my terms or did you come to teach me a lesson?" He did not reply. "If you notice I have not yet sent for my archers. Shall I do so now?"

In answer, they suddenly lurched towards me. Had I been riding Star they might have caught me but Cooper was young and he was quick. More than that, he had drunk from the enchanted pool. I whipped his head around as Lann Aelle led the rest of my men to attack the Saxons. They were no longer tight and those who faced us were not the axe-wielding hearthweru. They were the lightly armed ceorls. My equites darted in and slashing left and right drove them back to their circle. Six of their number lay dead when the shields clattered shut.

"That was a risk, Warlord."

"And I will not take another."

As the afternoon wore on the Saxons became more nervous. Three could not resist the lure of the burn and they made a break for the water and the safety of the woods. They did not make it. Kay and four of his equites caught up with them before they reached the water and slew them. The others learned the lesson and they squatted down behind the shields.

Lann Aelle nudged his horse over to me as the afternoon wore on. "They will try another break soon."

"I know. As soon as their axe men are bought to the front of the wedge then we will know what they intend."

"Do we repeat the same manoeuvre?"

"Not this time. We fall back and make them charge again."

"Then the attack on the fort is over?"

"It is. The Ealdorman is looking for a way out which does not cost him more men. Owain and his archers will thin them out some more and we will follow." I turned to Llewellyn. "Have the squires bring out the spare horses."

We, unlike the Saxons, had our water skins and dried meat which we had eaten but it was our horses which needed some respite. We watched as the leaders held a conference in the middle of the circle to discuss what they might do. There was now no chance of taking the fort. The Ealdorman had gambled. He had seen the handful of equites I had taken with me to his stronghold and thought that was all that I had. When the squires brought out the horses the Saxons thought we were going to attack. They quickly formed up with their hearthweru who wielded axes at the front of a newly formed wedge with spears over and around them. They made the move slowly so that we could not attack. Even so, they nearly caught us out. We had just mounted when they charged. The charge of a wedge is like a fast walk. Our squires galloped our tired mounts back inside the fort and we fell back, down the hill towards the river.

The Saxons took heart and hurried after us. I heard orders shouted and they stopped pursuing and began to head back down the road towards their stronghold. That was twenty miles away but if they could make the Otter Burn then they would be able to defend themselves there. I allowed them to pass and then headed

Saxon Throne

back up the slope. We formed up behind them. The sun was already heading towards the west but we had a couple of hours of daylight left.

Three miles from the Walls of Brus our archers began to loose arrows. The first few found flesh and four men fell. The Saxons quickly brought up their shields. We pressed them close so that they could not go after the archers and over the next four miles before darkness fell Daffydd and his archers slew another eight.

When darkness fell, we halted the pursuit and I shouted, "Next time Ealdorman, bring more men! We thank you for the gift of the horses!"

We returned to Angus mac Angus. We were tired but we had not lost a man and yet the Saxons had not only had their pride damaged, but they had also lost men. That evening, as we ate, Angus asked me about my tactics. "Why did you not charge them?"

"The shield wall is the most effective defence against horsemen. Had I had more horsemen then I would have dismounted half and hacked my way into the heart of the wall. That day will come but I judged it not to be today. My men do not lack courage but I lack numbers. I must husband what I have."

The next day Mungo and his men arrived with the hostages. If the Eorledman came again we could take the fight to him. As events turned out he did not come but King Oswald did. Geraint brought me the news and we prepared our men for a battle. Now that we had Mungo's men as well as Angus' we were able to use my squires and my mounted archers. We took our position up to the north of the fort and we waited.

There was to be no battle. An emissary rode up and shouted, "Warlord of Rheged, King Oswald would speak with you. Truce?"

"Aye, truce. We will meet by the river yonder." I pointed down to the river below us. "He can bring two men with him."

I returned to the fort.

"Well?"

"We go to speak. If you two come with me, we will see what the Saxon wants."

I could see that Angus was disappointed. "We will not give anything away, Angus mac Angus. We buy time. I have sent for allies. This galls me as much as you but we do not have the luxury of great numbers."

Mungo said, "Listen to him, my friend. He speaks wisely."

"I will hold my tongue. I pray I can hold my hand."

The Eorledman and a thegn accompanied the King. I saw that King Oswald was angry but he held his temper in check. I said nothing. I had learned that being calm helped in such negotiations. Eventually, King Oswald broke the silence. He jabbed a finger at Mungo, "You have broken the truce!"

I saw Mungo begin to rise and I held up my hand. "No, he has not. Mungo mac Fergus has not broken the truce. He has brought the captives which I captured." I smiled at the King, "I have never made peace with you, Saxon! Even when I was in Ynys Môn I fought you. There will never be peace between us. Either you or I will die first and I have dreamed my death, Saxon and it is not at your hands nor of your assassins."

"You are an unbeliever! A pagan! You are the spawn of the devil!"

"Watch your words. Saxon Slayer itches for more royal blood. King Edwin found that to his cost. Of course, you were not at his side. You were hiding that day when we defeated Northumbria. You prefer women to do your work!"

I saw from his face that my barb had hit home.

"Come, King of, where is it now? Bernicia? Deira? I know not but be swift for I lose patience!"

The thegn stood and began to draw his sword. "This is too much to bear! Let me slay him, majesty."

I laughed, "Please, Oswald, let him do it. My sword has not tasted Saxon blood yet this day! Let us trade blows!"

The King said, "Sit, Athelward! This man has killed too many Saxons already. What is it you propose?"

"Send your captives to us and we will return yours."

"Send yours first."

I stared at Oswald and he actually shrank back.

"Very well and then you give up the Walls of Brus."

I laughed, "Why? Your Eorledman left a trail of dead on his way back to his castle. If you want it then take it but Angus mac Angus will show you how to defend a castle."

They were not happy but they had no choice, King Oswald said, "Agreed."

I stood, "Then as the air down here is foul we shall leave." I started to walk away and then I spun around and put my face close to King Oswald. "This is not finished and one day I will end this blood feud. Believe it!"

I led the other two back up to the fort. Angus said, "I did not understand it all but did the Warlord not put King Oswald firmly in his place."

Mungo laughed, "Aye. I crossed the Warlord once, Angus. I would not do so a second time."

We waited by the gate and thirty captives rushed towards us. They must have driven them hard from Din Guardi for they looked almost exhausted. I said, "Let the Saxons go." The captives which Mungo had brought rushed the other way.

"Is this over, Warlord?"

"No, Mungo but we are safe for a short time. Use the time well. Build up your armies and, Angus, do not relent. Keep up your vigilance."

"Trust me, Warlord. I have learned. We fight, or we die!"

Chapter 18

We returned to Civitas Carvetiorum. We used the road which ran to the south of the wall. It had been some time since I had sent Pol on his embassy. I wondered how he had fared. Lann Aelle was also reflective. "If we pin down five times our number with our equites then we need fear the Saxons no longer."

"We have never feared the Saxons Lann Aelle but there is a difference between pinning down and defeating. We would have suffered the same fate as Cadwallon had we charged them. We cannot break their shield wall with horses."

Llenlleog said, "Perhaps then we ask the wizard for some magic."

A thought came to me, "That is not a bad idea Llenlleog although the magic we require I have seen already. They have something in the east called Greek fire. It burns, even on water. If Myrddyn and Gawan could make it then we could burn the shield walls."

Kay snorted, "Then why not just fire? We can make fire without worrying wizards."

"The trouble is, old friend, that we need to make the shields burn. We require something which will keep the fire burning longer."

"You are right Lann Aelle. Hot pig fat would work."

"And all that we would need, cousin, is a way of delivering it." I could see Lann Aelle's mind working. He was almost as clever as Gawan. "If we had small amphorae filled with red hot fat and we had a cord around the neck we could throw the amphora high in the air. It would smash on the shields. Then a burning torch would ignite it."

"That might well work. We will speak with Myrddyn. That could be a task for the squires." Lann Aelle was right; if the equites could pin down the shield wall then we could use fire to destroy them.

The discussion as we rode the last few miles home was lively as my equites worked out new ways of defeating Saxons. Their axes could spell doom for our horses. Even the new ones we were breeding would not be strong enough to carry mail. I knew that in the east they had warriors called Kataphractoi who rode such horses. We could only dream of such animals.

Pol had not returned when we reached the fort but Gawan and Myrddyn were walking the river bank. I sent the men, along with my horse, inside while I joined the two of them.

"The training is finished?"

Myrddyn shook his head, "A wizard, unlike a warrior, never ceases training. Even I am still training. The day you stop is the day you lose. We have reached the point where Gawan can start to use his powers. That way he will learn their limits and then extend them. How went the campaign?"

"You did not see it?"

"Our minds were focused within and not without. Come tell us all."

I told them what we had done. I waited for censure from Myrddyn but, surprisingly, he nodded and a ghost of a smile played on his wrinkled face. "Wise indeed. You have reined in Oswald and yet you have lost no men."

I went on to tell him our plans for defeating a shield wall. "We would use spears but I fear that the force needed to penetrate a shield wall would unbalance us and we would fall from our horses."

"You are right. Your idea would work. Another method would be to make a small onager such as the Romans used but that would slow you down. We could build them for use inside your walls." He actually smiled, "I think I would enjoy making those. You would also need Daffydd to teach his men how to make and use fire arrows. As I recall they do not fly as far as regular arrows and their flight is more erratic but, then again, a shield wall is a large target. Come, I have ideas. I wish to put them into practice."

He turned, abruptly, and headed towards the gates. Despite his age, he hurried ahead of us and I turned to Gawan. "How is the old man?"

"Just that, old. His mind is as sharp as ever but he eats like a bird and each day becomes smaller. I swear that one day he will simply disappear and become a wraith!"

I nodded, "I remember a time when he was like our father and as tall. Now he has shrunk. Perhaps that happens to all who become old."

"You may be right. Father was also beginning to shrink. Remember how he handed power to you. He knew his end was coming."

For the first time, I felt a cold hand on my shoulder. "Brother, I have dreamed my death but when will that day come?"

"I know not. We both know that you will have to be within sight of Wyddfa first. Take hope from that."

"I worry about who will be warlord when I am gone." I looked at Gawan. "You?"

"That is not my path, brother and we both know it. Let us leave that for the spirits. It is not our choice. Our father was chosen by the sword. Let the sword choose."

I took out the sword. Until we had used the water to test it I suppose I had taken it for granted. I thought it was a weapon to kill Saxons. Now I knew it was more. It was not only a symbol it was a link to the past. As I gripped the handle I had a sudden flash in my head, a picture. It was the dream, "I throw the sword away before I die!"

"The sword will choose the next warrior to wield it. When Father found it, the sword had lain in the earth since the time of the Roman legions. That was generations. Perhaps the land will have to wait for more generations."

"That is a depressing thought."

"No brother, it is hopeful. There is a force at work and it works for our people. The Saxons like Oswald are the invaders. They are like a dark cloud which comes on a sunny day. Eventually, the sun will drive them away." We had just walked through the gates and I was greeted with the clang of metal as Garth of Elmet hammered out another sword. "Not all Saxons are like Oswald. Look at Garth. He is one of our people now. He is of Rheged."

I put my arm around his shoulder, "And you have grown too. Myrddyn has changed you."

"I know. It is a great responsibility. I now understand the weight you bear upon your shoulders. You carry the expectations of the people to be as our father was. I now have the expectation of being Myrddyn."

"No, Gawan, I am not father and you will not be Myrddyn. The world changes and we change with it. Those who follow us will not be the same as us. They will be different but their goals will be the same." I spread my arm, "The safety of this land and its people."

Pol arrived back when the leaves began to fall from the trees. He looked weary. "Come we will take a bath, the three of us, and you can tell all."

He nodded, "I could do with that. I must reek for the Saxons do not bathe. I suppose I must be used to the smell."

Gawan nodded, "You are a little pungent."

"What of Myrddyn? Will he not join us?"

"The old man is busy designing war machines to defend our walls. He and Daffydd ap Miach spend hours each day. They are both happy. We will tell him this evening when we eat."

As we lay in the tepidarium he told us of his travels. "At first King Penda was lukewarm about the idea of a campaign to fight Oswald. He had other concerns closer to home. He sent me away to speak with Powys and Gwynedd. He wished time to consider our proposals."

"At least they were not rejected out of hand."

"You are right, Gawan. However, I began to think that my task was hopeless when I visited Aberffraw. King Cadafael of Gwynedd is called Cadafael Cadomedd behind his back."

"The battle decliner?"

"Aye. Many blame him for the defeat of King Cadwallon. We know different but they are right in one respect. He is a spineless jellyfish. He is no warrior. He wishes to sit beneath Wyddfa and let others fight the Saxons. He is no ally. King Cadwallon's son, Cadwaladr, is in Powys with King Cynddylan ap Cyndrwyn. It was at his court in Rhuthun that I began to see hope. The two of them swore that they would be your allies should you need them."

"Excellent!"

"However, Powys has not enough men to come to our aid. Should Oswald be foolish enough to attack close to their land they will fight."

Gawan must have seen the look on my face. "Remember how father nurtured Cadfan ap Iago? I see hope in Cadwaladr. Perhaps with the help of Powys, he will regain the throne of Gwynedd."

"Have you seen that yet?"

"Myrddyn and I have been looking east and not south. One enemy at a time, brother."

Pol added, "Besides that was like a stone falling down a mountain. I returned to the court of King Penda. In my absence, there had been a falling out. His brother, Eowa, broke faith with King Penda. He has fled Mercia, with his hearthweru."

"To the East Angles?"

"No, Warlord, to Northumbria. He is now an ally of King Oswald and King Penda has sworn that he will attack them. He and his army will be heading north."

I suddenly felt hope. Oswald's power could only be curtailed if another Saxon fought him. "When?"

"It will be next year. He has to build up his army for Eowa took some thegns and ealdormen with him."

Gawan interjected a word of caution. "That means, brother, that for a time at least, Oswald will be even more powerful. We will have to be even more vigilant."

Myrddyn added even more caution when we told him of our new alliance. "Mercia is many miles from here. I take more hope that Cadwaladr has a supporter. If Powys and Gwynedd ally, then there is hope." He pointed to my standard in the corner. "I dreamed last night of your dragon. I saw it flying over this land."

"Then we win!"

"It was not horsemen who carried it. They were shape shifters! They were those who can become wolves."

"I do not understand. We fight on horses and ride beneath the dragon of the Romans."

"I do not make the future I see it. Your ancestor, the one who first used the sword was given it by a Queen. You saw that in the water." I nodded. "Where did she get the sword? Perhaps those who used it first also fought on foot. Perhaps they were shape shifters too and the sword is going back to its home. You do not own the sword, Warlord, it allows you to use it. It has its own purpose and you, like your father, are merely a servant of the sword and the sword serves the land."

I pushed my goblet away, "I must have had too much wine. My head spins. I do not understand this. I thought that I, like my father, fought for Rheged."

Infuriatingly he smiled and just said, "Then you were wrong."

"I do not fight for Rheged?"

"No. Explain it to him Gawan. Talking with warriors tires me out. Besides I need to dream."

He left and I turned to Gawan, "Well?"

"Do you remember when you and Pol visited Constantinopolis?" I nodded, "And you studied in the libraries there. You read of this land before the Romans came. Was it called Rheged?"

Pol said, "No it was something like the land of the Brigantes or Brigantia."

"Exactly and the sword came from there. The names we call the land do not matter. It is the land itself which does. You fight, brother, for the land. These Saxons wish to change our land. Your... our task is to save the land. That is all. This future warlord will do the same. I have not seen him yet but I will dream and I will turn my mind to him. I am intrigued." He pointed to the wolf skin which hung on the wall. I only used it in the winter when it was cold outside. "When you slew the male wolf and took the skin I wondered at that. Now I see that it was *wyrd*. Do not try to see the purposes of the spirits. Just know that they are the force of good. With their power behind us we cannot lose, not in the long run, anyway. We may have reverses but ultimately we will win."

That was the trouble with wizards and mystics; they lived in a misty world. Pol and I lived in the real world. We would be the ones fighting the Saxons and, when it came down to it there would be a battle not in the spirit world but on a battlefield with sword against sword. I would leave the philosophy to those two. I needed to stay in the real world.

We had more than enough to occupy us. The new foals began to be born not long before Yule. Their training began as soon as they could stand. We also had squires who were ready to become equites and that necessitated manufacturing more mail and swords. Garth's forge was white-hot with heat. The war machines were finished and men were trained to use them. Women were employed to make pots to carry the pig fat. The pigs which we salted were now also used to render the fat. It was like gold. That would be the weapon which would tear open the shield wall and allow my equites to destroy the Saxon's most powerful weapon.

We also had messages from Gwyneth and Arturus in the east. They would be returning home within the next year. Arturus was on the cusp of manhood and his education was finished. When he returned, Pol would train him as a warrior.

I spent some time speaking with Daffydd, my captain. He was our link with the outside world. "How goes it in the east?"

Emperor Heraclius still rules with an iron fist. He is a bad enemy but, thanks to you and your father, we, here in the west, are highly thought of. The Lady Gwyneth is also held in high regard as is your nephew. I benefit by being given good berths and the customs officials treat us kindly."

"And does the Empire flourish?"

He shook his head, "They have lost Syria. It is not only here where we suffer from barbarian attacks."

Later as I sat alone looking out of the west tower I realised that we were using many of the practices the Emperor used. Not having enough men meant having to rely on well-chosen allies. I hoped that I had not made a mistake by allying with King Penda. Vortigern had invited the Saxons over to help him fight enemies at home and now they ruled the east and the south. I had much responsibility.

Perhaps that was the kick I needed. Even though it was winter and snow lay on the ground I took some equites, scouts and archers to visit Bors, Kay and Lann. I used the new equites along with Pelas, Llenlleog and Llewellyn. There was peace in the land and the three experienced equites were the best of models.

First, we headed east to Kay. Not surprisingly he had not been resting during the winter. He had travelled as far as the high passes. "We caught a few Saxon scouts. Before they died they told us all that they knew. King Oswald and his new Mercian ally are building up their forces."

"The question is, do they attack us in the spring or King Penda?"

"I have more of the farmers trained to fight and we have a signal tower. If I light it then they come here with their families. We can stay protected in our walls."

"Then do not forget to tell me if danger comes."

He pointed to a half dozen small, long-haired ponies. "I have some of the young sons of my equites. They will bring you the news."

I told him of our plans to destroy the shield walls. "We will try them out if the Saxons decide to attack us first."

"Do you think they will?"

"I would. If Oswald could conquer this land, then he could determine which route the Mercians would take and be able to fight them on ground of his choosing."

We travelled down the narrow road close to the place the locals called wolf mountain. It was hard going. Running north to south meant that the snow lasted longer in this part of the world and the folk who chose to live there were hardy. These people had the fewest Saxon incomers. It did not suit farming. They fished and they hunted. If King Oswald made the mistake of attacking down that valley, then they would leave a trail of bones behind them.

Once we reached the fort on the water it felt almost balmy in comparison to the wolf valley. Lann Aelle had finally taken a woman. She was a Saxon from Elmet but she was comely. I saw that she was with child already. "Will it be a son, cousin?"

"I hope so. I would like to leave one of my blood in this land." He smiled at his wife, Freja, "And it is right that she is of the Saxon people. My grandmother was too, I believe. Perhaps we are the new people of Rheged."

"Myrddyn has put me in my place over that. The name matters not it is the hearts of the people which count."

Lann Aelle laughed, "Old age has not mellowed him then?"

"He is worse than ever but I mind not for he is the hand which ever guides us. I feel happier since his return for our luck has changed."

"*Wyrd.*"

"You are right cousin." We went on to discuss the new alliance and I told him the same as I told Kay, that we needed to be vigilant.

As we headed west we crossed the valley which always intrigued me. If I was spared death in battle and had the chance, then I would live in the valley. It was strangely beautiful and appeared to be filled with a power I did not understand. I resolved to talk of this with Myrddyn and Gawan when I returned home.

The high pass of Hardknott almost defeated us. The snow had drifted as high as a horse and Llenlleog and I, having the biggest horses and being the largest warriors, had to force our way through. Once we did and started to drop down it was as though we were in a different land. The snow was but a thin covering and the air was warm. It was what Pasgen had said of his land, to the south. The gods favoured this coast.

Bors had not been idle. He now had a stone wall facing the sea and he had built a sturdy tower. His castle had been expanded to the landward side so that he and his equites could practise inside his walls. I had not seen him for almost a year and we had much to speak of. The journey through the snow had been hard on the horses and so we stayed for an extra night. There was no hurry to get home.

Sometimes decisions which are made have a greater impact than others. This was one such decision. As we rose, ready to travel north one of the sentries shouted, "Sails to the west. It is a fleet of pirates! We are under attack."

I had wanted to test my new equites. Now we would and it would be in battle.

Chapter 19

There were ten ships which were heading for the coast. Those who lived close by were already streaming towards the castle. They knew what this meant. The pirates were coming for animals and for slaves. Bors had built fire pits on the stone walls over his gates and they were lit. He had two commodities in abundance: sea water and sand. He had the sand in hessian sacks ready to be heated. When that was all gone, he would use the sea water. The attackers would have a hot reception.

We stood on his gate and watched them as they closed with the shore. With my men, we had in the garrison, twelve equites, fourteen squires and fifteen archers. The people of the town and the farmers brought the number of defenders up to eighty. Not a huge number but it would have to do.

"This seems a strange time to come, Bors."

"The ships which have called in to trade speak of much rain in the land of Hibernia. There are huge areas which are flooded. The crops they counted on are destroyed. They are starving. They have disease. These are desperate people Warlord."

I looked down the walls which were being filled with equites, squires and archers. "Do they have machines of war?"

"No, lord. They will use raw courage to scale our walls." He pointed inland. They may try to get to the farms which lie some way to the east. There are few animals there. It is this coastal strip which has the greatest numbers of animals and they are now being brought inside my walls. I told them all what they must do and they have obeyed me."

"Even as we watched the boats disembark their warriors, farmers were using the east and south gate to bring their animals to safety. The noise from the beasts was incredible. Guards stood outside the gates ready to slam them shut should any pirates be foolish enough to rush them.

"Do you have javelins?"

"We have some but the pirates have a habit of using them to throw back at us. We keep them as a last resort."

As the pirates swarmed ashore I was better able to estimate their numbers. I guessed that there were about a hundred and fifty of them. None wore mail and the few who wore helmets were their chiefs. Some had shields but they varied in size. There were a variety of weapons from swords to bill hooks. These were desperate men.

Agramaine brought me my shield. "Will you need your mace, lord?"

"No, Agramaine. These pirates wear no mail but they are wild. You watch yourself today Agramaine. Keep them at a distance and expect the unexpected."

He nodded and watched as they formed up on the beaches and prepared to move toward us. "They do not look as well-armed and organised as the Saxons."

"They are not and that is what makes them dangerous. You can predict what a Saxon will do. These will not use a shield wall but anything else is possible. They want your sword, helmet and shield. If they win them then they will go home and become a chief."

"He is right, son of Kay. I prefer Saxons. You know where you are with Saxons."

Once they had all landed each boat's crew began to shout and cheer. Agramaine asked, "What are they doing? Arguing?"

"No, they are getting their blood worked up telling each other what they will do to us. It is a typical barbarian tactic. They hope to frighten us. They tattoo their faces and wear war paint to terrify us. This cheering makes them closer, like brothers. It is like the equites with the warlord but we make less noise!"

Suddenly the warbands ran at our walls. This was Bors' castle and I let him give the orders, "Archers! Release!"

This was not a rain of arrows. The archers chose the leaders and the chiefs. They had no mail to avoid. Wherever they hit would be flesh. Even so, some of the warriors were struck with arrows and they kept coming. Bors had made a good ditch. It was deep and had deadly stakes embedded in the bottom. Some of the warriors tried to leap the ditch and they writhed at the bottom when they fell on the stakes. Others took advantage of the bodies and used them as a springboard to reach the walls.

Neither the water nor the sand was hot enough yet to be used and so the archers and the slingers continued to target the warriors.

"You should have had rocks and stones too, Bors."

"I know, lord. I will get some for the next raid."

I smiled, Bors was confident enough to believe we would survive this one. I picked up a javelin. Had they been the Roman ones they would have had a piece of wood close to the head which would have broken when it struck. It prevented the javelins from being thrown back. I took the risk for I saw a chief with limed hair ordering his men on. He was less than twenty paces from me and a tempting target. I threw it and it struck him in the shoulder and transfixed his body. It was a mortal wound but he seemed oblivious to it. He turned and, seeing me, hurled his throwing hammer at my head. I barely had time to deflect it with my shield. When I looked down I saw that he had sunk to his knees in a widening puddle of blood.

More men were close to the walls and they had shields held up to protect them. As some began to hack at the gate others started to climb. They had not brought ladders but they made a human pyramid. "Llenlleog, take some men down the wall and discourage those climbers eh."

"Aye Warlord."

That left Bors, Llewellyn and Pelas with me along with the squires. "Have you men guarding the gates below us?"

"Aye, Warlord. If they break through, then they will get a warm welcome."

"Speaking of warm, how goes the sand and the sea water?"

"Almost ready." Bors pointed to the Irish ships. Another three had landed and disgorged their warriors. "When we have enough below we can do more damage to them."

I glanced down the wall and saw that Llenlleog and my new equites were engaging those who had tried to scale the walls. They were using javelins like thrusting spears and toppling the men at the top of the pyramids. The ones who fell were either wounded or hurt as they crashed onto those below.

A voice from below warned Bors of the dangers there. "My lord the gate shows daylight."

Bors nodded, "Then we had best see if the sand is hot enough. The water always takes longer." He held his hand over the sand

and pulled it away quickly. "It is ready!" His men had made the cauldron so that it could be tipped by using two wooden levers. There were two metal rings at the side of the metal vessel. He and his squire put in the wooden levers and began to exert pressure. The edge of the cauldron began to move towards the chute which had been built into the wall. I saw the strain on the faces of the two men but gradually the weight in the cauldron shifted and the contents were dumped below. There were screams and cries as the red-hot sand struck bare flesh. One of the warriors had limed hair and his head caught fire. He ran towards the sea. He did not reach it. The ones below one side of the gate fled. All had burns from the sand. Some would be mortal but all were burned.

Bors said, "Now the water!"

He and his squire hurried to the other side of the gate and put the levers in place. It was easy to see that this was ready for it bubbled and steamed. This time the weight shifted quicker and the deluge of boiling sea water cascaded below. There were more screams and, once again, the survivors fled.

The walls had been cleared and huddles of warriors gathered out of bow range. "I think it is time for the equites, Bors."

"Aye lord. Get the horses. Archers and slingers keep them at bay! Equites and squires, we ride to glory!"

We hurried down to the stables and mounted. We all took a pair of javelins from the stacks. Outside we heard the shouts and cheers as the pirates prepared themselves for another attack. The gate was wide enough for four men. Bors and I took the middle with Llenlleog on Bors' right and Pelas on my left. The rest formed up behind us. Bors said to his gatemen, "Now!"

The opening of the gates caught the pirates by surprise. They were preparing to charge again. The arrows in their shields and bodies was testament to the skill of our archers. We rode knee to knee towards them. This was no solid shield wall. These were individual warriors, each of whom would try to kill one of these vaunted horsemen and take his mail. To them it was worth more than gold.

The dangerous ones were the ones with the axes. I saw three who swung their double-handed axes in a figure of eight. They occupied a space which was wider than our four horses. There was no possibility of us passing them without our horses being hurt. I pulled back my arm and flung the javelin. It was struck by one of the axes but Bors and Llenlleog's found flesh. I threw my second and this one flew true. The three men who had been a barrier were trampled underfoot as we headed towards the rest of the pirates.

I drew my sword and swung it overhand to smash the skull of the warrior who was trying to spear Bors. His falling body made a gap between Bors and me but it did not matter now. We were amongst the warband and the gaps were filled by equites who followed us. We had killed enough of the chiefs and heroes so that some of the pirates raced back to their ships. They had had enough. The panic spread like a heath wildfire. The braver ones who stood and faced us were hacked and slashed by our swords. The ones who ran were caught and trampled. The first of the ships with those who had succeeded in escaping began to pull away from the shore.

It then became like a hunt. We sought the survivors and chased them down. We took no prisoners. We needed no pirates as slaves. Better that they died and did not return to try a second time. By the time the sun began to set we had captured five of their boats for they had been pulled onto the beaches and not a single pirate lived.

Bors ordered his men from the port to strip the bodies and load them on one of the pirate ships. It was dangerously overloaded but it did not matter. We laid faggots on the bodies and, lowering the sail, allowed the wind to take it west towards the setting sun. Our archers launched fire arrows and we watched as the burning ship headed back to Hibernia. The pirates who had fled were still in sight and I wondered what they thought. A mile offshore and the ship was engulfed in flames. It sank lower into the water until it disappeared. Their bodies would feed the fishes and the fishermen of Alavna would enjoy better catches.

We left the next day. Two of the new equites had badges of honour for they had been wounded. Their mail protected them from cuts but not from the blows of hammers and axe heads. They would learn from the blows and wounds they had suffered. We rode along the coast for I wanted to see the land the way the pirates might. We passed the remains of old Roman watch towers. The Romans had been clever people and I decided to have them repaired and manned. We did not want a repetition of the attack. We had been lucky. Had I not stayed an extra day then Bors would have struggled to man his walls. It had been a lesson for him too. He had thought his defences were perfect: they were not.

Myrddyn and Gawan had continued their work. I was noticing a change in my little brother. He looked different. His eyes were somehow sharper. It was a characteristic I had seen in Myrddyn. I also saw that he looked leaner. I supposed that was because he ate when Myrddyn did, which was not very often. He might be developing into a powerful wizard but he would no longer be an equite on whom I could rely. My equites trained each day and we all had arms like oak tree branches. As Gawan and Myrddyn approached me I saw that my brother was now a little more willowy.

I dismounted and Agramaine led Copper to the stables. "You have had trouble brother."

It was not a question. "Aye, you dreamed?"

"No but you are late and I see that some of your equites are moving a little gingerly. But our sleep was disturbed. We knew that you were in danger."

"Pirates raided Bors while we were there. We sent them to the Otherworld." I led them indoors and told them how we defended the port. "I think we need some of the engines of war which you and Daffydd built for us here, Myrddyn."

"Daffydd can build them without my assistance. We have refined the design. We must turn our thoughts to Morgana and Morwenna. We cannot hope to defeat Oswald while they weave their magic."

"Do we even know where they are?"

"They are with King Oswald in Din Guardi. It is his stronghold and he is safest there."

"Then how do we get to the witches?"

"We draw Oswald out. He will bring them with him. When King Penda comes north you must persuade him to bring Oswald to battle."

"Penda is a cautious king. He will want to be sure of victory."

Gawan took out a map of Northumbria. "It is our horsemen which will encourage King Penda to attack. Here, north or Eoforwic is a good place. South of the Dunum, the land suits our horsemen. If King Penda cuts Eoforwic off from Oswald, then the Northumbrians will have to come south to relieve the siege. Osric's memory will be fresh in Oswald's mind. He will not wish Deira to split from him again. His son, Oswine lives yet."

Myrddyn shook his head, "I am surprised that Oswald has let him live."

Gawan said, "I have heard that Oswine is a quiet and thoughtful man."

"Perhaps he hides away from Oswald's men. Oswald is known to be treacherous."

Pol had joined us and he added, "King Penda is worried about Eowa. He will not engage in battle with Oswald if Eowa is not with him."

"Then we must find out exactly where they are. Fetch Geraint and Tadgh."

Myrddyn smiled, "I know what you plan, Warlord. There was a time when you would have used me."

"As I recall my father sent you into the camp of Aella where you were his healer for a while."

"I was. Your scouts will have to be careful. They do not have my skills."

"They have others, wizard. They are good at becoming invisible; without the aid of magic."

When the two arrived I said, "I wish you to travel into the kingdom of Northumbria. We need to know where King Oswald and his hearthweru are. We also need to know the whereabouts of Eowa, the Mercian. We think they are at Din Guardi."

My two chief scouts were rarely surprised by my orders. "We will do as you command Warlord. Do you wish us to find out where he has his army?"

"If you can then that will be welcome information but it is more important that you return with the whereabouts of Oswald and Eowa."

Myrddyn said, "Beware Geraint and Tadgh. This Saxon has two powerful witches."

"Like the one who caused the death of Aedh and Lord Lann?"

"Just so."

"Then we will be careful. I can fight any warrior who wields a weapon but a witch is a different matter."

After they left us I asked, "How will you defeat them?"

"They are powerful and they are clever but they rely too much on the power of poison. They have also failed to realise that Gawan has powers too. Thanks to your use of him as an equite they have dismissed him from their minds. They search for my mind only. So far, I have been submissive. When the time is right then Gawan and I will combine the powers of our minds and the spirit world. We will fill them with fog as they did to me."

"Can they be killed with mortal weapons?"

Gawan nodded, "They can, brother, but they will be enchantresses. Remember their sister Morgause. She took in all of us and used her charms to seduce us. They are like Medusa. If they have you in their stare and glare, then you are a dead man walking."

"I think I am old enough now to ignore their charms. Let me get within a sword length of them and they shall die. I am no wizard, brother, but we now know the power of the sword I wield. That may be the magic to end their lives."

Gawan looked doubtful but, for the first time in a long time, Myrddyn smiled, "Of course. I am getting old! In your dream, a queen came to you. This sword was wielded by a warrior queen. Give me the blade, warlord."

I handed him the sword. It seemed to dwarf the old man. He laid it on his lap and, closing his eyes, ran his hands over it. He touched the blue and green stones on the pommel and smiled again. Opening his eyes, he said, "I should have done this years ago. I forgot the power of the sword."

"What do you mean?"

"When Morcar stole the sword and poisoned the blade it gave him no help. It did not harm you. In fact, it returned to you so that you could kill him. The sword has a spirit. It is the spirit of a murdered queen. She lives within the blade and she seeks revenge."

I was confused. "Myrddyn, that was hundreds of years ago. Revenge? On whom?"

"On the two witches. They are the last spawn of the one who poisoned her. The stone which was dropped into the water is still sending ripples out. They are just harder to see. This is the sword which will slay the witches. When it does then the spirit of the queen can rest."

"How did you discover this?"

"I knew some from the time I spent in the cave at Wyddfa. While I waited for you at the Lough Rigg I was visited by spirits. The pool in the cave was also magic and the spirit of a woman came to me from its black waters and told me to test the sword. You said it yourself, the sword was magic. When I held it, my mind knew the right questions. There can be no doubt. Saxon Slayer is the only way to destroy the witches and with them King Oswald."

Chapter 20

The worst of the winter was behind us and soon the land became warmer. We had new birth throughout the land. More foals, calves and lambs were born. We added to the numbers of men who could fight and we waited for King Penda to come.

Geraint and Tadgh had been gone for a month when a Mercian messenger arrived. It was a thegn escorted by two warriors. I knew him. He had been there when I had slain Edwin. Penda was careful. He sent someone he knew I would trust.

"Edward of Namentwihc, it is good to see you."

"And I, you, lord. My king sends you word that he brings thirty warbands north. He heads for Eoforwic."

"Come, Edward, let us speak with Myrddyn and Gawan."

"Myrddyn lives?"

"He does and we have much to tell you."

When we were in my hall I said, "Advise your king not to try to take Eoforwic. He will lose too many men. It will be better if we block the road north. Eoforwic is a holy place to the Christians and they will not wish to lose it. If we can draw King Oswald down to meet you then I can use my horsemen to catch him in the vale."

"You wish to use King Penda as bait?"

"No, I wish to use Eoforwic as bait. It is in no one's interests if King Penda loses his best warriors taking stone walls."

Edward nodded, "He will be unhappy to lose the treasures of that city."

"If we defeat King Oswald close to the Dunum then the city will surrender. He should know that Oswald has a tenuous grip on his kingdom. He has combined two thrones but there are those who still support the family of Osric."

"It is Eowa he fears. His brother has eorledmen and thegns who follow him."

"I have my men seeking him. I know what King Penda wants." I put my arm around his shoulder and led him to my walls. I wished to learn of our other erstwhile allies. "What of the men of Gwynedd?"

"Their king is not called battle shirker for naught. He waits and he watches. I do not trust him. King Cadwallon was a king whose word meant something. I am sad that he fell in battle. It was a grievous loss."

"It was *wyrd*."

We headed back to his horse. "I needs must return to King Penda quickly. He worries about advancing so far from home."

"Know you that I will ensure that he has no enemies to the west. I will make my camp at the old fortress of Stanwyck. I can watch the crossing of the Dunum from there. I will wait for King Penda's decision. If he has another plan for me to consider then I will do so."

Once the thegn had left I set about ordering my equites to join me. I used Caradog, a reliable scout, to take a message to Mungo and Angus. It was courtesy to let them know what I intended. I also wished them to watch my flank. Then I addressed the problem of Myrddyn. We needed the wizard with us. He and Gawan would be needed to counter the magic of the witches but he was old and he appeared frail. He and Gawan were in their tower.

"King Penda has asked for us to aid him."

"And you wonder if this old man can travel across the country; is that not so Hogan Lann?"

I laughed, "I should have known."

"Yes, you should." He wagged a finger at me. "I will tell you if I cannot travel! Find me a horse and a soft saddle, that is all I ask."

"When do we leave, brother?"

"As soon as my equites arrive. I plan to use Stanwyck as a camp. It is well protected and close to both the Roman Road and the bridge over the Dunum."

Myrddyn nodded, "A good choice. You do well to go where the spirits are strong. The queen who used the sword had her palace there."

I looked at the old man, "A palace? All that I saw were ditches and ramparts."

"The Romans destroyed all trace of it for it was made of wood. The old people did not use stone. That is why so few traces remain on the land. But the spirits of the dead are there.

Gawan and I will be comfortable and the spirits will watch over us."

Daffydd had not yet left for Bors' castle. "Your work at Alavna will have to wait. I leave you in command of the castle. Let Bors know where we will be. I know not how long we will be away. That all depends upon King Penda and King Oswald. You can make any decisions you deem necessary."

"I will do so, Warlord. Be careful. Saxons are treacherous."

"You mean Northumbrians?"

"I mean all Saxons!"

It took two days for my men to gather and for us to have the baggage loaded. We had our pots and pig fat to transport as well as the new fire arrows. We had more servants and guards for our horses than we normally took. I would take no chances. It took us longer to cross the high divide. We arrived at Stanwyck after a long day's journey over the windswept top of Rheged. The green shoots in the valleys said that Spring was well on its way but the mountain tops still felt like winter.

As we set up camp I confided in Gawan, "I am worried about Geraint and Tadgh. They are both good scouts but there are witches. I thought they would have returned before now."

"They knew what to expect. I am not worried yet, brother. They will return. Better that they come with information than return early with nothing."

"You may be right. Will you ride with me tomorrow when I ride toward Eoforwic? I wish to visit King Penda. I prefer speaking face to face than through intermediaries."

"I will." He pointed to Myrddyn who was examining the defences of the old fort. "I think that Myrddyn will be busy speaking with the spirits of the dead."

"Do you not wish to speak to them too?"

He lowered his voice although Myrddyn was too far away to hear, "Myrddyn is busy preparing to join the spirits. I hope to have a longer life before I need to speak so frequently with the dead."

I took a good escort for this was Deira. We struck the Roman Road and saw Saxon refugees fleeing north. When they saw us on the skyline they ran even faster for the Dunum. We let them go. We did not need to wage war on families. They would be more mouths for King Oswald to feed. They would spread the terror of our presence far better than any trumpet of war. "Llewellyn, unfurl the standard. Let the dragon roar."

Kay burst out laughing as he watched the refugees leave the road and seek cover, "If we chose to chase them they would die of fear. We would not need to use a weapon."

We discovered the reason for the flight of the refugees when we reached Easingwold. Mercian warriors were burning the huts and slaughtering the animals for meat. Their weapons were pointed at us until I was recognised.

"Warlord, Thegn Edward said you would be here. He and the King have made their camp on the road from Eoforwic."

King Penda, son of Pybba, had brought many warriors but, apart from his thegns and Eorledman, the only ones who wore mail were the hearthweru. The other weakness of the Mercian army was its lack of horsemen. It moved at the speed of men in mail. King Penda was pleased to see me. He took off his helmet and came over to give me a bear hug after I had dismounted.

"Warlord! I am pleased to see you! I had thought us alone in this war!"

"I told you when Pol visited you that I wished an alliance."

He shook his head, "I am sorry. My experience with other leaders makes me suspicious of such offers."

"I never break my word."

"I know. Come sit." His men had hewn logs to make crude benches and we sat upon them. "Thegn Edward tells me you do not wish me to attack the walls of Eoforwic? Why? Do you wish the treasure for yourself?"

"You should know me better than that. I look beyond this war. Oswine of Deira lives still and he is less likely to be an aggressive neighbour. If we defeat King Oswald, then we break Northumbria and perhaps Deira will be less of a threat."

"I see you have put thought into this."

"Our aim is to defeat Oswald and Eowa is it not?"

"It is. My brother has converted to Christianity just to make an ally of Oswald. Some who left my brother tell me that Oswald sees himself as High King of this land."

"That was always King Cadwallon's dream."

"And it cost him his life. I just want a strong Mercia which is not raided. My land is rich. We have iron as well as fine land for farming." He waved a hand to the hills which were to the east and west of where we stood. "Apart from this vale, this is a wasteland." I did not agree but it suited me that he did not desire this land. "So, now what? We wait here for Oswald?"

"We have seen refugees fleeing north. It is two days to Din Guardi. That gives us two or three days to prepare a welcome for him. North of here, closer to the Dunum, there is a ridge which can be defended by your men. It controls the road to Eoforwic. He cannot pass the ridge without giving battle. You hold him and my horsemen will do the rest. Once we defeat him and he flees north we pursue him."

"Perhaps we can defeat him here and have done with him. One battle to end it all."

"That would be the best outcome but he is cunning and he has two witches with him."

"A Christian who associates with witches?"

"I think Oswald likes the support the church gives him. He will use anything he can to gain power. I think he sees religion as a weapon. As a Christian, he has the support of the church. He has two faces. His father was a pagan. It suits his ambitions."

"How far would we have to march?"

"It is but fifteen Roman miles. It is not far from Aelfere. I expect the people will flee when you arrive. I will keep my equites by the Dunum and let you know when they are heading in your direction."

"You return now?"

"We have preparations to make."

He clasped my arm, " A new alliance then!"

"A new alliance."

As we rode north I asked Gawan, "What did his thoughts tell you?"

"That it is Eowa who is his enemy. If he kills Eowa then he will return to Mercia."

I nodded, "Then we know where we stand. We must hope that Oswald is defeated."

I sent Caradog to the Dunum. Until Geraint and Tadgh returned we were limited in our scouts. I had archers who could scout but my scouts knew exactly what sort of information I needed.

I gathered my equites as we sat around our campfire. "We move north tomorrow. Oswald will have to cross the Dunum at the Roman fort. There are places we can watch where we will not be seen. We will then follow the Northumbrians and make sure that they meet with King Penda. Pelas, I want you to use the squires to attack their baggage. The archers will be with the equites. I intend to attack their flank. The archers can ensure that we are not outflanked ourselves. We will need fire in case they use a shield wall."

Owain ap Daffydd said, "And would you wish us to have the horses with the pig fat and the pots."

"Yes."

"We will need to make a fire to heat the fat. That will take the archers away from their job."

"Once the fat is heated it needs but one man to watch it and fill the pots."

I could tell that he was not convinced that it would work. Gawan said, "Myrddyn and I will watch the fire."

"You will be with us?" Owain was in awe of the wizard.

"I fought Saxons alongside your grandfather, Owain ap Daffydd, do not worry about me."

I had just turned in when I heard shouts from the sentries. I grabbed my sword and raced out. It was Geraint and Tadgh. Their horses showed that they had ridden hard.

"Sorry that it took so long Warlord. We rode first to Civitas."

"It matters not how long it took. Have you the knowledge which we need?"

Geraint nodded. "They are at Din Guardi. The Mercian, Eowa is with King Oswald. We saw the two men hunting. They did not see us." That did not surprise me. "Eowa has brought with him over a hundred men. King Oswald had not called out the fyrd. There were just the warriors of his hearthweru with him."

"Good. And the witches?" Gawan and Myrddyn had come from their shelters and were listening carefully.

"We saw them once. They were on the beach and were collecting seaweed."

I looked at Gawan. He nodded and said, "It is used in certain spells and potions."

"You have done well. Now rest. I have sent Caradog north of the Dunum to watch for Oswald."

"King Oswald had not stirred when we left but that was two days since."

"He will know, by now, that King Penda is here."

I joined my wizards. "Will he bring the witches with him?"

"Only if he brings his army. If he comes with just Eowa and his hearthweru then he will not."

"Why should he do that Myrddyn?"

"He may be cautious and suspect a trap. Gawan and I will try a spell of concealment. The witches will seek your thoughts. We will put a fog twixt us."

The Northumbrians came three days later. I kept a nervous King Penda informed as my scouts watched the road well to the north of the Dunum. When they told us, the witches were with them then we knew that they had brought their whole army. King Oswald had not raised the fyrd but he had brought every warrior from Bernicia and some Irish mercenaries. Along with the Mercians under Eowa he had a powerful army. I led my equites and we waited in the wood which rose above the Dunum and was close to the Roman bridge and fort. Gawan and Myrddyn were with me for their powers were needed.

We were concealed by the new growth on the trees but we kept our horses well away from the edge. We did not want them to give us away. Oswald had his own scouts out but they were on the road and they were not mounted. His hearthweru marched next followed by the King and Eowa. The two witches were with them too. Guards surrounded them but I saw that they had donned the garb of nuns. That showed that Oswald was deceiving his ally too. I turned as I heard Myrddyn and Gawan chanting quietly. When I looked back I saw that the horses ridden by the witches were skittish. As it was when they were crossing the bridge no one would think anything untoward but the two women had to concentrate on controlling their mounts. Their thoughts were not on me!

The host passed us and I estimated that there were almost three hundred in the column. Not all were what I would call battle-hardened warriors but he had numbers. We let them pass and I walked back to Gawan and Myrddyn. "Thank you for the spell."

"It was easier to make the horses become distracted than keep up a fogging of the mind. We now need to work out how to rid ourselves of these witches." Myrddyn's voice sounded harsh. This was not like him.

We allowed them to travel down the road before we left to parallel their course in the woods to the west. The folds in the hills meant that they would struggle to see us. Our camp was not far away either but they kept heading down the Roman Road. They would have to camp somewhere in the next few hours. The afternoon was getting on. There was an old Roman fort at Cataractonium. No one lived there but the walls would give shelter. The hall at Gilling might have been used but the Eorledman who lived there was an ally of Oswine. I did not think that Oswald would wish to risk a visit to a hall where there might be assassins. From Cataractonium they would head towards King Penda and his men. It was a mere twelve miles.

"Geraint, ride to the King and tell him that his enemy will be there by morning. Tadgh and Caradog keep a watch on Oswald. Let me know when he camps."

We returned to our own camp. Agramaine groomed Copper and made sure that his hooves were clean. He fed him grain and gave him much water before tethering him in the bottom of one of the central ditches where the grass was thick and lush. He then sharpened my daggers before asking, "Warlord. Do you wish me to sharpen Saxon Slayer?"

"Of course. And then you had better oil and polish my mail and my helmet."

He happily took them away. The other squires were doing the same for their equites but they all envied Agramaine for he got to touch the mystical sword. Gawan and Myrddyn were resting for they would need all their strength, both physical and mental the next day. Owain took the cauldron, pig fat and pots. He and his archers rode, as darkness fell, to the place where they would wait. On the rise above the road was a wood and, just to the west, a hollow. They would light the fire there and heat the cauldron. By the time morning came, the fat would be bubbling.

The archers would have to manage the heat until the battle began. Then it would be the responsibility of Myrddyn and Gawan.

The equites kept their own counsel. We were not barbarians who needed to build themselves up to fight. We were equites. One or two of the new equites took out their maces and practised with them. Those like Lann Aelle, Kay and Pol needed no such practice. When Agramaine returned with Saxon Slayer he helped me out of my mail so that he could oil and polish it. The shinier and more oiled it was the less chance I had of suffering a wound for weapons would slide off it. As he did so I sat with Saxon Slayer on my knee. If Myrddyn was right, and I had never known him to be wrong, then this sword had lived in this hill fort. The queen had held the sword in her hand. I almost sniffed the handle to see if any of her presence remained upon it. Foolish. However, when I put my hand on the hilt I felt a surge of power.

I opened my palm and looked at it. The hilt, as it had with my father, fitted it perfectly. Either the queen had had large hands or she had used the weapon two handed. It made no difference but I felt as though the sword was speaking with me. It was the only sword I had seen which had a channel in the blade to allow the blood to run away. It also made it slightly lighter than swords of a similar length. Whoever had made this, hundreds of years ago had known their craft.

I had thought that Myrddyn and Gawan were resting but when I sheathed my sword and stood I saw that they were lying on their backs and looking up into the sky. I was intrigued and walked over. Their eyes looked up but they had a glazed look. They were no longer in our world. They were with the spirits. I sat nearby and waited. Gawan was the first to raise his head and look at me. He saw Myrddyn was still in a trance and he sat next to me. He gave me a wan smile. Finally, Myrddyn sat up.

"Warlord we have dreamed your queen. This was her land and she was a powerful woman who was murdered by a witch." He paused, "It was poison."

I looked at Gawan, "Poison?"

"Not only that brother but I fear it was a similar poison to the one Morgause used."

Myrddyn stood. He looked animated for the first time since his return, "And thus we have an advantage. We will make the antidote to that poison. It is likely that they may well try to poison again. We are forewarned. I shall gather the ingredients now."

"Are you not tired, Myrddyn? Do you not wish to sleep?"

"My time for sleeping on this earth is coming to an end."

I looked at Gawan who nodded, "He dreamed his death while you were fighting the pirates. He is content. His work here is done."

Change was never a good thing, in my opinion. Changes brought death and loss. I could not lose Myrddyn. He had been ever-present since I had been a child.

Chapter 21

We left for the ridge before dawn. We could see the fires of the Saxons away to the east. When we reached the ridge, the cauldron was bubbling away but it was not yet boiling.

Owain pointed to the pot, "We delayed putting the oil in. By the time it is dawn, then it should be ready. We laid out the pots ready to be filled yonder and my archers all have two fire arrows each."

"Good. Pelas, take the squires. You know what you have to do."

"Yes, Warlord."

We dismounted, to save our horses, and we waited. The sun came up in the east and when it had cleared the hills opposite our position we saw the Saxon scouts as they hurried down the road. Soon they would see the shield wall of King Penda. The hearthweru of King Oswald came next closely followed by that of Eowa son of Pybba. I saw the great mass of warriors following the two witches dressed as nuns. Perhaps King Oswald's warriors thought that they would bring God's help.

A young Saxon boy came from the direction of King Penda's camp. Myrddyn and Gawan looked up at him. He was little more than a boy. He did not even have a seax. "Where are you from, boy?"

Kay's gruff voice normally frightened the young but the boy just smiled. "I have come from King Penda."

Myrddyn chuckled, "Well I would not go that way." He pointed to the north. "King Oswald lies yonder."

The Saxon's eyes widened in wonder, "Are you Myrddyn, the great wizard?"

Myrddyn nodded, "I am."

To Myrddyn's great amusement he dropped to his knees and kissed the hem of the wizard's tunic. "This is a great honour." He stood. "I was going to return to King Penda but may I serve you during the battle. It will be a tale to tell to my children."

Kay laughed, "Have you the parts to make a child yet?"

Myrddyn said irritably, "Kay!" Turning to the boy Myrddyn said, "Aye, you can for it will be safer here. We will be tending the pig fat. You can bring me water to drink."

The boy ran to the skin and clutched it as though it was a crown of gold. It was a good omen.

We went back to our horses and mounted leaving our scouts hidden and watching for the Saxons. We could hear, from the dell, when the scouts returned and reported the presence of King Penda. Even without the reports of our scouts, I knew what would be happening. The hearthweru would form a shield wall. That would not be to attack necessarily but to provide protection for Eowa and Oswald. Then he would assess if it was worth advancing or waiting for King Penda. Battles between shield walls were like two stags rutting. There was a great deal of posturing before the battle would be engaged.

Tadgh came over to us. "They are making a shield wall of the warbands who have shields and spears. It looks like Eorledman Ida is leading them." Ida was an old grizzled warrior. He had managed to survive King Edwin's disaster. He would be keen to prove himself against King Penda. "The hearthweru are ready to follow up, lord."

"Good. Prepare!" We had to time our charge to strike at the perfect moment. If we appeared too soon then King Oswald and Eowa might withdraw and we would not have them. We needed the hearthweru to be committed before we unleashed the thirty equites who would, hopefully, tear into their right flank. Their right flank would have no shields. Their right hands held their weapons.

We moved forward to line up just below the ridgeline. I risked nudging Copper forward so that I could watch the battle. King Penda had a triple wall of shields. It meant that they were overlapped by the Northumbrian line but it would be hard to break. Shield wall against shield wall was a slogging match. The two lines ebbed and flowed and then I heard a horn. The Northumbrians began to withdraw. I saw the field littered with their dead but Ida still remained alive. They walked back and then parted to allow the hearthweru to advance. Although smaller in number the hearthweru would be heavier and better armed. King Oswald had used his inferior warriors to weaken

King Penda. Now his hearthweru would advance and they were a more potent force.

They were committed. King Oswald's best troops were moving away from the King, Eowa and the witches. As they moved up the slope towards the Mercians I said, "Forward." We lined up on the ridge. "Llewellyn, sound the horn!" When the horn sounded Pelas would attack the baggage. As soon as the notes rang out Ida and his battered men looked around.

"Forward for Rheged!"

I had chosen this place because the slope was gentle and the turf was without obstacles. Eorledman Ida tried to turn his battered warriors to face us but for some, we were too great a threat and weaker warriors ran. We carried three javelins each. I hurled my first one when we were twenty paces from the wavering line of Northumbrians. It struck a warrior in the foot. I already had my second ready and I threw it at a warrior who was close to Eorledman Ida. This time it hit the warrior in the thigh and he dropped to one knee. I used the last one as a thrusting spear and stabbed down at Eorledman Ida. He brought his shield up to counter the blow and my javelin stuck in. I kicked Copper in the flanks and he kept going. Since he had drunk from the enchanted pool he seemed to anticipate my every command. The javelin became embedded in the shield and Ida had to move his feet quickly to keep his balance.

We had broken through their flimsy line but they outnumbered us. I drew Saxon Slayer and felt its power in my hand. I wheeled Copper so that I faced Ida's sword. I brought Saxon Slayer down hard. He tried to pull his shield around but the javelin embedded in it made that almost impossible. My sword struck his and rang out. I lifted it up and, this time angled it from the right to strike at his throat. Once again, he tried to block with his shield. He failed and my sword ripped into his cloak, chopping his brooch in two. His cloak fell awkwardly. It would now be an encumbrance

"You are a trickster! Come down from that horse and fight me like a man!"

I suddenly wheeled Copper across his front and punched with my shield. He was already off-balance and his feet caught in his cloak. He tumbled backwards. His shield fell from his hand. He leapt to his feet and, tearing his ripped cloak from his shoulder, ran at me. I think he intended to strike Copper but he was an agile mount and he danced out of the way of the clumsy blow. With no shield to protect him, I was able to hack at his left arm. Saxon Slayer bit into the upper arm, driving mail rings into his flesh. He was tough and he raised his right hand to bring down his sword. Instead of pulling Saxon Slayer back, I flicked it to the right and the tip ripped across his throat. It was not a deep wound. It did not need to be. It tore the artery and blood flooded out. He held his hand there for a heartbeat and then crumpled to the ground.

His death saw the warriors begin to fall back. My equites ruthlessly chased them down until we heard a Saxon horn. I watched as the hearthweru, who looked to have been on the brink of victory began to move backwards. I saw King Oswald and Eowa as they rallied the warriors who were fleeing our blades. I turned to Llewellyn, "Lead us back up the slope."

I saw that some of the horses had suffered wounds. We had no spares with us. Our squires were busy in the rear of the Northumbrian host. The hearthweru moved steadily backwards. I watched from the top of the ridge as King Penda rallied his own men.

King Oswald and Eowa began to form a new wedge made up of those hearthweru who were without wounds and the best warriors who remained from Ida's band. I rode to the cauldron. "It is time for the pig fat."

While Myrddyn and Gawan began to fill the pots, I shouted, "Owain ap Daffydd. Encourage them to make a shield wall!" I noticed the young Saxon boy still clutched Myrddyn's water skin. He seemed unafraid of the advancing Saxons.

"Aye lord."

The archers rose from where they had been lying and, in one practised motion knocked and then released their arrows down the slope. I rode with Llewellyn and my standard, to stand amongst them. It was a well-made shield wall which advanced up the slope. They had two rows of shields forty men wide. Spears protruded from them. To charge would have invited disaster.

"Owain, ready your fire arrows."

He turned, "Dai fetch a brand from the fire."

The shield wall was moving slowly but relentlessly towards us. They were not afraid. We could do nothing. We were too few to outflank them and their shields and spears were too great a barrier. They would destroy us and then return to finish off King Penda.

My equites appeared behind me. The Northumbrians must have wondered why they did not hold a sword in their hands. I shouted, "Charge"

The Saxons stopped and braced for our strike. We wheeled at the last moment and the rest of my equites threw their pots of boiling pig fat. Only Llewellyn and I held our weapons. Then twenty flaming arrows cracked into the shields. Not all ignited but the ones which did had a terrifying effect. A wall of flames leapt up. My equites raced back and I rode along their line taunting them.

"This is wizard's fire! Your God cannot help you now!" Myrddyn had added a powder which made the flames bluer and greener than normal. It looked like a magic fire.

My archers were aiming at the gaps which appeared as burning men fell. I heard a thegn shout, "Reform! Reform!"

They tried and then Pol led my equites with a second shower of boiling fat. This time the flames which burned ignited the liquid and we needed no more fire arrows. Then my men drew their swords and we charged, not those who were on fire but the ones who had reeled and recoiled from the flames. They were without protection. There was no shield wall.

Our appearance through the smoke and the flames came as a real shock to them. Saxon Slayer took a man's arm off just below the shoulder. Copper's hooves caught another and he was trampled to death. A Saxon made the mistake of turning from me and I brought my sword across his back. It did not penetrate his leather byrnie but it knocked him to the ground.

They broke. Their best warriors lay writhing as they burned. The shield wall was destroyed and my archers had too many targets before them. When King Penda led his warriors forward it proved too much for an army attacked by wizard's fire. The army of Oswald and Eowa evaporated. They disappeared like early morning mist. The two Saxon leaders, along with the witches, led the way. I could not allow the witches to escape. "Equites! Follow me. Let us avenge my father!"

Lann Aelle and Pol were the first to reach me. Iago, Llenlleog and Kay followed quickly. We headed for the four horses which were already racing up the road to Aelfere. Brave knots of men foolishly tried to stand in our way. Had they moved aside they would have lived but they did not and they died. I felt a heavy blow and looked down. A Saxon had hacked at my leg with an axe. If I had not been wearing greaves I would have lost the limb. As it was the head had become entangled with the splints of the greave. He tried to pull it away. Saxon Slayer took his head in one blow. I looked up the road. The men we had slain had bought the fugitives enough time so that we would not catch them. They had not been fighting and our horses all carried a heavy mailed warrior. Pelas and the squires might have been able to but they were busy slaying the fleeing warriors. They could not have seen the King, his ally and his witches. They had escaped. We had won but it was not the victory I had hoped.

I reined in, "There is little point in killing our horses. We know where he will go. He will head to Din Guardi."

Pol nodded, "The pig fat worked."

"It did but next time they will know what to expect."

"It was a great victory, Warlord."

"If King Oswald and the witches had died then I would agree but we still have work to do."

My three scouts galloped up as I checked Copper to ensure that he had not suffered any wounds. "You wish us to follow them, Warlord?"

"Yes, Geraint. I think they head for Din Guardi. I will see King Penda and we will follow with the army."

There were occasional cries from the field as the wounded were despatched but, as the rest of the warriors were chasing the Saxons, it felt eerily peaceful. Pol had just finished examining his horse and he came over. "The fire pots worked as we thought, warlord, you should be pleased with the victory and yet you look sad."

"We missed the chance to end it today."

"There was nothing we could have done."

I pointed to Pelas and the squires who were still in the Saxon baggage. "Pelas obeyed my orders. I should have said that I wished him to stop the witches and Oswald from leaving."

"When we look in the past it is always easier to see what we should have done. It was the right decision to attack their baggage. This army is finished. They cannot campaign again this year. You have made Rheged safe."

"I know but what of next year. Oswald will raise a bigger army and Eowa is still a threat to Penda. We cannot afford a long siege. The pirate raid showed us that."

"Come, let us find your brother. Perhaps he has words of comfort."

When we reached the ridgeline, I saw Gawan kneeling over Myrddyn. I leapt from my horse. "What is it?"

"At the moment of victory, he slumped to the ground. He breathes and I can find no wound but he is not in this world."

"Why did you not send the Saxon boy for us?"

Gawan looked around, "He has gone! I did not see him go. I have a bad feeling about this."

"Pol, find a cart amongst the Saxon baggage. Bring it here."

He galloped off and Gawan stood. "I fear this is the work of the witches. He fell at the moment of victory. I saw the witches turn." He shook his head. "I was too busy watching the battle. Myrddyn alone was wrestling with the witches. They have done something to him. He is enchanted."

"Gawan, use your mind. How do I get close to the witches and kill them?" I pointed to Myrddyn. "This way we are just waiting for them to hurt us. If they try it enough times, then they will succeed."

He strode to the ridgeline. He looked to the west and then to the north. When he turned to face me, he looked animated. "Water, we must use water."

"Water?"

"The sword has an affinity for water. We showed that at Civitas Carvetiorum. We must use water to negate the power of the witches. They go to Din Guardi and there the castle is surrounded by water. There the sword will have superiority over the power of the witches."

"And there they will be protected by King Oswald and his army."

"Father and Myrddyn did it once."

"But they never told us how."

"Then I must heal Myrddyn and we can ask him."

A cart, pulled by two horses, raced up to the ridge. Pol had Pelas and eight squires with him. Pelas dropped to his knees, "I am sorry, Warlord, I have failed you. I should have stopped the King and the witches from leaving."

"No Pelas. Had you tried you would have died. I see now that I must either kill the witches or be killed by them. I want three squires to watch and guard Myrddyn and my brother. We go to Din Guardi and they must keep them safe."

We met King Penda four miles north of Aelfere. He looked excited, "A great victory!"

"It is not finished yet, King Penda. They will go to Din Guardi. We must rid ourselves of as many of his warriors as we can on the journey between here and there."

He frowned, "Why? It is just a castle. We can take it."

"Wait until you see it and then tell me if we can take it."

We camped at the fort on the Dunum. I guessed that the four on horses would kill their mounts to reach Din Guardi. Perhaps they would have other horses waiting for them. I did not expect to catch them. They would not rest and they would not camp. Nor could we divide our forces. We were going into the heart of Northumbria. The Saxons there would not just let us walk through their land.

When we reached the Dunum Gawan walked down to the river. The rest of the army was busy cooking and examining the treasures they had taken from the dead. I followed him down to the river. The water only came up to his waist and Gawan waded across to the island. Intrigued, I followed him. He knelt, once on the island and began to scrabble in the sand. His hand suddenly emerged, triumphantly and he held a small metal figure. It was about as long as his finger.

"What is it?"

"This is from the time before the Romans. It is a shrine to Icaunus, the river god. The Romans must have used it too for this is Roman." He stood and, cupping his hands, shouted. "Pelas, have your squires bring Myrddyn here."

"Here brother?"

"This is a holy place. We need either a cave in a mountain or such a shrine. The water will protect Myrddyn from the power of the witches and Icaunus will heal him." He suddenly looked doubtful. "At least I believe it will."

I looked into the woods. "This is where father found the sword. The fort was where he found other weapons. This is *wyrd*. I know what to do." Six squires carried Myrddyn. He was not heavy and I daresay that Pelas could have done so alone. Pelas and Pol had burning torches with them for it was getting darker.

"Lay him in the sand so that his head faces west and his feet east." They did so and stood in silence, wondering, no doubt, what we would do next. Gawan knelt and folded the wizard's hands across his middle. He went to the river and, cupping his hands, gathered some water. He sprinkled it on Myrddyn's face and then stood. "I have done all that I can. What was your idea, brother?"

I drew Saxon Slayer and placed the hilt in Myrddyn's hands. I stood and said, "Great queen of this land, use your power and your sword to heal Myrddyn."

I stepped back and the ten of us made a circle around the body. Penda and his Mercians must have thought that we were burying the wizard. Nothing happened at first and then a breeze came from the west. It was a warm breeze. I could smell pine. The wind grew stronger. The torches flickered and Pelas and Pol had to use their bodies to shelter them from the wind. Suddenly from the shore, close to the fort came a howl. I looked over fearfully. What had we conjured? And then I knew what it was; Llewellyn had planted my standard and the wind had blown through it. The wind grew stronger and the howling with it. I had never heard it as loud and then just as quickly as it had begun the wind died away and there was silence. I could hear the murmur of voices from the fort but none of us turned. We stared at Myrddyn.

There was a plop in the water to my right as a fish broached. I could not help glancing away. I saw the ripples in the torchlight.

One of the ripples touched the island and I heard a gasp. I turned and saw that Myrddyn's eyes were open. He looked as though he had awoken from a deep sleep.

He smiled, "The sons of Lord Lann have saved the life of Myrddyn. I know what we must do. I have spoken with Icaunus and the queen." He began to rise, still clutching the sword. He pointed it towards the spot the fish had broached. "Your work is almost finished my queen and soon you can rest. Your death will finally be avenged."

He handed me the sword, "You are healed?"

"I am healed long enough to do what I must do." He looked at Pelas and the squires. "Well, what are you standing around for. You carried me here. You do not expect an old man to get wet, do you?"

I laughed, "Myrddyn is back. Carry him back to the fort."

Chapter 22

When we reached the fort the King and all of his thegns were looking at us as though we were ghosts. "What happened Warlord?"

Myrddyn smiled, "The sword and the god Icaunus have healed me. Now give me air and fetch me some ale I am thirsty."

When they had all gone Gawan said, "The boy?"

Myrddyn nodded, "I have been duped again. The witches are clever. They sent an innocent young boy knowing that I would be less suspicious."

I shook my head, "From now on, old man, we slay those who come close to you. We trust no one."

"When I was in the Otherworld I was told that my time is nigh. Like your father, my death will serve a purpose. You, Gawan, will benefit the most from my death. My spirit will be within you. I will die but be reborn in you. You will become Myrddyn."

"But he will still be Gawan." I did not want to lose my brother.

"Of course, on the outside and inside too but there will be a part of him, deep down, which will be me. Remember that I must be taken to my cave. You will swear."

Gawan and I nodded, "We swear."

"Not you, Warlord, for your work is unfinished. It is Gawan who will take me back. He will know what to do with my body."

Pelas brought him the ale and he drank it. "That was a cunning potion. It was in water and yet I did not taste it. Perhaps that was why it did not kill me or perhaps they wanted me out of the battle."

"We must find a way to destroy them."

"And I have one, Warlord. I am tired now. By the time we reach Din Guardi, you will know."

It took two days to reach Din Guardi. Had I taken my equites we could have reached the castle in one day but King Penda needed us to protect his flanks as his column raided and pillaged every church and monastery on our march north. There were many of them. We caught some of the priests with their books and their relics. We took them to the King. He had had them hammered onto crosses. He could be a cruel man and he hated the followers of the White Christ. I did not hate them, I just did not understand them.

We arrived much richer but King Oswald had had time to rid himself of the mouths he did not wish to feed and to stock up with both food and warriors. There were just warriors within the walls. The women and the old fled north when we arrived. It would have been hard enough to winkle him out before, now it would be almost impossible.

When King Penda saw the fortress rising out of the sea, he saw his dilemma. He and his thegns rode around it looking for weaknesses. Myrddyn took Gawan and me to the headland to the north where we could look almost down on the walls. "It matters not what King Penda will do. You will slay King Oswald, Warlord. I have dreamed that. These walls will not fall to that butcher of holy men. We are here so that you may kill the witches with Saxon Slayer."

Even Gawan looked surprised. "But how? The walls are high and the gate well guarded."

Myrddyn tapped his nose. "You forget the stories you heard as children. Your father gained entry and he killed a king. You, Warlord, will gain entry and kill the witches."

"If I am to gain entry why cannot I kill King Penda and Eowa too?"

"It is not meant to be. If you tried, then you would die and that would not suit the spirits for you have dreamed your death. Your death must serve a purpose as will mine."

"Then tell me what I must do?"

"There is a cave beneath the castle walls. You follow it and it becomes a tunnel and, finally, a door which leads into the bowels of the castle. We need to find a time when there is a low tide and no moon. That will be in twenty days. We have until then to work out where they will be and who you should take with you."

"What if the door has been sealed? Or the tunnel collapsed? What if the cave is no longer there?"

Myrddyn looked at me impassively, "It will be as I have said. This will be my last magic trick. It will be remembered. We will give Penda things to occupy him while we wait for the best time." He stood and looked west. "When this is over Gawan will take me back to Wyddfa and your father's tomb."

"Just Gawan?"

Myrddyn looked at me with sadness in his eyes, "It must be so Warlord. The next time you see the tomb your own death will be imminent. Your time is not yet. You have work to do in Rheged before the end."

We returned to the camp. King Penda was not happy. "How do we scale those walls? We could not build ladders long enough."

Myrddyn rubbed his hands, "And that is why you have a wizard. Have your men go to the forests and cut down some trees for me. We will show you how to make some engines of war. We will make stone and fire throwers. The foundations of the castle are stone but some of the ramparts and the warrior hall are made of wood."

Penda laughed, "Excellent! That will show these priests that our ways are better." He went off eagerly. He had something to do.

Myrddyn said, "It will not work for the lower parts are all made of stone and the heart of the castle is also stone. Still, it will stop him wasting his men on fruitless attacks and keep him occupied."

While the Mercians got on with cutting down trees and jumping to obey Myrddyn's many brusque commands I spent time with Llenlleog, Pol, Pelas and Agramaine. We went to the headland where Myrddyn had told me what I needed to do. It was windswept but it afforded a view all the way down the coast.

"I have brought you here to tell you how we will gain entry to the castle and find and kill the witches."

I had stunned them with my words. "Witches?"

"Do not worry Agramaine, I shall be killing the witches. Your task is to make sure I stay alive long enough to do this. We will be in a castle full of warriors, all of whom will be as angry as wasps in a shaken wasps' nest if they find us."

"Why us?"

"I need equites who can think and who can adapt. It may well be that we have to find another way out. You are the ones who could do that."

"And how do we get in?"

"A good question, Llenlleog. We have to enter a cave and then a tunnel before we open a hidden door in the heart of the castle. What we do not know yet is where the witches will be found."

"Do we not need a wizard for this?"

"No, Pelas for the witches would sense their presence, Myrddyn and Gawan will be here, on this headland, using their minds to confuse them."

They were silent as they took in what I had said. I did not doubt that they would follow me but each one must have thought that none of us would emerge alive. Pol asked, "Warlord, must it be you who slays them?"

I took out Saxon Slayer, "This must kill them. This is witch bane. The sword has magical powers. It brought back Myrddyn from the Otherworld. If I fall then one of you must kill them for if you do not then Gawan, his wife and his son are all in danger." I did not tell them that I would not fall. Not unless the spirits had tired of me. My death would be in the west of the land.

Pol said, "We will not let you down."

The siege was a strange one. Penda made no attempt to attack the walls and the garrison could do nothing about our presence. They taunted and insulted us. Our men challenged them but they stayed within their walls and we without. My archers and scouts brought in plenty of game. We ate well. Once the war machines were under way Myrddyn said, "Warlord let us fetch a boat from the beach. I would have fish. Have your men row us."

It was a strange request but I knew him well enough to comply. I took the men who would be coming within the cave. Gawan stayed close to the castle where he would battle with the witches. We had discovered that they were in the north tower. It overlooked the sea and was the highest one. He stood on the headland. As an added precaution, he held Saxon Slayer. I would not need it in the boat.

We rowed out to sea. To the north of us was the monastery on the island the monks called Holy Island. We saw seals basking on the beach. So far King Penda had resisted levelling it. When we were a mile offshore Myrddyn had us throw the net over the side. I noticed that the tide and the current took us south. We would have to row hard to return to the small bay from whence we had left. We hauled some fish aboard but Myrddyn seemed indifferent to the quality of the catch. He kept staring west, to the shore.

"Have we enough fish yet Myrddyn?"

He looked at Pelas, "Fish? Oh, yes. That will do but throw the net over a few more times. We do not want those on the shore to become suspicious, do we?"

When we had drifted beyond the castle he said, "Now we can row! Head back to the camp but watch the castle. The tide is low and I will show you where the cave's entrance is to be found."

I saw nothing and I wondered if I had been right and the tunnel had been covered. Myrddyn said, "Do you see that large rock with the reddish hue?"

"Yes, Myrddyn."

"Just above it and to the right is the entrance. At high tide, it is below the sea. Even now the water will be lapping in the entrance. You will climb up and then climb down. You will need to leave someone on the beach to keep watch."

I added, "Each of you must remember the rock for when we enter it will be dark."

Agramaine asked, "Will we have torches to light our way?"

Myrddyn laughed, "I should keep you around, Agramaine. You amuse me. Perhaps all wizards should employ a fool to ask such questions! How can you light a torch? It will be seen from the castle. The water will be in the cave and will douse a light. You will be in the dark and you will use your hands."

Agramaine looked abashed. He was obviously frightened of the dark. This would be a greater test of his courage that any combat. When you faced your fears then you knew your limits.

The four stone-throwers were ready two days later. There were still seven days to go before we entered the castle. We needed the moonless night. Myrddyn was keen for us to begin an assault and keep the Northumbrian's eyes on the land and not the sea. King Penda had watched the machines grow with increasing impatience. However, once they were ready he became excited.

He could hardly wait for Myrddyn to show his men how to use them.

"First, your men need to bring rocks from the shore. They should not be too big else we will damage the machine. The size of a man's head would do."

It took another day to gather them by which time we had ringed two sides, the landward side, with willow shields and our few archers. The Mercians, like all Saxons, were poor archers. Myrddyn did not think that the stone-throwers would do much damage but he wanted to make the Northumbrians fearful that they would. He had all four of them placed close together. Penda had assigned men to operate them. Myrddyn told them to choose a slightly smaller rock than King Penda might have wished. I knew it would be to get the range.

"Release!"

The stone flew high, clearing the gatehouse and landing, with a crash, inside the fortress walls. We heard shouts from within. It had done some damage.

Myrddyn went to the next machine. "Use a larger stone." They manhandled the stone into the basket. Myrddyn had them move it slightly to the left and then said, "Release."

It may have been luck or perhaps the wizard really knew what he was doing for the stone rose high and then struck the top of the stone wall. Splinters flew off showering the faces of the warriors standing close by and the stone itself bounced up and took off a warrior's head. It was a spectacular hit. The Mercians roared and banged their shields.

King Penda pounded the shoulder of Edward of Namentwihc. "This will fall within the day!"

Myrddyn had little respect for any king, especially a Saxon one. "That was luck and knocking a few chips of stone from the wall will not gain us entry. At least they will shelter now."

He was right for there were no heads to be seen.

"Let us try all four at once and then we will try one at a time again." Myrddyn did not want to break the machines. The more they were used then the quicker they would break. "Release!"

Myrddyn's warnings were justified for although the four stones all rose at the same time the machines differed. One stone smashed into the gate. One, which had not yet been used, sent its missile into the castle itself. The other two hit the stone walls. A small crack appeared but that was all.

"There, you see. This will take time. They are not going anywhere and they will be getting hungry. A few days of this and they might weaken."

Neither of us believed that but if I could get inside and kill the witches then that might change everything. Over the next few hours' stone after stone was hurled at the walls. It became a monotonous drumbeat. Sometimes it was a sharp crack and crash as it hit stone while at other times it was a dull thump as it hit the wood. Despite Myrddyn's gloomy prognostications, we knew that we were having an effect when we heard hammering as they shored up the gate which had shown signs of cracking.

Towards evening the wear and tear took their toll and two of the machines broke. Myrddyn, who was tiring himself, ordered that we cease the attack while the machines were repaired.

"We have made a good start, King Penda. We will not use them during the day tomorrow, we will let them think they are broken but we will use fire in the nighttime. They will lose sleep and use up precious water." Of course, Myrddyn knew that at high tide they had access to the sea and that the castle had a well. King Penda was happy for the memory of the decapitated Saxon was spoke of as we sat around fires and ate Northumbrian boar and venison.

Iago was impressed by the machines. "Why do we not use them more?"

"Because, thankfully, fortresses such as Din Guardi are rare. As you saw today they break down easily. Myrddyn built them well but the strain of use damages them."

We had thought Myrddyn was asleep but he opened his eyes. "If we used metal parts to support the wood and if he had seasoned wood they would last longer. The ones we have at Civitas Carvetiorum will last much longer. We had more time to build them."

It was almost amusing to see the Northumbrians trying to hide behind their walls and watch us at the same time. They were frightened of the stones striking them. As the day drew to a close we lit huge fires. Myrddyn had had the men collect dried animal dung and straw. Using fresh animal dung, he had them make them into skull sized balls. He made a hole in each one and placed in some kindling. He added a powder.

"What is that Myrddyn?"

"It is something which will make the fire burn and light the rest of the incendiary." He handed Gawan a small box. "I will tell you where you collect the rock which makes this and how to grind it up." He pointed to the strange missiles. "Some of these may not burn but as long as a few do then it will be effective. Tomorrow we return to using rocks. This is too time-consuming."

As soon as it was dark he took a torch and lit the kindling. There was a flash of green and blue and it caught fire. "Release!"

It was spectacular. The flaming missile rose high in the sky. It looked like a shooting star and it left a blue and green trail. It smashed on top of the wall and showered those who were round about. They ran in fear. We managed to send eight such flaming objects at the walls and gate before one of the machines burst into flames because the man loading it was careless. We had to move the others out of the way. The assault ended. It had been effective for the gate had caught fire. The shoring up of the inside meant that they did not realise their danger until the gate was well alight. It took many buckets of sea water to douse the flames.

The next morning, we saw the blackened stain on the door and the charred timbers. It had worked. The three remaining machines lobbed stones for half a day until they required a repair. The gate was battered and one corner of the gatehouse had a large crack while some of the stones had fallen down. That night we heard them as they hammered wood into place to replace the damaged stone.

And then the witches began to use their powers. Gawan and Myrddyn began to feel pains in their heads. Myrddyn knew the cause and he and Gawan withdrew to the headland. It was the end of the siege engines but King Penda had taken heart and he planned a nighttime assault on the gates. I thought it was a mistake but he would not be dissuaded. It suited me for the next night was the dark of moon and the low tide. The next night would see us enter the witches' lair and I would kill them or we would die in the attempt.

We gave as much advice as we could to the men chosen to attack the gates. It was not as daunting a prospect as when we had first arrived. The gate and gatehouse had been weakened. It would be low tide when they attacked and my archers could give some help. Even so, I did not envy them. Our use of pig fat had shown them a weapon of which they may have been unaware.

An Eorledman from the land close to Gwynedd, Humptwauld, led them. They all bore axes and black cloaks. That had been our idea. They needed to be invisible for as long as possible. My equites were not fighting but we were brothers in arms and we went with them to the ramp which led to the gate to give them support. All was silent as they climbed with shields held above their heads. Owain and his best archers watched. It would be hard to see a target; they would be aiming at shadows but they watched and waited anyway.

The gods favoured them for they made the gate unseen. As soon as they began to hack at the charred wood the alarm was sounded and stones and javelins were hurled down at them. When my archers saw a target, it was felled but the defenders held the advantage. I began to wonder if they might succeed when flaming torches were thrown on the shields below them and pig fat dropped. The shields erupted in flames. We had told the Mercians to soak them in water and that saved many lives. Throwing away the flaming shields they ran.

Eorledman Humptwauld was not so lucky. He had been looking up and his whole upper body was encased in flames. He ran towards the sea but he died before he could reach it. He had been a brave man but the attack failed.

Chapter 23

"King Penda, we wish you to use the war machines again tonight."

"But one caught fire."

Myrddyn shook his head, "It doesn't matter. If they break tonight then I will show your men how to make more tomorrow, but your men must use them alone. Gawan and I have to battle the powers of the witches."

King Penda was a shrewd man, "And what else, Warlord?"

"I intend to get into the castle this night and slay the witches. With their power broken we have a chance to defeat King Oswald."

He and his leading thegns stared at me, "How will you do that?"

"Myrddyn has devised a way."

"But if you die then what of the alliance?"

"I will not die. We may fail to kill the witches but I will not die."

"Then we will attack."

"Do not risk your men. We just need their attention on this side of the castle and away from the tower where the witches reside."

"If you survive, Warlord, this will be a tale to tell around the fireside."

Edward of Namentwihc shook his head, "Even if it fails then it is a tale of great glory. I wish that I was going with you."

"It must be my oathsworn. We go to battle witches and I would not risk the life of a warrior who had not sworn an oath to me. We will go now to prepare."

We would not be taking shields or helmets. We would have to do with our mail coif. We each took a Saxon seax as our second weapon. In confined spaces, they were deadly. Myrddyn and Gawan waited with us as we checked that we had everything we needed. Myrddyn handed us each a small stoppered amphora. "Take this. It is an antidote to the poison favoured by the witches. It is the sister's weapon of choice. The blades they use may be tainted. If you are cut by the witches' weapons, then drink it immediately. If it gets to your heart, then you will die."

I saw Agramaine and Pelas staring at the amphora as though it would bite them.

Gawan smiled, "It will save you; not hurt you. "We must go now to the headland. Tonight, we will have a battle of wills. If they keep their minds on us, then they will not see you when you enter."

Myrddyn said, "The stairs from the tunnel come out close to a storage room, as I recall. Do not go in that door but ascend the stairs to the right. The danger comes when you leave the stairs and enter the corridor. It is close to the King's quarters. The tower you seek should be ten paces to your right. Move as quickly as you can. I hope there is no guard on the door of their quarters. If there is then you must move like lightning. You will only have a short time in the castle before the tide will return and will flood the tunnel. Unless you wish a watery grave then do the deed and get out as quickly as you can." He looked like a grandfather as he spoke. There was genuine compassion for us. "May the Allfather be with you."

They left and I sensed that Agramaine and Pelas were becoming worried. That could be dangerous. "You should all know that your task is not to face the witches and their poison but to protect me from warriors. Do that and we will survive. Their best warriors will be on the walls waiting for another attack by the Mercians."

We slipped out of the camp and headed south. We waited, hidden in the sand dunes until the sun dipped over the high ground to the west. Had I brought Geraint or Tadgh then we would have found the stone quicker. As it was it did not take us as much time as it might. In the dark, the reddish hue was hard to see but there was something about the rock formation which I recognised.

I clambered up over the rock and make my way down the tumble of rocks on the other side. It was what Myrddyn had said but I could not see the entrance and then I saw a stream of water and it was flowing from beneath the fortress. As I moved along its line I saw a dark maw ahead of me. I had to move like a spider using both my hands and my feet. When I reached it, I felt air on my face and it was coming from the hole. We had found the tunnel.

The others joined me and I pointed to Agramaine. We had identified him as the sentry. He nodded. I had to force my body into the entrance. There must have been a rock fall since my father and Myrddyn had been here. It explained why it had not been discovered. Once I was through I clambered down until my feet splashed in water. I put my fingers down and put some to my lips. It was sea water. The water surged back and forth and its noise hid any sound we might make. I used my hand to touch the side of the cave and I put a hand above me to warn me of a shelving roof. I headed into the dark. It was a moonless night but there was a slight glow from the entrance. It was either that or Myrddyn had used his magic somehow. I heard my equites' feet as they splashed in the water and we headed deeper into the cave.

My left hand touched the roof. I hissed, "Tunnel!"

I found I had to bow my head. Alarmingly the tunnel began to narrow and now that the entrance to the cave was hidden by the turns in the cave we were blind. It was frightening. I lost all sense of both direction and space. Suppose a hole had appeared in the ground below me? We would plummet to the depths of the earth. I mentally berated myself. There was still water beneath my feet. I was as nervous as Agramaine and Pelas. I shook myself, I was Warlord! I steeled myself and carried on. The tunnel seemed interminable.

Suddenly the hand above my head touched not rock but air. I was able to stand and the relief was beyond measure. Llenlleog bumped into my back. There was hardly any sound beneath my feet and when I reached down I touched damp sand.

"I think we are close," I said quietly. This part of the tunnel appeared wider and Llenlleog went to the left to ascertain its dimensions. While Pol did the same with the right I edged forward with my hands before me. I stumbled on a rock in the sand and I fell forward. It would have been a disaster had I not had my hands before me. My fall was arrested by the wooden door. We had found the hidden way into the stronghold.

"Found it!"

I used my hands to explore the wood. I had hoped that my eyes would have adjusted to the dark but it was so black that we could see nothing. I moved my hands around the edges to find the edges of the door. I was looking for a handle of some kind. The door was slimy. Weed clung to it. I found nothing and so I took out my seax and began to scrape away the weed from the edges in the middle. If there was a handle, then that is where it would be found. As I scraped the side close to my left hand my blade jarred on something metal. I redoubled my efforts and found a latch. I could not move it with my hand. Perhaps it had rusted. I slid the seax into the gap between the door and the frame and moved it up until it touched the metal of the latch. I had to use two hands and I thought it would not budge but it suddenly moved up. I used my seax to prise open the reluctant door. Warmth filled my face as the door slowly opened.

Even more joyous was the light which was before us. It was not a light in the truest sense of the word but my eyes could make out the floor, the walls and the ceiling. After the dark and the gloom of the tunnel, it felt like daylight. Once we had the door open I switched my seax to my right hand and I began to walk down the low corridor. The floor had a covering of both sand and dead, dried seaweed. The sea had come in before now. The stones rose as we walked. The corridor turned as we walked. It was not a long walk and we turned a corner and saw a door to our left. The light was brighter here and as we moved past the door I saw a sconce to my right and stairs leading up.

I moved slowly up the stairs. I could now hear noises above me. We were in the castle. They were distant. There were shouts and cries. I saw the door ahead. I placed my ear to the door. I heard footsteps thunder past and then silence. It was the time for action. I opened the door and stepped into the corridor. After the dimly lit stairs, it was like a bright sun. I stepped out and moved quickly to my right until I found the door Myrddyn had said. I opened it and waved my men through. Pelas and I had just entered and I had shut it when I heard shouts and then more footsteps.

"Fetch more wood from the store. The west tower is in danger of collapse!"

"Those machines of the devil will destroy us."

"Fool, there is but one left!"

And then the Saxon voices went from my earshot. Pol led us up the narrow stair. I felt cool night air and we stepped out onto the battlements. Luckily there were no sentries. They were busy fighting King Penda. I saw the door to the tower. Sheathing my seax I took out Saxon Slayer. I know not why but something made me raise it to my lips and kiss it. I stepped back to look at the top of the tower. It rose about six paces above my head and the top part was wood. We had seen sentries on the top when we had sailed the coast. Now, like the ramparts, it was empty. There would just be the witches within.

I nodded to Pol and he went to the door. He held the handle. He looked at me and then jerked it open. I leapt inside. It was an anti-climax. There was a ladder which led to the top of the tower and another door. Before we could do anything, the door opened and I saw the boy who had come to us before the battle. Pelas was the one who reacted the quickest. He burst through the door and into the room.

The two young women, the witches, were naked. They turned and stared at us. The boy backed off fearfully. His eyes were wide with terror. I saw too that the women looked terrified. They did not look like witches. What if Myrddyn was wrong? I found myself doubting the wizard.

"Why are you here, Warlord? We mean you no harm. King Oswald took us against our will."

The second took a step towards me, "Why have you drawn your sword? Would you do harm to orphans? My sister Morwenna and I mean you no harm."

I tried to turn my gaze from them but their eyes seemed hypnotic. I saw that my equites had lowered their swords. The two women came closer. I saw that they held out their right hands as though in supplication. Their voices were musical and pleasant. Myrddyn was wrong. His time alone had addled his brain. I felt my sword tip lowering.

"We will leave with you and join you and King Penda. King Oswald is Christian. We worship the mother."

Their words were reassuring. I could smell the perfume they wore and it was intoxicating. Their eyes were wide and innocent. We could not kill them. They were two paces from me and I noticed that the youth was also closer.

Suddenly a voice in my head said, *'Brother, they enchant you. Close your eyes and hold the sword!'*

As soon as I did so I saw them, in my mind's eye. They were not beautiful innocent women. I saw beneath their flesh and they were creatures of the dead. Their eyes burned with fire and their smiles were snarls. Their hands were not delicate but were claws. I lunged forward and plunged my sword into the middle of Morgana. Even as I did so she hurled something from her hand at me. My brother's warning had saved me. I ripped out my blade and was about to do the same to Morwenna when she hurled powder at Pol. He fell to the ground screaming. I brought my sword over and hacked across her neck. Her head rolled to the side and she was dead. I opened my eyes for the vision disappeared.

Pol was writhing around on the floor. "Llenlleog, get water and wash out Pol's eyes."

"Aye."

"Pelas, watch the boy."

"He is harmless."

Even as I turned to look at the two sisters a blade appeared in the boy's hand and he slashed it across Pelas' forearm. "You little..." Pelas plunged his sword into the chest of the boy.

"Come, the shouts will have aroused the garrison. Llenlleog help Pol. Pelas watch the rear. I will lead."

This was a disaster. With Pol wounded and Llenlleog having to help him that left just me and Pelas to fight off any of the garrison who had heard the cry. I hurried down the stairs with my seax and Saxon Slayer in my hands. When I reached the bottom two Northumbrian warriors were running towards the door. I had been expecting someone and they had not. Neither wore armour and when they saw the mailed warrior emerge from the door they stood in surprise. I leapt at them stabbing one with Saxon Slayer and ripping the seax across the throat of the second.

The one I had stabbed shouted, "Enemies in the east tower!" He fell at my feet.

"Llenlleog, hurry."

I stood in the corridor facing the direction of the gate. I glanced over my shoulder and saw Llenlleog leading a blinded

Pol. Pelas stumbled out. The cut must have been worse than I had thought. I could not carry him. "Pelas, lead the way and I will guard the rear."

"I will Warlord. I just feel a little weak!"

Three Saxons appeared. One wore mail, "The Warlord!"

I had to buy my men time, "It is! Come and face your doom for this is Saxon Slayer and it has tasted blood already. Let it feed on yours." I leapt at them slashing at the mailed warrior. His shield came up and deflected my sword so that it caught his fellow on the shoulder. I lunged forward with my seax and whipped it sideways. It tore open the stomach of the third. I felt a blow to my right shoulder as the mailed warrior hit me with his sword. Had I not worn the mail I had then I would have been hurt. As it was the mail rings bent a little. I stepped back quickly to give myself room to swing.

The mailed warrior saw this as a weakness and he lumbered towards me. I let him come and, with my back to the wall deflected his sword with my seax and then hit him in the face with my sword. It was not a clean blow but Agramaine had sharpened the sword to the hilt and the edge tore across the face and nose of the warrior. The guard rammed into his eye. The warrior whom I had slashed in the shoulder struck at me with his sword. I twisted my body and the sword slid along the mail links. I rammed the seax into his throat and, as he fell, pulled Saxon Slayer back and rammed it into his middle. It tore through the links. He was wounded but I had no time to finish him off. Already I saw more men coming down the corridor. I turned and ran.

When I reached the door, I shut it. There was no lock. I took the stairs two at a time. As I reached the corridor leading to the tunnel I found Pelas lying in a heap. He looked up and gave me a sad smile, "I fear the blade was poisoned."

"Have you taken the antidote?"

He held the empty jar, "I was too late. Leave me here and I will slow them down."

"We leave no one behind." I put my sword away and lifted him up. I heard noises behind me. I hurried down to the door leading to the cave. I used my foot to kick open the door and manhandled him through it. Once through I put my weight on the door and then rammed my seax into the tiny gap between the door and the frame. It would hold, albeit briefly. As I lifted Pelas again I realised the water was now up to my ankles. The tide had turned.

It was hard wading through the icy waters carrying a warrior who was barely conscious but I was determined that I would not leave him behind. We had saved Myrddyn, Myrddyn would save him. It was slightly easier going this way for the sea bed sloped but the water grew deeper. When I saw the lighter area ahead I knew the entrance was close.

"Agramaine!" He did not appear, "Agramaine!"

His face appeared, "Yes Warlord!"

"Help me, Pelas is wounded."

He clambered towards me for I had to climb up over the rocks and the sea was now up to my chest. I worried that Pelas might drown before I could get him out. Behind me I heard shouts as the Saxons breached the door. As Agramaine reached me a huge wave broke and drenched me. It was much easier to haul him up with the two of us and when Llenlleog appeared we pulled him over the top of the rocks. Another huge wave struck us and I was unbalanced. I tumbled back into the swirling waters. Luckily, I hit water and not a rock. The water surged and I spluttered to my feet.

One of the Saxons had got ahead of the others and he lurched at me with his sword. The water was up to our chests and he tried to swing the sword over his head. It clattered on the roof. I had no seax and Saxon Slayer would not aid me and so I grabbed his head and, pulling it towards me, head-butted him. His eyes rolled up into his head. I dropped my hands to his neck and started to squeeze. I forced his head below the water. His hands scrabbled around as he tried to fight me off but the blow to his head and my strength meant he failed. When he went limp in my hands I let go.

The water was now up to my neck and my armour was pulling me down. I forced my legs forwards. I stepped onto a rock and pushed myself up. I was about to tumble backwards when Agramaine and Llenlleog's hands grasped mine and pulled me from the surf. I sprang out like a cork.

"Hurry Warlord or we will not make the dunes."

I saw that Pol, blinded though he was, was holding Pelas upright although his body looked limp. "Go help Pol and Pelas. I can stand now and I will make my way across."

The tide was coming in but the hollow below the cave was deeper than the passage to the beach. Even so, the waters came up to our waists. I slipped and slid across slimy rocks and found my feet on the sand. It sucked a little but it was more secure than the weed-covered rocks. I waded ashore and found Pelas lying on his back. I thought he was dead but, as I leaned over him, he opened his eyes.

"Lord, you are safe! Thank you for trying to save me." He closed his eyes and winced in pain. "Such a little scratch and yet it has killed me. I am honoured to have served you and I will wait for you in the Otherworld."

"Pelas you were the best of squires and you would have been the best of equites."

He said nothing and Agramaine said, "He is dead, lord."

"Let us carry his body back for I will bury him with honour." Between us we lifted him and Pol was led by Llenlleog. "How are the eyes, Pol?"

"They burn, lord. I fear my days as an equite are gone. Those witches have done for Pelas and for me."

"But their evil is gone. Saxon Slayer has destroyed them."

Kay and my equites were waiting in the sand dunes. They took our burdens from us. I felt weary as we made our way back to the camp. When we reached it, I felt as though I had the weight of the world upon my shoulders for lying there, surrounded by my squires and archers lay Myrddyn. He was still and Gawan's face, in the firelight, looked pained.

He looked up when he saw us. "What ails Pelas and Pol, brother?"

"Pelas is in the Otherworld but the witches threw something in Pol's eyes. He is blind."

Pol said, "Llenlleog tried to wash them out but they still burn."

"Let me look." He led Pol to the firelight.

I turned to Kay, "And the attack?"

"The King just used the machines. They did some damage but are now broken."

"They did what they had to for the witches are dead."

Kay shook his head, "And Myrddyn has not moved since we brought him down from the headland."

I wanted to ask Gawan what had happened but Pol's life was still in the balance. My brother laid Pol down next to the fire and then he reached into Myrddyn's leather bag. I saw that he now wore it about his shoulders. That was an ominous sign. He took out a jar and scraped out some of the ointment. He smeared it on Pol's eyes.

"That soothes, Gawan."

"Good. I hope it works. Myrddyn cannot tell me if what I do is right. I just have his thoughts in my head. I hope that it is the right ointment. I still have much to learn. It feels right."

Pol said, quietly, "I trust you, old friend."

Gawan tied a bandage around it and said, "Here drink this. It will help you sleep and aid the healing." He handed him a beaker. Pol drank. "Llenlleog and Agramaine, lead him to his tent and watch him. He needs sleep." He smiled, "As do you two."

Llenlleog shook his head, "We will watch!"

I led Gawan away. "What happened?"

"We wrestled with the witches. They sensed your presence and there was a third power."

"Their brother, the boy who poisoned Myrddyn and who killed Pelas."

"That explains it. It was too much for Myrddyn. They destroyed his mind and I wrestled alone. You saved my life, brother when you slew them."

"Destroyed his mind?"

"He breathes but his mind is in the Otherworld. He will continue to live until I take him to his tomb. The wizard is gone. I am now Myrddyn." He tapped the side of his head. "His knowledge is growing in my mind but I have much to assimilate."

"What will you do?"

"Tomorrow I must leave with Myrddyn. We will travel to Civitas Carvetiorum and thence to Wyddfa."

I would have to leave the siege and escort the wizard. I owed him that much.

Saxon Throne

Gawan shook his head, "You cannot come, brother. Wyddfa is your doom. Myrddyn would not wish it. Give me Kay, Lann Aelle and ten equites. That is an escort for a wizard."

"Aye, I will."

I was weary but I had to find King Penda. He and his men were celebrating the success of the machines for Kay had told me that one of the corners of the gate was almost down. He greeted me with a bear hug, "Warlord! Did you succeed?"

"Aye the witches are dead but I lost a warrior and Myrddyn is as good as dead. It has cost us."

"Aye but now we can take this castle with steel and iron!"

"King Penda, my men and I must leave for a while. The Northumbrians are trapped within their walls and you need not my horses. We will be away but a month and then we will return with more machines. Myrddyn is gone but I have a builder at my home who can make them."

He clapped me on my back and said, "We will not need them. We will take this castle before the new moon rises!"

I did not share his confidence. I did not sleep that night but I kept vigil over Pol. I felt responsible for his injury. Pol was my oldest friend. I had lost my first squire, I had lost my father, I had lost my wizard; Pol would be a step too far.

It was noon when Pol stirred. Gawan was waiting to escort Myrddyn home but he would not leave until he knew the results of his treatment. Pol coughed, "You are awake?"

"Aye lord." He sat up. He began to take off the bandage.

"Stay your hand. Let me send for Gawan."

"I will disobey you, Warlord. I like not this dark. The tunnel was bad enough but this is worse than death. If I cannot see, then I want to know as soon as I can. I will have to learn to live with blindness but I will know." He tore the bandages. His eyes were red and inflamed and they were closed. I saw his lips moving as he silently chanted the help of the gods. He slowly opened them and blinked. I waited. Could he see?

"Well, Pol, what do you see?"

He smiled, "I see a Warlord and I see a friend. Gawan has saved my eyes."

We walked over to the wagon in which Myrddyn lay. Pol said, "Not Myrddyn too?"

237

Gawan said, "You see again. I am pleased. Yes, old friend, Myrddyn is not yet dead but he waits between our world and the next. We will take him to the tomb he built for our father and himself."

"The world is changing."

"That is ever the way and yet the earth stays the same."

He clasped my arm, "Take care while I am gone, brother. The Warlord needs not only warriors to watch him but also his brother. Myrddyn's power now makes me stronger."

I nodded and walked over to Myrddyn. I had known him almost my whole life. I had thought he would never go. I touched his cheek; it was warm and proof that he lived still. I put my mouth close to his ear, "Myrddyn, old friend, like my father I never told you while you were with us that I thought you one of the two greatest men who ever lived. I tell you now for my brother says you live still. I take comfort from the thought that your powers lie with Gawan but I shall miss you for your wit, and your humour and your mischief. The world will never see your like again and it will talk for generations as yet unborn of the things that you have done. Farewell. I would not be who I am but for you."

I was suddenly aware that the world was silent. I turned and every equite, squire and archer stood with their heads bowed. I stepped back and drawing Saxon Slayer, Witches' Bane I raised it aloft, "Myrddyn the Great!"

There was a hissing sound as all drew a sword and roared, "Myrddyn the Great!"

A great flock of gulls which had landed on the beach all took to flight. It seemed to be symbolic. It was like Myrddyn's spirit leaving us.

Gawan came to me and I saw his eyes were wet, tears coursed down his cheeks, "That was well said, brother. One chapter has now ended and, when I return, another will begin."

I nodded. I did not risk speaking for my heart was full. I mounted Copper which Agramaine had thoughtfully brought and I rode with the wagon until we were over the hill which led west. I sat and watched as the wagon and escort of equites disappeared into the west. Myrddyn was going home. The next time I saw his home would be the end of my life too.

Saxon Throne

As we headed west I decided to honour the men of Gwynedd who had died fighting for Cadwallon. We stopped at the battlefield now filled with bleaching bones. With Iago, I went to the place where Dai and the oathsworn had fallen. We gathered the bones that were there and the two of us dug a hole as deep as my arm and placed the bones within. Then I took the dragon necklace which King Cadwallon had given me to show his authority. We placed it on the top. After we had piled the earth back on top my men brought a large slab of stone and laid it upon the top.

"Brothers we could not do you honour when you fell but we do so now. You fulfilled your oath and you did your duty. No man can do more. Sleep now with the dragon of Cymru and one day a warrior will come to reclaim the dragon and to avenge your death."

I took out my seax and carved the outline of a dragon on the rock.

Iago asked, "Why do you do that, lord?"

"Gawan has told me that one of his descendants will save the land of Rheged. It is a sign for him."

"But how do you know he will find it and know what it means?"

"I do not but the spirits do and my brother does. I trust them. It is *wyrd*."

Epilogue

In the end, we did not return to Din Guardi. While we were away King Penda lost too many men in fruitless assaults. He lost his temper and raided the churches and monasteries. King Oswald did not stir to stop him and the Mercians returned home richer but with two deadly enemies still in the north. That error would cost King Penda in the end but he rode south triumphantly having defeated King Oswald in battle.

We returned to Civitas Carvetiorum where Pol recovered and we resumed our vigilance for enemies. When Gawan and my equites returned at harvest time my brother looked almost ancient. His hair appeared to have begun to turn white. He, Kay and Lann Aelle stayed with me for we had things to say. The four of us along with Pol ate alone and Gawan told me of Myrddyn's end.

"He lived until we reached Wyddfa. We camped outside his tomb, with the wolf's eyes and gaping mouth. As we camped and sat around the fire he opened his eyes and smiling said, *'It is done. My time is over and yours has come.'* He folded his arms, closed his eyes and stopped breathing. He chose to die. I prepared his body as he had told me and we carried him that night into his tomb. He had his niche prepared and the wall above had his name. We laid him in the tomb and the others left. I kept vigil as he had told me and I dreamed. I saw the future and I saw my death. I saw Rheged die and I saw a child of my child bear a child. He turned into a wolf and drove the Saxons hence. When I came out my hair was this colour."

"Then all that we do is in vain. Rheged dies no matter what we do?"

"Did you not hear me, brother? It will be saved by our blood. The Saxons will lose. Not today and not tomorrow but someday and it will be the power that we have in our veins that helps the wolf warrior who carries the dragon that will prevail. This is not the end, this is just the beginning. Pol said it, *'the world is changing'* but in the end, it stays the same."

I was not certain I understood what he meant but I did take heart from the fact that someone with our blood would avenge our defeat one day. We would keep on fighting even though we knew that we would lose. We were warriors and that is what warriors do.

The End

Glossary

Name-Explanation
Abbatis Villa- Abbeville –Northern France
Aengus Finn mac Fergus Dubdétach-Irish mercenary
Aelfere-Northallerton
Aelle-Monca's son and Hogan Lann's uncle
Aileen- Fergus' sister, a mystic
Alavna-Maryport Cumbria
Artorius-King Arthur
Banna-Birdoswald
Belatu-Cadros -God of war
Belerion-Land's End (Cornwall)
Bilhaugh Forest –Sherwood Forest
Bone fire- the burning of the waste material after the slaughter of the animals at the end of October. (Bonfire night)
Bors- son of Mungo war chief of Strathclyde
Bro Waroc'h- one of the Brythionic tribes who settled in Brittany
Byrnie – mail shirt
Caedwalestate-Cadishead near Salford
Caer Daun- Doncaster
Caergybi-Holyhead
Cadwallon ap Cadfan- King of Gwynedd
Caldarium- the hot room in a Roman bathhouse
Ceorl- Commoner, an ordinary soldier
Civitas Carvetiorum-Carlisle
Constantinopolis-Constantinople (modern Istanbul)
Cymri- Welsh
Cymru-Wales
Cynfarch Oer-Descendant of Coel Hen (King Cole)
Dál Riata-land in the southwest of Scotland
Daffydd ap Gwynfor-Lann's chief sea captain
Daffydd ap Miach-Miach's son
Dai ap Gruffyd-King Cadfan's squire
Delbchaem Lann-Lann's daughter
Din Guardi-Bamburgh Castle
Dùn Èideann -Edinburgh
Dunum-River Tees
Dux Britannica-The Roman British leader after the Romans left (King Arthur?)
Edwin-King of Bernicia, Deira and Northumbria

Saxon Throne

Eoforwic - York (Eboracum)
Erecura-Goddess of the earth
Fanum Cocidii-Bewcastle
Fiachnae mac Báetáin- King of Strathclyde
Fiachnae mac Demmáin - King of the Dál Fiatach
Freja-Saxon captive and Aelle's wife
Gammer- Old English for mother
Gareth-Harbour master Caergybi
Gallóglaigh-Irish mercenary
Gawan Lann-Lann's son
Gesith- Saxon chieftain
Glanibanta- Ambleside
Gwynfor-Headman at Caergybi
Gwyr-The land close to Swansea
Hagustaldes-ham - Hexham
Halvelyn- Helvellyn
Haordine-Hawarden Cheshire
hearthweru - King's bodyguard (the precursor of the housecarl)
Hen Ogledd-Northern England and Southern Scotland
Hogan Lann-Lann's son and Warlord
Icaunus-River god
Ituna- River Solway
King Ywain Rheged-Eldest son of King Urien
Lann- First Warlord of Rheged and Dux Britannica
Llenlleog- 'Leaping one' (Lancelot)
Loge-God of trickery
Ladenses- Leeds
Loidis-Leeds
Maeresea-River Mersey
Manau- Isle of Man
Mare Nostrum-Mediterranean Sea
Metcauld- Lindisfarne
Myfanwy-the Warlord's stepmother
Myrddyn-Welsh wizard fighting for Rheged
Nanna Lann-Lann's daughter, wife to King Cadwallon
Namentwihc –Nantwich, Cheshire
Nithing-A man without honour
Nodens-God of hunting
Oppidum- hill fort
Paulinus of Eboracum- The Pope's representative in Britannia
Penrhyd- Penrith, Cumbria
Penrhyn Llŷn- Llŷn Peninsula
pharos- lighthouse

Saxon Throne

Pol-Equite and strategos
Prestune-Preston Lancashire
Roman Bridge-Piercebridge (Durham)
Roman Soldiers- the mountains around Scafell Pike
Rhuthun -Ruthin North Wales
Scillonia Insula-Scilly Isles
Solar-West facing room in a castle
Spæwīfe- Old English for witch
Sucellos-God of love and time
Táin Bó- Irish for cattle raid
Tatenhale- Tattenhall near Chester
Tepidarium- the warm room in a Roman Bathhouse
The Narrows-The Menaii Straits
Treffynnon-Holywell (North Wales)
Tuanthal-Leader of the Warlord's horse warriors
Vectis-Isle of Wight
Vindonnus-God of hunting
Wachanglen-Wakefield
Walls of Brus- Wark on Tyne (Northumberland)
War shits- dysentery
Wrecsam- Wrexham
wapentake- Muster of an army
Wide Water-Windermere
Wyddfa-Snowdon
Wyrd-Fate
Y Fflint- Flint (North Wales)
Ynys Enlli- Bardsey Island
Ynys Môn- Anglesey
Yr Wyddgrug- Mold (North Wales)
Zatrikion- an early form of Greek chess

Historical note

There is evidence that the Saxons withdrew from Rheged in the early years of the seventh century and never dominated that land again. It seems that warriors from Wales reclaimed that land. I have used Lord Lann as that instrument. King Edwin did usurp Aethelfrith. Edwin was allied to both Mercia and East Anglia.

There is a cave in North Yorkshire called Mother Shipton's cave. It has a petrifying well within. Objects left there become covered, over time, with a stone exterior. In the seventeenth century, a witch was reputed to live there. I created an earlier witch to allow the Roman sword to be discovered and to create a link with my earlier Roman series.

The Saxons and Britons all valued swords and cherished them. They were passed from father to son. The use of rings on the hilts of great swords was a common practice and showed the prowess of the warrior in battle. I do not subscribe to Brian Sykes' theory that the Saxons merely assimilated into the existing people. One only has to look at the place names and listen to the language of the north and northwestern part of England. You can still hear anomalies. Perhaps that is because I come from the north but all of my reading leads me to believe that the Anglo-Saxons were intent upon conquest. The Norse invaders were different and they did assimilate but the Saxons were fighting for their lives and it did not pay to be kind. The people of Rheged were the last survivors of Roman Britain and I have given them all of the characteristics they would have had. They were educated and ingenious. The Dark Ages was the time when much knowledge was lost and would not reappear until Constantinople fell. This period was also the time when the old ways changed and Britain became Christian. This was a source of conflict as well as growth.

It was at the beginning of the sixth century that King Aethelfrith was killed in battle. His sons, Eanforth, Oswiu and Oswald became famous and outshone both their father and King

Edwin. Although Edwin became king he did not have the three brothers killed and they had an uneasy alliance.

King Cadwallon became the last great British leader until modern times. Alfred ruled the Saxons but no one held such sway over the country from Scotland to Cornwall in the same way that King Cadwallon did. He did this not by feat of arms alone but by using alliances. He even allied with the Mercians to ensure security for his land. His death saw the end of the hopes of the native Britons. They would survive but they would never reconquer their land. I have invented a Warlord to aid him but that is backed up by the few writings we have. Dux Britannicus and Arthur are both shadowy figures who crop up in what we now term, the Dark Ages.

King Edwin's life was saved by Bishop Paulinus who had been sent by the Pope to convert the Northumbrians to Christianity. The act made King Edwin order all of his people to convert. I have used Paulinus as a sort of villain. I have no doubt that the Church at the time thought they were doing good work but like the Spanish Inquisition a thousand years later they were not averse to using any means possible when dealing with what they deemed pagans. King Cadwallon did convert to Christianity but still fought King Edwin. Bede, the Northumbrian propagandist, portrayed Cadwallon as a cruel man who destroyed the Christian kingdom of Northumbria. Perhaps that was because King Edwin became an early Christian martyr. History is written by the winners and the Anglo-Saxons did win, albeit briefly before the Norse and the Bretons combined to reconquer England in 1066.

The people of Brittany did arrive there as stated in the novel. I have obviously invented both names and events to suit my story but the background is accurate. They spoke a variation of Welsh/Cornish. There was a famous witch who lived on one of the islands of Scilly. Although this was in the Viking age a century or so later I can see no reason why mystics did not choose to live there.

The horses used by William the Conqueror at Hastings were about fifteen and a half hands high. The largest contingent of non-Norman knights who accompanied him were the Bretons and their horses were marginally bigger. It is ironic that the

Saxon Throne

people of Britain came back to defeat the Saxons. It was a mixture of Briton and Viking (Norman) who finally conquered Britain. (*Wyrd*!)

The stirrup was unknown in Britain at this time. I can find no explanation for this. It strikes me that someone would have invented it. However, it seems they did not and so the Warlord and his men can't use the lance or the spear. The impact of the weapon would have knocked them from the saddle. Charlemagne and his armies had the stirrup. That, however, was a century after this period in British history.

The battle of Hatfield took place on the River Don close to Doncaster. It was fought on a swamp in a bend of the river. It was in the early 630s. King Edwin was killed at the battle and the leaders of the victorious armies were named as Penda and Cadwallon. It marked a reversal in fortunes for the Saxons. They were forced to retreat further north and Eanfrith, the eldest of Aethelfrith's children became king of Deira. He was also killed by Cadwallon and Oswald became king. The kingdom of Northumbria would never be as powerful again until the Vikings conquered it in the ninth century. Bernicia and Deira emerged as minor kingdoms. King Cadwallon had a brief year of glory when he rampaged through the land of Bernicia. It was not to last.

The Viking name for Helvellyn was wolf mountain and there were many such animals there. Wolves were so prevalent in the north of England that William the Conqueror actually stipulated that his new lords of the manor had a duty to hunt and exterminate them. The last ones were only killed in the sixteenth century.

The change in King Cadwallon is attested to by Bede. Given that the priest was writing as someone who believed King Edwin was a saint we should perhaps take his testimony with a pinch of salt but Cadwallon was a Christian king. He said that King Cadwallon ravaged, *"provinces of the Northumbrians"* for a year, *"not like a victorious king, but like a rapacious and bloody tyrant."* The priest also said, *"though he bore the name and professed himself a Christian, was so barbarous in his disposition and behaviour, that he neither spared the female sex, nor the innocent age of children, but with savage cruelty put them to tormenting deaths, ravaging all their country for a long time, and resolving to cut off all the race of the English within the borders of Britain."* We see this change during this novel. Perhaps it is not to be seen as unusual. Alexander the Great was viewed in a similar way. Perhaps it is success which breeds such changes.

Osric, the King of Deira, did try to take a large walled town in which King Cadwallon waited. The army sortied and slaughtered all of them. Eanfrith did try to negotiate with King Cadwallon. It is said, by Bede, that he went to speak with King Cadwallon along with twelve warriors and he never returned. In many ways, it was ironic for his successor, Oswald, fought and killed King Cadwallon at the Battle of Heavenfield (Hexham) and then completely destroyed the Welsh army. King Cadwallon's reign as High King lasted less than two years and enabled the Saxons to rule Britain until the Vikings arrived.

The bubonic plague was first brought to Britain in the sixth century. It was called Justinian's Plague. It devastated Wales on a number of occasions. Famously in 642, the year of the Battle of Maserfield, it is reputed to have taken King Cadafael. King Penda did, indeed defeat and kill Oswald at Maserfield and he did it with an alliance of the Welsh and Brythionic people. It was the monk Bede who tells us of the events of this time and they should be taken with as much salt as possible! King Oswald was Christian and Penda was a pagan. Bede was an excellent propagandist! That story will be in my next book-sorry for the spoiler!

King Penda invaded Northumbria sometime in 636 or 637 and besieged Din Guardi. He was there for some months but he could not manage to break down the defenders' resistance. It proved too great a nut to crack and after laying waste to the land around the stronghold he eventually returned to Mercia. Oswald then spent the next few years building up his army before he and Eowa invaded Mercia in 642. However, that is meat for the next novel and the next and final instalment in the story of the Warlord of Rheged.

A Punic Ditch was invented by the Romans and it was almost impossible for someone trapped in it to escape.

The shrine on the Tees was part of the Time Team programme.

I used many books to research the material. The first was the excellent Michael Wood's book "*In Search of the Dark Ages*" and the second was "*The Middle Ages*" Edited by Robert Fossier. The third was the Osprey Book- "*Saxon, Viking and Norman*" by Terence Wise. I also used Brian Sykes' book, "*Blood of the Isles*" for reference. "*Arthur and the Anglo-Saxon Wars*" by David Nicholle was useful. "*Anglo Saxon Thegn*" by Mark Harrison gave an insight into the way the minor chiefs ruled their lands. In addition, I searched online for more obscure information. All the place names are accurate, as far as I know, and I have researched the names of the characters to reflect the period. My apologies if I have made a mistake.

Griff Hosker
February 2016

Other books by Griff Hosker

If you enjoyed reading this book, then why not read another one by the author?

Ancient History

The Sword of Cartimandua Series
(Germania and Britannia 50 A.D. – 128 A.D.)
Ulpius Felix- Roman Warrior (prequel)
The Sword of Cartimandua
The Horse Warriors
Invasion Caledonia
Roman Retreat
Revolt of the Red Witch
Druid's Gold
Trajan's Hunters
The Last Frontier
Hero of Rome
Roman Hawk
Roman Treachery
Roman Wall
Roman Courage

The Wolf Warrior series
(Britain in the late 6th Century)
Saxon Dawn
Saxon Revenge
Saxon England
Saxon Blood
Saxon Slayer
Saxon Slaughter
Saxon Bane
Saxon Fall: Rise of the Warlord
Saxon Throne
Saxon Sword

Saxon Throne

Medieval History

The Dragon Heart Series
Viking Slave
Viking Warrior
Viking Jarl
Viking Kingdom
Viking Wolf
Viking War
Viking Sword
Viking Wrath
Viking Raid
Viking Legend
Viking Vengeance
Viking Dragon
Viking Treasure
Viking Enemy
Viking Witch
Viking Blood
Viking Weregeld
Viking Storm
Viking Warband
Viking Shadow
Viking Legacy
Viking Clan
Viking Bravery

The Norman Genesis Series
Hrolf the Viking
Horseman
The Battle for a Home
Revenge of the Franks
The Land of the Northmen
Ragnvald Hrolfsson
Brothers in Blood
Lord of Rouen
Drekar in the Seine
Duke of Normandy

Saxon Throne

The Duke and the King

Danelaw
(England and Denmark in the 11th Century)
Dragon Sword
Oathsword
Bloodsword

New World Series
Blood on the Blade
Across the Seas
The Savage Wilderness
The Bear and the Wolf
Erik The Navigator
Erik's Clan

The Vengeance Trail

The Reconquista Chronicles
Castilian Knight
El Campeador
The Lord of Valencia

The Aelfraed Series
(Britain and Byzantium 1050 A.D. - 1085 A.D.)
Housecarl
Outlaw
Varangian

The Anarchy Series England 1120-1180
English Knight
Knight of the Empress
Northern Knight
Baron of the North
Earl
King Henry's Champion
The King is Dead
Warlord of the North

Saxon Throne

Enemy at the Gate
The Fallen Crown
Warlord's War
Kingmaker
Henry II
Crusader
The Welsh Marches
Irish War
Poisonous Plots
The Princes' Revolt
Earl Marshal
The Perfect Knight

**Border Knight
1182-1300**
Sword for Hire
Return of the Knight
Baron's War
Magna Carta
Welsh Wars
Henry III
The Bloody Border
Baron's Crusade
Sentinel of the North
War in the West
Debt of Honour
The Blood of the Warlord

**Sir John Hawkwood Series
France and Italy 1339- 1387**
Crécy: The Age of the Archer
Man At Arms
The White Company
Leader of Men

Lord Edward's Archer
Lord Edward's Archer
King in Waiting
An Archer's Crusade

Saxon Throne

Targets of Treachery
The Great Cause

**Struggle for a Crown
1360- 1485**
Blood on the Crown
To Murder a King
The Throne
King Henry IV
The Road to Agincourt
St Crispin's Day
The Battle for France
The Last Knight
Queen's Knight

Tales from the Sword I
(Short stories from the Medieval period)

**Tudor Warrior series
England and Scotland in the late 14th and early 15th century**
Tudor Warrior

**Conquistador
England and America in the 16th Century**
Conquistador

Modern History

The Napoleonic Horseman Series
Chasseur à Cheval
Napoleon's Guard
British Light Dragoon
Soldier Spy
1808: The Road to Coruña
Talavera
The Lines of Torres Vedras
Bloody Badajoz
The Road to France

Saxon Throne

Waterloo

The Lucky Jack American Civil War series
Rebel Raiders
Confederate Rangers
The Road to Gettysburg

Soldier of the Queen series
Soldier of the Queen

The British Ace Series
1914
1915 Fokker Scourge
1916 Angels over the Somme
1917 Eagles Fall
1918 We will remember them
From Arctic Snow to Desert Sand
Wings over Persia

Combined Operations series
1940-1945
Commando
Raider
Behind Enemy Lines
Dieppe
Toehold in Europe
Sword Beach
Breakout
The Battle for Antwerp
King Tiger
Beyond the Rhine
Korea
Korean Winter

Tales from the Sword II
(Short stories from the Modern period)

Other Books
Great Granny's Ghost (Aimed at 9-14-year-old young people)

For more information on all of the books then please visit the author's website at www.griffhosker.com where there is a link to contact him or visit his Facebook page: GriffHosker at Sword Books